The Difference Between

by

LETA BLAKE

An Original Publication from Leta Blake Books

The Difference Between

Written by Leta Blake
Cover by Dar Albert
Formatted by BB eBooks

First Digital Edition, 2016
Second Digital Edition, 2020

ISBN: 979-8-88841-038-7

For JR, even after everything.

Wade Maguire and Russ Paulson are in love. After a year of passion and happiness, they're buying a home and moving in together. Everything is rosy for them—until a jealous and insane ex from Wade's past puts all of that to the test.

After being kidnapped and tortured by his deranged former lover, Wade loses his ability to engage with his own sexuality or with Russ. With the help of a psychologist, EMDR therapy, and a sex plan, they work together to overcome the damage inflicted. In the process, they discover wells of love they've never known before.

As passion is reborn and their sex life reignited, Wade realizes a need to re-experience certain events in Russ's loving arms. For Wade, the difference between pain and pleasure is love, and the difference between rape and rough sex is consent.

Dark, and yet ultimately hopeful, this book contains many emotional and graphic sex scenes, as well as some scenes of torture. *Proceed with care.*

Stand-alone with a happy ending.

Author Note

I defeated some big personal demons when writing this book. I hope it will help others defeat their demons too.

IMPORTANT TRIGGER WARNING

CAUTION!

Chapters 2 & 3 of this book contain graphic descriptions of torture and rape. If you want to read this book without the most graphic descriptions of these events, **please read Chapter 1 and then skip to Chapter 4**. In addition, throughout the book there are less graphic descriptions of the rape and torture. Please do not continue this book at all if that isn't a safe topic for you.

PART ONE

Chapter One

Los Angeles in May was beautiful. The jacarandas were in
bloom and the sky was an endless dazzle of clear blue that
lifted Wade's spirits. Waiting outside his hotel for his ex-friend-
with-benefits, Owen, to pick him up, Wade basked in the
gorgeous weather. It was a sweet reprieve from the already
suffocating heat of his home in Atlanta, Georgia.

Leaning back against a decorative pillar near the hotel entrance, Wade watched BMWs and Porches pull in to the circle in
front of him. Bellboys hopped to action emptying the cars of
people and luggage. A clump of women, wearing tight designer
jeans that probably cost as much as Wade's monthly rent back
before he moved in with his boyfriend Russ, stood in a tight knot
waiting for a valet to return with their car.

One of them whispered, nodding in his direction, "Isn't he
that gay actor? I think he is?"

"No, he's too short."

He wasn't too short, actually—six feet even—but he wasn't
the actor they were thinking of either. In fact, he wasn't an actor
at all. He was just a lowly waiter-turned-manny for his best
friend's kids. Still, he'd heard a lot over the last few years, ever
since the movie *A Single Man* had come out, about his resem-
blance to one of the side characters. His best friend Kari had gone
on and on about it: "You've got the same thick, dark eyebrows
and high, sexy cheekbones! And those moody hazel eyes of yours!

Oh and that messy brown hair that always looks like you just crawled out of bed!"

Wade rolled his eyes remembering how she'd rubbed her hands through his carefully mussed hair, making it stick up in all the wrong directions. His just-woken-up look wasn't easy to come by and she knew it. Kari loved to tease him and anyone else she could find to poke at. Her husband Doug couldn't make her behave. No one could.

"He's certainly dressed like an actor," another woman said, looking him over from head to toe.

Wade snorted under his breath. Apparently worn jeans from Target, leather flip-flops, and a t-shirt he'd had since his senior year in high school was the fashion du jour for not-so-famous actors these days. He wondered what the women would've said if he'd worn one of the expensive outfits Russ had gifted him with over the last year. Probably the same thing. The women were convinced he was the actor he resembled and they'd see what they wanted to see.

The women piled into a BMW M5 and a hired driver got in with them.

Wade blinked his eyes in the bright sun, amazed again by the wealth surrounding him. The gorgeous, cream-colored hotel rose up fourteen stories in the bright sunshine. Every secret corner of it was well appointed and the lobby even smelled like a crisp designer scent created just for the hotel. Such glamor didn't reflect his usual digs when traveling, but his boyfriend Russ had surprised him the day before he flew out with reservations for the Four Seasons.

"Moira handled the details," Russ had said, brushing a hand over his neatly trimmed, ash-brown hair and dismissively crediting his assistant as he frowned over a case brief. "It'll be better than a Best Western or Owen's couch." He'd glanced up, a spark of jealousy glinting in his eyes. "Or Owen's bed."

A California breeze flitted through Wade's hair and he sighed. Russ had nothing to worry about. He'd never loved Owen. Not romantically. What'd been between them had only consisted of years of friendship and hard-up horniness, nothing more.

Besides, Owen was so conflicted over his bisexuality, specifically his desire for men, they could never have made it work anyway. Wade was determined to live out, proud, and loud. Owen, shamed by his military father and uber-religious upbringing, had wanted Wade to quietly suck his cock on the sly and then be a-okay with Owen beating himself up for weeks afterward, making them both miserable.

That was the main reason they'd never moved into 'boyfriend' territory. Well, that and Wade just hadn't felt *romantic love* for Owen. He was handsome enough—six-two to Wade's six foot, with blond, curly hair, and broad shoulders. And there was no doubt he was a steadfast, if emotionally unpredictable, friend. But, despite all of his good qualities, he'd never made Wade's heart go pitter-pat.

Or, as in the case of Russ, ka-*boom*.

Speaking of…ka-boom was what'd happened to his and Owen's friendship, once Wade put an end to their hook-ups to go all in with Russ. It'd been an ugly scene. Owen had lost it, shouting at Wade for over an hour about how arrogant, pushy, demanding, and *short* Russ Paulson was, and how awful. (Short! As if being three inches shorter than Wade was a deal-breaker when Russ's cock was thick enough to make Wade see God every time they fucked. Owen had all the wrong priorities.)

"He's not the right man for you," Owen had shouted.

"Oh, and you are? Every time I suck you off, you lose your mind for a week. You don't want a relationship with me, but you don't want me having one with anyone else."

"That's not true! I don't want you having one with my fucking dickwad boss!"

Wade had rolled his eyes. "What you need is someone to help you get past your hang-ups."

That'd gone over like a lead balloon. Eventually Owen had grown so angry Wade was forced to step back from their friendship. It'd hurt, since they'd been close friends since eighth grade, but Russ was the man Wade had fallen in love with, and Owen needed to accept it.

That'd taken a year apparently. And this trip out to L.A. put all past resentment to rest. It'd required an entire country between them, but the sting had finally faded, and Owen was ready to be friends again.

Watching a handsome man in a suit—not unlike the kind Russ wore for important days at court—step out of a Porsche and into the sunshine, Wade allowed some hope for his oldest friend. Maybe in sunny La-La-Land, Owen had found a boyfriend—or a girlfriend—he could truly love and who loved him back. Wade wasn't picky about the gender. His only desire for Owen was happiness. That was all he'd ever wanted for him.

Rolling up the short sleeves of his cream-colored t-shirt, Wade exposed his toned, lightly-freckled biceps to catch some extra Vitamin D until Owen arrived. Which, glancing quickly at his phone, shouldn't be too long. Owen was always punctual. Wade was the one who was usually late.

Checking his messages, he frowned. No response from Russ yet, either. Wade had texted as soon as his flight had touched ground (*Hey babe. I'm in L.A. safely.*) and again after checking into Four Seasons (*The room is great. Thanks for treating me like a prince.*), but Russ must have been in court or tied up with a client.

He ran a hand into his dark hair and sighed. It was ridiculous to miss Russ already, but he did. It was too bad they hadn't made the trip together. They could have taken a few extra days to drive the 101 up to San Francisco, stopping along the way at various seaside resorts to rest and make love. But Russ's workload at the law firm made that impossible.

"I'll make it up to you," Russ had promised the night before, running his hands into Wade's wavy hair, and peering up at him with his slate-gray eyes. "Next fall, we'll travel to Upstate New York to see the leaf show and pick some apples."

"No cell phone?"

"No cell phone, no clients, just you and me alone. We'll hike, bike, and fuck under the autumn blue sky until we're exhausted."

California sun in his eyes, Wade grinned, his cock thickening against his thigh as he remembered Russ waxing lyrical, using his smooth 'trust me, I'm an excellent attorney' voice.

"Does Moira know about this plan?" Wade'd asked, leaning down to rub his stubble against Russ's freshly shaven cheek.

"Of course. It'd never happen if she didn't."

"She knows about us fucking under the, how did you put it? Autumn blue sky?"

"She'd guess that part even if I didn't tell her."

Then Russ had kissed him and all worry about vacation planning was wiped from his mind.

As another round of cars, drivers, and valets did their dance, Wade laughed to himself at the backwards way he and Russ had done everything in their relationship: fucking before dating, living together and buying a house before they'd even gone away on a trip. He'd never known love could happen the way it had between them—so consuming and so fast. It'd been a whirlwind.

"Everything okay, sir?" a beautiful, blonde hotel manager with a name-tag reading *Audra* asked. Her red lipsticked mouth stretched around white teeth. "You've been waiting here a long time. Can we help you arrange transportation?"

"No, thank you," Wade said, smiling. "I'm waiting on a friend."

She nodded and said, "If you need anything at all, directions or restaurant recommendations, go inside to speak to a concierge. We're always happy to help." Then she walked toward the employee's parking area, either leaving for the day or taking a lunch break.

Surprised that Owen was actually late now, Wade tucked his phone back in his hip pocket and moved to lean against the exterior wall next to the entrance. Maybe the move to California had loosened Owen up after all. As the son of a strict military man (Wade could never remember which branch), Owen had always been judgmental about Wade's tardiness before. "It's disrespectful and shows your lack of discipline."

Wade had always assumed that his mediocre grades and general lack of occupational direction was a better indicator that he lacked discipline, but he'd let Owen blame it on his tendency to slide into any event six to eight minutes late. Why not?

An older gay couple walked out of the hotel, holding hands, and laughing. The taller gentleman looked quite dashing in a scarf and hat, and the shorter man wore Bermuda shorts and a Polo shirt. They exuded a comfort with each other that could only come with years. Wade wanted that for himself one day. His stomach tugged with longing for Russ, as if he hadn't seen him less than eight hours earlier.

He supposed it was good that his first reunion with Owen was alone, though. The history between Russ and Owen was complicated at best, and hostile at worst. Russ had been Owen's boss, and maybe it did kind of suck that Wade had slept with him. It certainly hadn't helped what had already been a strained relationship.

A year and a half earlier, Wade had worked as a waiter at Early Risers, a breakfast joint, in the morning, and as a bartender at Rolling Wilds at night. Owen had worked as a clerk for Russ's law firm, Zachary, Ulster, and Paulson. Most evenings, when Owen was finally released from the so-called hell of his job, he'd stop by Rolling Wilds for a beer and to unload about his awful boss—a boorish, arrogant man with unrealistic expectations.

From the start, Wade had been sympathetic but intrigued. The parallels between this asshole Russ Paulson and Owen's tough father couldn't be ignored. The stories Owen spun seemed colored by that lens, like he'd put all the anger and hate he couldn't heap on his father onto his boss instead.

Eventually Owen had asked Wade to be his plus one to the law firm's holiday party. ("Just as friends! No one can know what we do together!") And Wade agreed to go as much out of curiosity about the nightmare boss as out of generosity to a friend.

When the night came, he'd dressed in a red sweater and tight black trousers, met Owen at Rolling Wilds, and they'd traveled together in the same car to the law offices where the party was being held. Wade couldn't wait to finally meet the monster Owen had kvetched about for almost a year.

When they walked in, a strange fission ran through him, a premonition perhaps, and his heart beat quickly. The lobby was packed with people in suits. Wade supposed any one of them could have been the evil, heartless attorney who made Owen's work life miserable, but then he'd locked eyes with a man across the room and in an instant he'd known.

Only five-nine or so in height and thirty-three at the youngest, Russ Paulson stood dressed in a dark suit with a tasteful green and red tie his only nod to the holidays. His muscled arms folded over his broad chest, and his bronzed skin, chiseled chin and fine nose, set off his luminous, deep gray eyes. Wade's breath caught as those eyes landed on him with immediate interest. The kind of interest Wade understood from nights in clubs and gay bars. He'd licked his lips and smiled encouragingly.

"What are you looking at?" Owen had hissed. "That's him. That's my dickhead boss."

"The raging asshole?"

"Yeah. Obviously."

Wade'd swallowed roughly, grabbed a drink from a passing waiter, and made it his mission to get close enough to hear every arrogant word out of Russ Paulson's sexy, smirky mouth. And he'd succeeded. What he uncovered was that Russ was indeed intense, cunning, demanding, and brash, but he wasn't cruel. Owen was wrong about that.

Still, people clearly feared Russ as much as they admired him. Every glance he shot Wade's way gave him chills—both good and bad. Something loomed between them and Wade wanted to run away from it and wanted to crash into it headlong.

So it was a surprise and not a surprise at all when, at the end of the night, Russ had unceremoniously sent Owen home alone, and escorted Wade into his plush office. There Wade had willingly bent over the wide, wooden desk, taking Russ's fat cock like a greedy cum dumpter vying to be the world champion of cum dumpters.

No condoms. No real preparation.

Just a wild, dirty, insane fuck culminating in an earth-shattering orgasm.

It'd been the best sex of Wade's then almost twenty-six years of life.

The next day he'd written it off as a super slutty one-night stand (made possible by his prescription for PrEP). It was bound to have awkward consequences for his friendship with Owen.

But, as far as he knew then, nothing life-altering had taken place.

But a week later, after making up with Owen (it'd taken multiple *mea culpas* and a promise to never abandon him at a party to fuck his boss again), Wade dropped by Zachary, Ulster, and Paulson after his shift at Early Risers to ask Owen if he wanted to grab an early dinner.

He never saw Owen.

Because Russ spotted him in the lobby before the receptionist had the chance to call Owen out, and instead of getting food with his friend, he'd sucked Russ's delicious cock hungrily and gobbled down his cum. Then he'd been fucked bare until he'd cum his brains out again.

"Why do you smell like maple syrup?" Russ had asked, as they'd cleaned up in his private executive bathroom.

Wade blushed telling him about his job as a waiter at Early Risers, but Russ hadn't blinked twice. "I see. Well, I have work to deal with now. Come again tomorrow," he'd said, smoothly, like there was no question at all.

"Okay," Wade had agreed. Because there wasn't. He'd never shot off so hard in his life as he did with Russ. It was stunning. As far as he was concerned, he'd stop by whenever Russ asked. "Can I have your number?"

Russ handed a business card over saying, "For booty calls only, okay?"

It became an almost daily thing. If Russ wasn't with a client or in court, he'd text Wade to come over when his shift ended at Early Risers. Russ's assistant would wave him through and Wade would spend a half-hour riding Russ's cock in his huge leather chair. And every single time it was so damn good Wade thought he'd died, and every single time Russ took it farther, made it nastier, and hotter.

When Russ started showing up at Early Risers for breakfast

most mornings, paying the hostess to seat him at one of Wade's tables, and when he dropped by Rolling Wilds to nurse a beer for a few hours in the evenings while Wade worked, it started to dawn on him that Russ might have changed his mind about 'booty calls only'.

And when Russ asked him out on real dates to places like the High Museum of Art and the Atlanta symphony, he finally started to embrace the idea that Russ thought of him as more than a super-good hookup.

And then just as unexpectedly they'd fallen in love.

The transition from being Russ's eager bottom boy to his devoted boyfriend came in the wake of a massive career disappointment. Russ failed to clear the name of a young man, just eighteen years old, who'd participated in a crime while high on meth and under duress from his drug-dealer stepfather. Despite Russ's best efforts, the judge came down hard, sentencing the young man to fifteen years in prison.

That night when Wade left Rolling Wilds, he found Russ waiting in his Porsche outside. "Come home with me?" he'd asked, and, for the first time, Wade accompanied him to his posh apartment in Berkshire Terminus.

On the plush (and surprisingly fussy) couch, decorated with multiple throw-pillows, Wade had listened as Russ spilled his guts, amazed to be trusted with his lover's unbridled frustration and anger.

"I couldn't save him. I tried. I did my best. He's not going make it in there. He's small and not very smart. It's over for him. I failed."

In a flash, like in a movie or a love song, Wade fell hard. The fan of wrinkles beneath Russ's lashes, his tousled ash-brown hair, and his strong jaw were no longer just attractive, they were beautiful and sexy and worthy of adoration. He gave into his desire to care for Russ, to be more than a quick orgasm or a fun friend, and he kissed every dimple and angle of Russ's face.

Russ had kissed him back, whispering, "Where did you come from? Where have you been? I've needed you, dammit."

After that night, he'd given Russ his heart.

And, to his shock, Russ confessed that Wade had already had his, citing a moment in the High when Wade had declared they should call the modern rooms Trash Art and be done with it. "I knew then. And your ass…" Russ had smiled wickedly. "What don't I love about your ass?"

When Russ discovered that Wade had no family, having disowned his felon father, and been left orphaned by his mother and step-father, he'd promised to take care of Wade no matter what. Within a few more months, he'd asked Wade to move in and started taking care of him in ways Wade had never known before. He'd never felt so safe.

Russ loved him and showed him every day.

And now they'd bought a house together with half of Wade's inheritance and a lot of Russ's savings. The contractors still had work to do, but they'd be moved in by the end of summer.

That was their story. It was one Wade loved to ruminate on and polish. It was special.

Owen, for his part, had taken a separate path.

He'd quit his job at the law firm after trying to get Russ in trouble with the other partners for fucking Wade. He'd failed. Apparently, since Wade wasn't an employee and not technically Owen's boyfriend, there was no real impropriety beyond the obvious. Then, when Owen's father had died in L.A. Owen left to deal with all of that. In the end, he'd decided to stay on the West Coast and cut all ties. It'd been painful but for the best.

Painful because Owen had been there when Wade's biological father had gone to jail for drugs, and he'd been there when his mother and his step-father had died. Owen might not have been able to cope with Wade sucking his dick now and again, but he'd held Wade while he sobbed, raw and terrified, and that was something Wade couldn't forget.

A car horn blared, jolting him back to the present. The sunshine was butter yellow and warm, a good omen for the day ahead. Wade checked his watch again. Owen was officially forty minutes late. He sighed, restlessness growing.

Rocking back and forth on his heels, he remembered the massive kiss Russ had given him at the airport.

"If Owen starts to give you any crap about me, or us, or drags up the past at all, come home."

"Okay."

"Don't think you have to sit there and let him say whatever he wants. It's not worth it. Not even to be his friend," Russ had instructed as he pulled up to the airport departures drop-off.

"Gee, you've got so much faith in me, don't you?"

Russ had taken Wade's chin in his fingers, and said, "Yeah, I do. I've got a lot of faith in you."

"I guess you wouldn't let me go spend a week with an ex-lover if you didn't."

Russ had kissed him then, possessively, hungrily, and Wade had almost decided to chuck the whole trip and just stay home, because suddenly a week without seeing Russ, kissing him, having sex with him seemed like far too long.

"Go," Russ had said. "Let me know when you get there."

Breeze lifting his dark hair, Wade texted Russ again.

Waiting for Owen to pick me up. He's weirdly late. Love you.

Just as he hit send, a blue Honda Accord pulled up in front of the hotel, and Owen jumped out. His curly blond hair glinted in the sunshine and ginger-colored freckles sprinkled across his nose. Wearing a tight t-shirt that showed off his muscled arms and chest, as well as tight jeans that hugged the right places, he looked pretty great.

Wade had almost forgotten how attractive Owen could be. There was a reason he'd sucked the guy's cock so often despite the always-ugly fall-out.

"Wade!"

Breaking into a grin, he rushed to the curb to meet Owen as he came around the car and captured him in an embrace. "Owen, man. Wow. You look amazing!"

"So do you," Owen replied, tousling Wade's hair, and it didn't bug him the way it did when Kari did it. "You've let it grow out."

"Nah, just been lazy lately. Maybe you can hook me up with a celebrity stylist," Wade said, poking Owen in the stomach.

"No way. I like it. It's sexy."

Wade laughed.

"I can't believe you're really here! Did Russ give you a hard time about coming?" Owen asked, opening the passenger side door for Wade, and waving him in.

"No, of course not." Wade noted the car was a bit messy on the inside, not like the old Owen who kept his car like his apartment: neat as a pin. Settling in, he looked up, the sun backlighting Owen as he towered above with his hand on the door to shut it. "Honestly, I'm still surprised you asked me to come out here. I thought you'd decided to hate me forever because of how things ended."

"What? No. Are you kidding me?" Owen's deep voice pitched up in surprise. "I never hated you, Wade."

"Are you sure?"

"I was angry at the time. No denying that. But I'm over it

now." Owen shrugged. "Things have changed for me, too, you know. They've changed for both of us."

Owen shut the door to Wade's side and made his way around the car to climb in the driver's side.

As they pulled away from the curb, Wade's phone dinged with a message.

Love you, too. Have fun.

Wade grinned in satisfaction. Life was good. Everything was turning out to be very good.

THE TRAFFIC THINNED out after an abominably long time. Wade finished up the last of the stories he'd been telling Owen about Nicole and Eric, Kari and her husband Doug's kids, and his new job as their manny. Owen seemed distracted as he listened to Wade talk, but the traffic was insane, worse than Atlanta at rush hour even, and so Wade assumed he was concentrating on driving.

"Anyway, it's all thanks to Russ, of course. I couldn't have quit waiting tables if he hadn't asked me to move in. I'm thinking of going back to school in education next year."

Owen's hands tightened on the steering wheel. "That's great for you. I know you wanted to be a teacher once upon a time."

"Yeah. I never felt safe using the inheritance money before. You know, how steep tuition can be. But Russ says..." Wade trailed off, seeing Owen flinch, but then he went on with it anyway. "Russ says he can handle it for me."

"Generous."

"He wants me to follow my dreams. He's passionate about helping people, too. That's why he does what he does."

"Right." Owen's voice walked the line between sincere and sarcastic.

Wade decided to ignore it. "Kari's kids are great. They're already teaching me so much that'll come in handy when I'm in a classroom. Don't get me wrong. It's not always easy work."

"Oh yeah?"

"Some days things are so hectic getting them where they need to go and dealing with their dramas that, I swear, I miss waiting tables. But they're so cute and loving, and they look like little Kari and Dougs, so my heart melts whenever they give me those eyes. You know the eyes, right?"

Owen nodded. "I remember."

They'd been driving for a long time, it seemed, but with all of the traffic and being in an unfamiliar city, Wade wasn't sure just how far they'd gone.

"So, where are we headed?" He was hungry. By napping on the plane, he'd missed the in-flight snack service, and he'd been too nervous and excited since landing in L.A. to grab a bite. He hoped, wherever they were heading, they'd arrive soon.

"There's a place about an hour north of here. I know it's a drive, but it's got my favorite barbeque, and I knew we'd have plenty to talk about." Owen shot a glance over at him, his blue eyes sharp in the sunlight. "That's okay, right? You still like barbeque? I mean, that much hasn't changed, has it?"

"Love it!" Wade said, grinning. "I'm pretty hungry though. Didn't get to eat on the flight. Do you think we could pull in somewhere, get some take-out or something? I promise not to spoil my appetite."

Owen chuckled. "Nope, nope. I planned ahead. Here—" he waved toward a blue backpack in the backseat. "I made some cookies."

"Mm, you know my weakness."

"Yeah, I used Kari's lemon cookie recipe. I remembered how much you loved those. She gave it to me, oh, what was it now? Ten Christmases ago?"

Wade went warm with affection remembering. It'd been their senior year in high school and they'd convened at Kari's house to exchange presents. That'd been a fun night despite Kari's crazy mom implying they were all going to burn in hell. It was a real shame he and Owen ever let sex and bad feelings get in the way between them. They had so much history together.

"If anyone should be making a present of Kari's baking, it should have been me. I should have gotten her to make the snickerdoodles you love. I tell you what, I'll make you some tonight. I'll get her to text me the recipe."

Owen nodded. "Sure. I have a great kitchen at my place. I can buy the ingredients and we can make it together. Have a movie night like we used to."

Wade smiled again, reaching around to grab the backpack. Inside he found a Tupperware container with two bottles of water and lemon cookies inside. They looked just as good as Kari's. Wade handed one bottle to Owen who cracked it open, and took a sip, and then Wade opened the container of cookies. The sweet, sour scent made his mouth water, and he held one out to Owen.

"No, thanks," Owen said, checking his blind spot before moving into the next lane. "I already ate a ton of them this morning."

"Are you sure?" Wade asked. "You know how I am when I start on Kari's lemon cookies. I'll eat them all before you know it."

Owen grinned. "Oh, I remember! You can have them. Really. I made them for you."

Wade took a bite. So delicious. Not exactly the same as Kari's, though. Something was just a little off, but it was close enough. He polished off all four cookies quickly and downed half of the bottle of water.

"Good?" Owen asked.

"Perfect."

It only took a few minutes, though, before he regretted eating the cookies so fast. His stomach cramped and twisted, and sweat popped out on his upper lip. He rolled down his window to let in some cool air.

"Wade?" Owen asked. "You feeling okay? You look a little green."

"I think I'm getting car sick," he said, his tongue going thick and fuzzy. "That never happens."

"You're probably dehydrated," Owen said. "Drink some more water."

Wade nodded and rubbed his eyes. He almost finished the bottle and then pulled out his cell phone, to read the text from Russ again.

Love you, too.

"Hey, where are we going exactly?" he asked. His eyes couldn't focus on the phone.

"It's still a bit away."

He couldn't make his thumbs hit the right letters to text. He sighed and placed the call instead.

"Who are you calling?

"Kari."

"Why?"

"For the snickerdoodle recipe." Kari didn't answer. The world swooped and swirled. Wade disconnected the call. "Um, I feel really bad, man. I think you might need to pull over."

"Don't worry about it."

Wade's sight wavered, going dark at the edges.

"You don't need to worry about anything," Owen said, plucking the cell phone from Wade's hand and tossing it out the open window.

"What—?" Wade's pulse thudded and rang in his ears, and then everything went completely dark.

Chapter Two

OWEN GROANED AS he hefted Wade's limp body over the final threshold to the holding room. Wade was a couple of inches shorter and, despite working out, a good twenty pounds lighter. Still, Owen had always heard that dead weight was the hardest to carry, and it was true. Carrying Wade down the stairs to the basement was nearly impossible.

Letting Wade fall into a heap on the floor, Owen cradled his head so that it didn't bump too hard. Then he turned to lock the door behind him.

Wade was so handsome. Owen gazed down at him, letting himself really look for the first time since he'd picked him up. Wade's wavy, dark brown hair fluffed out in a mess around his face and head. His long, lanky limbs sprawled on the floor, and his beautifully formed fingers curled up next to his face. His full, pillow-like lips were parted and his long, brown lashes pressed against his high cheekbones obscuring the hazel eyes that Owen had yearned to see again for so long.

All of Wade was his now. Every last bit of him. He was his to save and his to finally love. He just had to do a few things first.

Owen looked around the room, taking in the bed in the corner—studded along the base with rings for easy restraint—and passed his gaze over the table in the middle of the room with the two bondage frames looming over it. The basic shower and toilet were built into the wall opposite.

The sidewall he'd decorated with paddles, crops, and flogs. He wondered how soon he'd get to use those. Knowing Wade, he'd fight the process. Owen sighed. It was a good thing he was up to the task.

Last year, he'd missed the signs of Russ's true nature. It should have been obvious from the way he'd seduced and infected Wade that very first night. There was no other explanation for the tie between the two men—one powerful and wealthy, the other so young and aimless. But now Owen understood. Russ was a portal opener and he'd turned Wade into a portal for demons.

What he needed to do to save Wade was brutal and terrifying, but it had to be done. He wasn't going to give up.

Even if it cost them both their lives.

Owen knelt down and stroked Wade's face tenderly. He touched Wade's soft, plump lips, ran his fingers through Wade's dark hair, and bent close to smell him. He coughed and pulled back. Wade wasn't wearing any cologne, but there was still a scent on him, something so vague that no one else would ever notice it, but Owen did. Owen sniffed again. The odor grew stronger and stronger. Foul, like rotten eggs, and Owen knew exactly what it was. Russ Paulson's semen—the demonic vehicle by which Russ had infected Wade, opened him up to possession by demons that would destroy him like a slow virus, rotting him from the inside out. His oldest friend and ex-lover's only hope was for Owen to drive them away.

One day, Wade would thank him for this. One day, Wade would be safe and he'd fall on his knees in gratitude and say he loved him.

Owen looked up and spoke to the big man in uniform standing beside him. "I'm strong enough, Dad. I can do this."

His father nodded. Owen took a deep breath and wished his Dad was still in his physical body so he could absorb some of his deep strength. But the Colonel was dead and Owen had to do this on his own.

His father had first appeared six months before. Drunk and wasted on the sofa of his father's military-sparse apartment, despairing at his life, alone without a family, without friends, and without Wade, he'd jerked upright when his father knelt down beside him and said, "Get yer ass up, boy."

At first, Owen hadn't believed the wavering image was really his dad. He'd ranted and railed at it, begged it to go away, but it'd been no use. Owen was forced to acknowledge the Colonel's presence now the same way he had when his father was alive. The man shadowed his every waking and sleeping hour. After Owen had accepted him as truly the spirit of his father the Colonel had made clear Wade's predicament. He'd explained in urgent terms that it was up to Owen to save Wade's life.

Once Owen knew and believed, a sense of safety and peace had descended on him for the first time in a very long while. It was then that he'd started to plan.

The fact that the Colonel had left Owen a healthy inheritance allowed for every piece of the puzzle to click together in Owen's brain. He'd begun searching for the perfect place to help Wade that very day.

Only two weeks had passed when he found it: a small house situated on the very outskirts of a Frazier Mountain community, away from civilization and nosy neighbors. He'd made the purchase in cash, using the identity he'd created for himself at his father's behest, grateful that even in death his father was watching out for him—and Wade. Most grateful that in death his father had accepted something he never had in life: his son's love for another man.

"Thank you, Dad," he said softly, smiling at the apparition in front of him. "I have him here with me now and I know what to do."

He stripped Wade's clothes, and put them to the side. He'd burn them later to drive the point home that Wade would no longer need them. He knew it was going to be hard to make Wade understand the urgency of the situation, to get him to believe that Russ was a demon, and that Wade had been compromised by his semen. It would be hard to convince Wade that he was hosting hundreds, if not thousands of vile creatures inside his body, and that Owen was the only one who knew, the only one that could save Wade from his fate.

He ran his hands slowly over Wade, feeling the warm flesh, enjoying the sensation of Wade's body hair under his palms, and he barely resisted touching Wade's flaccid cock. He wanted to feel it swell in his hand, to start the process of ridding Wade of some of the evil, but he knew what had to happen first, so he refrained.

Hefting Wade again, he managed to get him onto the bondage table, and then, with some effort, arranged his body the way it needed to be—with his ass at the edge, his arms tied back over his head and latched to the bolts on the wall, and his legs buckled into leather restraints on the bondage frame, sticking straight up into the air and spread apart. Owen shifted his hardening cock in his pants, breathing heavily. He swallowed hard, and nodded at his work.

"You were right, Dad. He's full of them."

He wasn't quite done, though. He went to the wall where he'd hung all of the accouterments he'd need, and took down the blindfold, a hip harness, and additional straps. He then opened a drawer in the chest beneath the wall, removing lubricant and a plug.

Returning to Wade, who was moaning a little, he petted his hair gently, and said, "It's going to be okay. I know what you need."

He fastened the straps around Wade's torso and added the harness around his hips, making sure to latch all of them to the table securely, so that Wade wouldn't make Owen's job any more difficult than it needed to be if he woke up before Owen was ready for him.

He then moved between Wade's legs, giving in and kissing his soft inner thighs, licking the dark brown hairs there, intimate in a way he'd never allowed himself before. Seeing Wade here, knowing he was at his mercy, dependent on Owen now for his very life, and that Owen alone could save him, somehow made every bit of him precious, and he wanted to own it, hurt it, lick it, bite it, and make it bleed.

But first things first.

He had to get rid of the odor that made him want to retch—the scent of the demon that covered Wade, and that Owen could smell most strongly emanating from Wade's asshole. Of course. That was where Russ would stick his penis—which wasn't a penis at all, but a gateway to hell—in order to flood Wade's body with demons. Owen had to clean it out first.

He unbuttoned his jeans, and freed his erect cock, pinching the head of it hard enough to hurt, hard enough to make his cock soften so he'd be able to do what he needed to do. He rubbed lube all over Wade's asshole first, and then smoothed lube all over the plug he'd chosen, before finally slicking the head of his cock, and lining up.

He didn't push in—not all the way—just enough to breach Wade's anus and get his pisshole aimed, and then he relaxed his bladder, hoping all the water he'd downed during the day would be enough. He groaned in pleasure as he sent a stream of urine into Wade's colon, and he pushed inside just a little more to make sure he got it as far inside as possible. He closed his eyes as the tight, clinging heat of Wade's asshole made him hard again, and he bit down on his own cheek to tamp back his arousal.

When piss started to pour out of Wade's ass and onto the floor, Owen pulled his dick free and fought hard to cut off the stream, wanting to save it for the rest of his task. Before more could leak out, he plugged Wade's asshole, twisting the anal plug in. Wade whimpered at the intrusion, but remained unconscious. Owen wasn't sure if he was glad or not. Part of him wanted Wade to be awake, to see how Owen was taking care of him, but a larger part dreaded how Wade would fight him.

Better to defeat some of the demons now, while Wade was asleep.

WADE CAME TO slowly. His body hurt all over, and his tongue felt thick, fuzzy, and strange. As he took a deep breath, the smell of urine was so overwhelming he gagged. He opened his eyes, but he couldn't see. Pitch black surrounded him. And then he felt it—a gut-churning, clenching pain in his abdomen, like strong cramps during a stomach virus—and he jerked entirely awake, suddenly realizing that he might crap himself if he didn't get to a toilet.

But he couldn't move. No matter hard he tried, he couldn't budge.

His hands were tied over his head with what felt like thick, wrapped ropes that pulled him taut, and his eyes were covered with a mask of some sort that had pads pressing against his lids so that he couldn't open them. Worse, he was naked, and his legs were tied to something that forced them both up, and apart, as though his ankles were bound to something tall. Thick straps wrapped around his chest and lower torso, holding him flat against a hard, ruthlessly unforgiving surface.

Wade's heart pounded, his stomach cramped again, and he gasped sharply, as panic ripped through him. He tried to jerk and pull, terrified sounds bursting out, but he was bound so tightly he had no room to maneuver. His mind scrambled. Where was he? How did he get here? Was he hurt? He didn't feel any pain except for the horrible cramps in his stomach. He screamed, but it was weak and sounded muffled to his own ears. He tried again, but the noise seemed to absorb instead of echo. He desperately searched his mind for a memory, anything at all.

He'd been with Owen. In Los Angeles. He'd come to visit. Russ had taken him to the airport, and he'd fallen asleep during a dumb comedy on the flight. He'd gone to his hotel, checked in, showered, and then met Owen. He'd had cookies. He'd started to feel sick.

His heart hammered so hard it felt like it would beat out of his chest, and he cried out as another painful cramp shot through him, tearing into him like being stabbed on the inside. Sweaty and sick, he struggled against the restraints, though every movement made his abdomen hurt more.

"Help!" he called out. "I don't want to do this anymore!"

He didn't know if he'd ever wanted to do this. It seemed unlikely. But he definitely didn't want it now. His mind supplied him with the sudden, terrifying understanding that he was tied up, naked, and in a position where he could easily be raped. If he hadn't been already. He listened hard. He seemed to be alone.

"Hello? Anyone? Help me! Please!"

Nothing happened. No one came. He didn't hear anyone else in the room. He tried yelling but the sound seemed muffled again, like screaming into a pillow.

Was he dead? Was he dreaming? A swirl of unreality washed over him, and he relaxed a little. It was a dream. He could wake up now. And he waited. But nothing happened except for another torturous stab of pain in his stomach.

It was real. Whatever was happening was real.

The pain was overwhelming, undeniable. He'd been with Owen. Had they been kidnapped? He hoped Owen was okay, that they hadn't hurt him. He groaned, thinking of Russ, his ash-brown hair in sunlight, his eyes when he'd kissed him goodbye. Was that the last time he'd see him? Was Wade going to be killed here? He screamed again, struggling. No. He wasn't ready to die. Their life together was just starting. He wasn't ready.

"If you want money. I have a lot of it," he bluffed. "I'll give it to you. However much you want. All of it," Wade offered, helplessly. There was no answer and wild hyperventilation took over. His body shook like it was coming apart. "Please."

His skin was sticky all over, like he was covered in a film of something half-dried, and his hair was wet. The stench of urine was strong, and he realized with another sickening jolt that he'd probably pissed himself.

There was the sound of a door opening and his heart leapt with fear and hope. Was someone going to help him? Kill him? Hurt him now?

"Who's there?" he asked, shaky and raw.

"Wade?"

Wade swallowed hard, relief flooding him. "Owen, thank God. Help me."

"You're waking up," Owen said.

Wade's mind jammed. Owen sounded…he sounded calm, and not at all surprised. "Owen?"

He heard footsteps, could feel the air particles move as Owen stood next to him, and Wade strained against everything holding him down. Owen didn't do anything to help him get free.

Wade's abdomen pierced again, and he felt an uncontrollable urge to push down, to expel the painful contents of his gut.

"Starting to hurt?" Owen asked, and Wade jerked at the sensation of Owen's hand pressing against his aching abdomen. "Go ahead and push. You won't get much out. Not with this in your ass."

Wade trembled as Owen's big hand ran down to cup a buttock, and then his fingers tapped against a thick, hard piece stuck there. Wade cried out. His ass was full with a plug. He'd been too scared before, and too desperate not to shit himself, to notice.

"And this harness holds it in," Owen went on, pulling on something that was wrapped very tightly around Wade's hips, something with straps. "You couldn't push it out if you tried."

Wade gasped and struggled. Horror filled him, as he started to understand. He'd been in the car with Owen. He ate cookies. He'd felt sick and wanted to call Kari. And Owen had thrown his phone out the window. That was the last thing he remembered.

Wade's blood ran cold.

"Owen, please. You don't have to do this. You're hurting me." It sounded pitiful and empty, and strangely muffled too.

"No, I do. I'm saving you," Owen said, caressing Wade's body with strong, firm, massaging strokes. It ached and hurt like hell when Owen pressed against his stomach.

"Saving me?" Wade sounded small to his own ears, small and very scared.

"I'll explain it all eventually. For now, just trust me. I'm doing this for you, and one day soon you'll thank me. And even if you never do, even if you fight me until the end, I'm not going to let you down, Wade. Because after everything, I realize now, I love you."

Wade's mind spun. He couldn't speak. He couldn't breathe. None of this could be real. It had to be a nightmare, because this kind of thing didn't happen. Not in real life. Not outside of scary movies.

"You're hurting me." He said it as reasonably as he could. "If this is a joke, it's not funny." Wade's mind whirled, dizzy with fear.

"I'll move you soon, don't worry. I'm sure your legs are starting to go numb." As Owen talked, he touched Wade, fondling and rubbing. "First I need to finish cleaning you so that we can close off the portal he started in your body."

Warm, wet liquid hit his chest and ran over him. He gagged. He hadn't pissed himself. He was covered in *Owen's* piss. From head to foot.

Owen hummed. "You wouldn't believe how much water I had to drink today," Owen said. "It's taking a lot of cleaning to get his scent off of you. I'm not surprised. He's dumped his cum in you for so long now. You're full of demons. Do you feel them dying, Wade? When I piss on you, does it burn your skin? Dad said it might burn, but it has to be done."

Wade was struck dumb with violation and horror. And Owen's dad? He was dead, wasn't he? He'd read the obituary and sent flowers. What was Owen talking about? He gagged again but didn't throw up.

"The demons fight the cleansing, Wade. But don't worry, when I'm done, we can release the demon carcasses from your ass. I pissed there first," Owen said.

Wade choked on vomit.

"Your colon is the place where the gateway opened. The greatest concentration of new demons will be there. Did he touch you this morning? I'm sure he did. He couldn't let you go without making sure the gateway was safe. They'll suck him back into hell if he lets them down. He doesn't want that."

Oh, God. Owen was *insane*, completely and totally fucked-up insane. The terror inside swelled—absolute and all consuming. Owen could do anything. Anything at all to him. Owen could kill him if he wanted to.

Wade struggled but it was useless. Piss poured on him. A hot, wet rush over Wade's abdomen, on his cock, and then in his hair again, and even in his ears, making a weird streaming, hissing sound that filled up his Eustachian tubes.

Another sharp pain in his stomach wrenched, and Owen murmured a comforting sound. "I know. I know it hurts. It's not like any other enema. The demons are dying and that's why it's so bad. Just breathe through it. I'll let you use the bathroom when I'm done. After we make love."

Piss everywhere. Even in his ass. And now Owen was talking about *making love?*

No. He was talking about *raping* him.

"Owen," Wade said, voice shaking. "Please stop. You're scaring me. Please. I don't want to do this."

"Shut up!" Owen grabbed Wade's face, and squeezed his cheeks hard. "New rules, Wade! You don't talk until I tell you to talk. You don't *shit* until I tell you to shit. You don't piss. You don't eat. You don't *breathe*. Do you understand?"

Owen pried open Wade's mouth as he fought to keep it closed. Pinching Wade's nose, cutting off his air, Owen pressed against Wade's face determinedly. Wade struggled for breath, and then his abdomen clenched again. A scream ripped from his throat. Owen forced a plastic ball-gag in his mouth.

Huffing through his nose, he struggled to keep from throwing up, his gag reflex triggered.

"This is all to help you," Owen said, sounding almost calm again. "I can't help you if you fight me."

Wade groaned, and tried to struggle, but the straps were too tight, cutting into him when he squirmed.

"This room's sound proof. It's underground. Padded thoroughly. No one even knows it exists. So you can yell as loud as you need to eventually. And you will. Getting the demons free is going to hurt a lot, and I'm sorry for that. But, right now, I can't stand to hear it." Owen's voice went soft. "I'm scared, too, you know. What if it doesn't work? I have to stay focused. I have to do this. I can't lose you again."

Wade yelled around the gag.

Owen slapped his face. "Shut up! I won't let the demons trick me. You want my help! The real you? Deep down inside? You know you need me to save you."

Wade shook his head frantically, trying to breathe but all he could do was hyperventilate. Dizziness and blue spots swirled, like he might pass out. He wanted to, if only to make it go away, but he was scared of what might happen if he did.

"I'm gonna make love to you now," Owen said, slipping into a stronger Southern accent. "I've waited a long time and he told me it was the best way to kill them. Semen of light to kill semen of darkness."

Wade shook his head. The blindfold was tight and no light peeked through. He felt Owen's hand trail down the side of his body, and he tried to shrink away, grunting a negative sound around the gag, but he couldn't escape his touch even a little.

Wade stiffened when Owen climbed onto the table. His heavy weight settled on Wade's body, covering him, putting pressure on his distended abdomen. He grunted, rage swelling in him when Owen's hard cock slotted in beside Wade's flaccid one. He tried to head-butt him, but had no force behind the impact, and Owen simply gripped handfuls of Wade's hair, holding his head still as he began to hump him.

Each forceful thrust pushed against his screaming gut, tearing at his insides, and Wade shrieked. The pain from his overfull and convulsing colon was so sharp and intense, he wailed on and on, shouting in agony. Owen's thrusts became increasingly rapid and harsh, and he whispered in Wade's ear, "Yes, that's it. Scream. I know it hurts. They're clawing you trying to get out. But I've got you."

Owen licked Wade's lips, slimy and wet. "I anoint your lips with my saliva, may it destroy the evil in your screams." He licked them again, and then spit on Wade's mouth, using his tongue to rub the glob around on his lips and face.

Wade's throat tore as he screamed louder and longer than he'd known possible, and then Owen moaned, and scrambled up. As the weight left his body, Wade groaned in relief, until he felt the hot, wet splash of Owen's cum on his face. It slipped down his cheeks and over his lips, spattered his chin and neck. Desperate sobs wracked him as the bitter taste flooded his mouth, and he had no idea when he'd begun to cry.

Owen hushed him. "That's good, Wade. It's just the beginning, but now we're getting somewhere." Owen rubbed his cum all over Wade's face, smearing it over his jaw, nose, forehead, and mouth, and even lifting the blindfold enough to smear some just under it, but not quite to Wade's eyes.

"Shut up, Dad!" Owen suddenly yelled, climbing down from the table. "I know what I'm doing! I *can*. I *will*. Get out!"

Wade listened for the sound of a door, for the sound of anyone else, but heard nothing. As he panted, Owen's hand moved down to grasp Wade's flaccid cock. Wade groaned as another cramp hit him, his body trying to dump his bowels but unable to expel it.

"Cum for me, and I'll let you take a crap, okay? It's as easy as that."

Wade grunted and shook his head. This was *not happening*.

But Owen's hand was on him, moving and pumping, and Wade's cock responded. Horrified, he realized he wasn't able to keep from getting hard, the pleasure joining and growing with the fear and disgust in Wade's mind.

"You were always such a slut," Owen whispered. "Getting on PrEP, fucking strangers raw, doing it with anyone at all."

Wade moaned.

"That's the reason I didn't fuck you. I didn't want to encourage your anal fixation. But I was wrong. I realize that now. If I'd kept you satisfied, you wouldn't have fallen into *his* bed, and he never could have used you, infected you the way he did."

Wade tried to move out of his skin, away from the hand that was bringing him up to an aching hardness. His mind went to Russ, and he wondered how much time had passed. If Russ might know that something was wrong yet. How long did he have to hang on until he could know for sure that Russ was looking for him?

"Don't fight it, Wade. You don't want your intestines to rupture, do you? A little orgasm for me, and you'll feel a lot better." Owen's hand moved quickly on Wade's cock. "Just let me make love to you."

Wade yelled as the hot, sweet pull of a hand job began to overtake him. He couldn't fight it. He needed to stop the pain. Cumming was his only way out. His mind scrambled to find something to focus on, something sexy and comforting, but as soon as he thought of Russ again, he instinctively pulled his mind away. No, Russ had nothing to do with this disturbing pleasure. Nothing to do with it at all.

No sooner had he refused to think of Russ, than he heard his voice in his head, crystal clear:

You have to get out of this Wade. Do what you need to do in order to get home to me. Let him get you off.

Wade gave in, letting his body respond, and when he got close to cumming, the table shifted, and the part under Wade's ass fell away. He groaned around the gag in his mouth, his abdomen clenching and spasming.

A rush of pleasure descended, whiting out the world as his orgasm unfurled, and then he screamed as Owen pulled the plug from his ass. Spurting wet, foul mess from his anus in relief, he skyrocketed into a blinding orgasm, shaking and shooting hot bursts of cum over Owen's hand, overwhelmed and consumed.

As Wade came down to find himself still horrifyingly trapped, still kidnapped and now raped by his oldest friend, Owen rubbed a soothing hand on his leg. "That was good. So much came out of you. We must have killed a lot of them."

Wade whimpered.

Owen sniffed at him. He felt Owen's nose running over his body, and suddenly Owen gagged. "I can still smell him!" Owen yelled. "I smell him on you."

Wade tongued the back of the ball gag, choking, tears running down his face, and he sucked in heaving, sick, breaths full of terror.

"It's okay, Wade," Owen said, his voice hard. "I'm not through with you yet. I'll never give up. No matter how long it takes."

Chapter Three

TIME PASSED. WADE had no idea how to measure it. For all he knew, he'd been at Owen's mercy for weeks.

Owen never left him alone for more than a few hours at a time, spending most of Wade's waking hours tormenting him and calling it love. Enduring Owen's attempts to drive out Russ's demons left Wade little time for thinking. Being tied to a wall and whipped from head to toe, and then pissed on before being forced to cum, required all of Wade's mental powers just to survive. Even then there were times when he blacked out from the pain and exhaustion.

He only tried to escape once. He took the opportunity of Owen unbuckling and unshackling him to try to knock him down, to punch him out in hopes of getting the key to the door and escaping. His punch had landed, but Wade was weak from lack of food, lack of sleep, and an overabundance of shocking pain. Owen just rubbed his jaw, frowned, and said the demons would pay for Wade's disobedience.

And he did pay. Hard.

Owen tied his arms with a long rope attached to some rings in the ceiling and forced a wide spacer bar between Wade's ankles. Pushing a vibrating prostate stimulator into Wade's ass to milk him of as much cum as possible, he continued with his delusional explanations, saying the demons couldn't live in Wade if all of Russ's semen was pumped out of his body. The fact that

Wade's semen was his own meant nothing to Owen, who told Wade only that he didn't understand how the demons work, and that Russ had infected him so that all the semen Wade made was actually Russ's. Wade stopped asking questions when Owen suggested that one permanent solution was to remove Wade's testicles so that the demons no longer had vehicle for reproducing their evil. He didn't want Owen giving that too much thought.

After stringing Wade up with the stimulator working in his ass, Owen flogged him until he was shaking and begging for mercy, bleeding from the barely healed places where his skin had broken during a prior attempt to beat out the demons. Then Owen left him alone, strung up and in pain, with his prostate being pounded by the vibrator until he screamed and screamed. He'd been milked so thoroughly that cum pooled on the floor between his feet. A long string of it attached to his hard cock and stretched to the shimmering, glossy puddle like a spider-web of forced pleasure.

His arms burned, stretched up so tightly and long, and his pelvis flared with shameful lust and over-stimulated agony. His body wasn't his own. It responded the way Owen wanted and his disgust and horror didn't make it stop. He needed to cum to get rest, but he hated cumming and the way it stripped him of everything he knew about himself. But when Owen finally returned, stroked a hand down Wade's side, and said with a hideous smirk, "Are you ready to let me help you?" there was nothing else Wade could do.

"Yes. Please let me cum. Please." He sobbed, broken and desperate.

Owen smiled, reaching for Wade's cock. He swirled his fingers over the head and smeared the pre-cum around. "See? That wasn't so hard, was it?"

He moved behind Wade, removed the vibrating plug, and

Wade almost cried in relief, until Owen thrust inside of him in one violent, dry fuck that made tears sting Wade's eyes and a new wave of sweat break out over his body.

"Ask me to fuck you. And say it nicely, Wade. Say it so that I know you love me."

Wade nearly vomited, but he said it. "Fuck me, Owen. Please fuck me. I love you."

"That's good, Wade. You're getting better all the time. Some day, you'll be fixed and it'll be just you in there."

He fucked Wade so roughly he saw stars behind his eyes. Owen reached around, jerking Wade's cock, and he cursed under his breath as he was fucked closer and closer to orgasm. A string of venomous hate left his mouth, until Owen put a hand around Wade's throat and squeezed his windpipe, cutting off Wade's breath and his words, saying, "Cum for me, you slut."

And Wade came.

He came so damn hard he lost the strength in his legs, collapsing down so that pain ripped through his shoulder blades, and he yelled as the agony only seemed to intensify the orgasm.

Owen shot his load up Wade's ass, biting his shoulder and slapping his hip hard.

When the convulsing was over for them both, Owen said, "That's right. You'll cum when I tell you to cum and never again with anyone else."

Wade readily agreed, knowing that was what Owen wanted to hear, but the words tasted like vomit.

Over time, the bizarre combination of nausea and orgasm became familiar to him, like breathing, and he lived in it for what seemed like a lifetime. The sexual agony and pleasure went on and on, long past his ability to cope, and Wade gratefully passed out after being hurt for hours, only to be wakened and forced to cum again.

The oblivion of orgasm became his mind's only escape.

OWEN COULDN'T GET Russ's smell off Wade no matter how hard he tried. It drove him crazy, making him itch all over and explode in rage he couldn't contain. He'd pissed on him, cum on him, cum *in* him, and pissed in his ass every day for almost two weeks now, but nothing defeated the sulfur stench of the demons living in Wade's body.

Owen was losing patience. He hated that smell. He hated how the demons inside of Wade tried to manipulate him into feeling sorry for their host, tried to convince him not to hurt Wade, even though Owen *had* to hurt him. It was the only way. He hated how, when he was fucking Wade, the demons would work on his cock from the inside, making it feel even better when Wade screamed, making Owen cum extra hard when he lurched and cried out in pain.

He suspected it was because he *liked* killing the demons that he was unsuccessful in destroying them for good. He knew if he enjoyed the demons' struggles to live in Wade that he would no longer be pure enough to defeat them entirely. The best he could hope for was to keep them at bay. His father was right. His lust for Wade made him weak.

Owen strapped Wade to the table, arms tied overhead, legs spread and shackled. He wrapped Wade's balls tightly with a long shoestring he'd brought down for this purpose. That morning Owen had been in the kitchen, looking out the big windows toward the view of the mountains, wondering if he was going to manage to win this fight before the police found them. He knew they were looking for Wade.

Probably.

It's not like he had family after all. Only Russ and Kari would notice or care.

"He makes too much of the demon seed," his father had said in his ear as he ate cereal and stared out the window. "Cut them off or tie them up. Slow the process down."

So Owen wrapped Wade's testicles up tight with a shoestring, until they shone purple and bright.

Wade cried, long, wild, shameless wailing sobs which made Owen's cock ache. He didn't beg anymore, or try to reason, and rarely did he plead for anything but to cum. It was working, though Wade sometimes still fought—if Owen made it hurt enough, if he shattered him with pain. Owen didn't tell his father, but he understood now why Wade had so easily succumbed to Russ and become a gateway for hell. Fucking felt so good. No girl's pussy had ever felt so tight or alive. And his orgasms were massive, intoxicating, and addictive.

Once Wade's balls were tied off, Owen lined Wade's body with clothespins on a string. He pinched the skin of Wade's cock and scrotum and nipples and then snapped the pin in place, dripping pre-cum when Wade screamed with each new addition. Finally, he was ready. He slid his cock into Wade's tight ass, holding it there while Wade sobbed, squirmed, and shook his head.

Owen had never felt anything like the ecstasy that pummeled him when he gave Wade pain. And nothing compared to the orgasm Owen experienced when he gripped the string and jerked backwards, wrenching all the clothespins free at once. Wade screamed in agony, his body arching against the restraints, his neck flexed and his eyes rolled back. His asshole clamped on Owen's cock, and he came and came. Owen collapsed on Wade as he filled his ass with cum again.

Pulling free, he shoved a plug up into him, a bigger one than he'd used before, and shivered when Wade screamed again. A trickle of blood slipped down the side of Wade's asscheek.

"You tore me," Wade whimpered, when he finally stopped yelling.

"Shut up," Owen answered. "That's the demon speaking."

He grabbed a riding crop, snapping it down on Wade's purple, restrained balls. Wade screamed again, and Owen paused to force in a ball-gag. Wade's entire body clenched and unclenched, straining against the ropes, flushed and sweaty with pain.

Owen's cock jerked and a small bit of pre-cum slid down the side of his shaft. He took the crop to Wade's balls again and again, screaming at the demons, commanding them to leave, to get out of Wade's body.

Wade convulsed, wailing. And then suddenly Wade went silent, and Owen saw he'd passed out again.

It infuriated him when that happened. He wasn't sure why. Part of him thought he could try to beat the demons out whether Wade was awake or not, and surely it would be kinder to Wade, so that he didn't have to endure the agony of the demons' deaths. But it wasn't as rewarding to Owen. He liked the satisfaction of hearing the demons' die as their screams came ripping out of Wade's throat.

He set aside the crop and went to the wall. There were things he could do to prepare for when Wade woke up. He took down the electrodes and retrieved the electrostim kit from a drawer. He'd read that the electrodes would burn the skin without the proper lubricant, but he didn't see any reason to worry about that. The real reason for the conduction lube was to increase the surface space of pain. The more pain he could summon in Wade, the less the demons would find his body a good home.

Owen placed the electrodes on Wade's tied balls, and up and down the length of Wade's cock. He glanced up as Wade groaned and snuffled, and waited patiently until Wade's hazel eyes opened and looked to him. The fear on his face made Owen's cock jerk again, and he had to reach a hand down to stroke it.

"This will end when you cum," Owen said, and he turned on the electricity, dialing it up to a level that made Wade's eyes fly wide, and his entire body flex and strain. Owen stroked his own cock watching Wade fight. Wade's eyes bulged, and his entire body jerked and writhed against the ropes. Owen's gaze went down to his cock, the red, tied length of it lifting and trembling with each jolt of electricity, and there was a new odor, a burning smell, and Owen smiled—he was scorching the demons out. The scent of their death.

"It's working," Owen said. "They're dying now. And when you cum, they'll be out of you. Maybe it's the last of them, and you'll finally be okay." He turned the knob one setting higher and Wade's broken scream pierced the air. He couldn't wait anymore. He pulled out the butt plug, positioned himself at Wade's hole, and rammed inside. It was a hard fit since Wade was so tense, but he forced it, and hot blood slicked the way. Wade's hole spasmed and jerked around him, massaging his cock.

Then he felt them. The demons. They sucked at his dick in greedy grabs, pulling him in more and more, trying to seduce him, to trick him into letting them stay, but he wouldn't have it. He turned the electricity up another notch and Wade's hole clenched around him hard. Owen slapped Wade's balls with his hand, reached up and pinched Wade's bruised and swollen nipples, digging in with his nails, and then screamed, "Cum, dammit! Cum! Get out of him! Get out!"

Wade jerked and jerked under the onslaught of the electricity, his cock streamed with pre-cum draining from him in copious amounts, but it wasn't enough. Russ's semen was endless inside him, and Owen lunged forward, grabbed Wade's throat with one hand, covered his ball-gagged mouth and nose with the other, and fucked into Wade's gripping ass, screaming, "Cum, or I'll let him die! I'll suffocate you demons out of him, you fucking monsters!"

Wade's eyes were wide and terrified, but then the wet, hot pulse of Wade's cock between them let Owen know he'd won. He'd defeated the demons again. But he kept his hands on Wade's mouth, nose, and throat as he fucked him hard, cumming in his ass, coating the demons inside with his powerful seed. It was glorious, and hard to handle, because it felt so good.

He struggled to catch his breath through the aftershocks, and only then let go of Wade, watching as Wade gulped in breath with a gratitude that made Owen proud.

He could do this. His father was wrong. Owen would absolutely win.

"PLEASE, OWEN," WADE said. "I need a break. Just a little break. I don't think I can cum again unless I rest."

He was strung up from the ceiling, his arms aching and his fingers gone numb. His legs were held apart with a spacer bar, and his dick was kept hard with a cock ring, so that no matter how many orgasms Owen managed to wrench from him, he never went completely flaccid.

Owen's eyes were cold, and he shook his head. "Shut up," he said. "You don't speak to me, Demon. Get out of Wade's body. It doesn't belong to you."

Wade panted softly, every part of him aching, sore, cut, or bruised. "Does it belong to you, Owen?" he asked, hoping to get through the insanity, to touch the man inside that Wade had cared for once. He had to be in there somewhere.

Owen's lips curled into a snarl, and his eyes lit with a rage so intense that Wade regretted his words. Owen grabbed his hair, pulled him forward and spit in his face. "Yes. He belongs to me, Demon. Get the hell out of him."

Wade groaned when Owen thrust him back, making him lose his balance so that a tearing pain in his arms wrenched him, and he closed his eyes and dug down deep for something to hold onto. An image of Russ swam to the surface of his mind.

Russ looking over legal briefs, frowning at whatever he saw there. Russ's quick smile when he laughed, the imperfections of his teeth, the tender way he stroked Wade's chin—

"What are you doing?" Owen whispered. "You're thinking of him. You crave him, don't you? You crave the demon's dick inside of you. You *want* to be hell's portal."

Wade kept his eyes closed, turned his mind away from Russ, because he wasn't welcome here in this place where Wade was in pain and scared. That wasn't where Russ belonged. He belonged to safety, and care, and love. So, he focused instead on what his body was feeling, the pain, the aches, and the horrible pleasure of his hard cock thudding with restricted blood. This was here. This was now, and he was going to try to live through it. Again.

Owen was close. He could feel Owen's breath on the side of his neck, feel his body heat and the movements behind him, but still Wade didn't open his eyes.

"Answer me," Owen said. "You want it. You want him."

Wade's breath came in harsh, hyperventilating puffs; he recognized the rising rage in Owen's tone. He knew there was no good answer. Yes would result in pain. No would result in pain. He didn't want to give Owen the satisfaction of speaking.

"Answer me!"

"I hate you," Wade muttered. It was only partially true. He hated Owen for hurting him, for making him cum, for torturing him. But he hated him the most for being insane, for having broken in such a way that he'd do this to Wade, so that Wade couldn't even blame him, because how do you blame a person who doesn't even know that they're wrong? And yet he hated him so damn much.

"That's a demon," Owen said. "Wade loves me. And when I get all of you out of him, he'll tell me how grateful he is. Tell me now, Wade! Thank me for helping you!"

Wade trembled and waited for the pain, and his fear escalated as nothing happened. And then he felt it—the bright, cold edge of a knife at his balls. He went very still, adrenaline shooting through him so hard and fast that he felt like the top of his head might burst off.

"Say it," Owen said, his voice deadly quiet. "Say it or I'll cut the demons out of you."

Wade whispered, "Thank you for helping me, Owen."

Owen was directly behind him now, and Wade fought the moan as he felt Owen push into his sore, torn ass. He whimpered as the blade scraped against his balls again, threatening in its continued presence.

Then Wade's blood ran cold as he felt another sharp knife at his throat.

Owen was pressed against Wade's back, his dick buried in Wade's ass, holding one knife to Wade's balls and another to his throat.

Wade slowly opened his eyes, taking in the dirty room around him. Everything was covered with piss, cum, shit, or blood, even his tiny bed in the corner where he barely spent any time. As Owen rocked in and out of Wade's ass, fucking him slowly, Wade wondered if this room would be the last thing he ever saw.

Owen's thrusts grew rapid and ragged, and Wade's eyes rolled up, his cock was sore and aching, his prostate horribly bruised, and the scrape of the knives on the skin of his scrotum and neck was terrifying.

"I'll slit his throat if I have to," Owen whispered. "I can do it, Dad. I have it in me."

Wade opened his mouth to speak, but the knife at his throat shoved tighter against his jugular, and he held himself as still as possible as Owen fucked into him.

"Cum for me," Owen said. "Cum for me or die on my cock."

Wade whimpered, his dick was hard, yes, but it was getting no stimulation, and he was so scared that he might pass out. He couldn't breathe with the knives against his skin, much less cum.

"Cum, Wade!" Owen yelled. "Get out of him, you bastards! I'll cut his balls off! I'll kill him!"

Blue and black spots swirled in Wade's vision, and he strained for some kind of feeling like orgasm, but there was nothing. His heart pounded, blood rushed in his ears, and he let himself think of Russ—intense, determined, handsome Russ. If he was going to die, then he wanted to go out with Russ in his mind, not this fear and terror, but then Owen screamed, an agonized yell.

Owen yelled in a crazed voice, almost like he couldn't believe it himself, but was determined none-the-less, "You have ten seconds, and if you're not out of him, I'll cut them off, and if that doesn't work, I *will* kill him."

Wade's mind exploded. A rushing sound in his ears overrode every other noise, except the countdown to his balls being severed and his throat slit.

He felt himself arcing up through layers of fear he'd never imagined, and suddenly, out of nowhere, as Owen said "four", Wade felt orgasm rip from him. His cock pulsed with a glory that consumed him. He screamed as Owen nicked his scrotum, pulling the knife tight, cumming in Wade's ass at the same time.

The door to the room kicked open, three policemen with guns pushed through the door, and Wade felt a sharp pain at his neck. Then there was nothing.

47

PART TWO

Chapter Four

Four Months Later

WADE DIDN'T KNOW how he felt about his psychologist. The guy was nice enough, he supposed, and had some good advice. But their daily two hours together were spent with Wade reliving the horror of the weeks he'd spent being tortured in an underground room in California. So it wasn't as though Wade really had positive feelings associated with the guy.

But Dr. Salinas was the best of the best when it came to trauma recovery. Russ had made sure of that when he scoured Atlanta to find the right doctor to work with Wade. That, Wade knew, was because Russ loved him and wanted him well, and so he appreciated his efforts even when he had no idea how he was ever going to be 'well' again. Sometimes he wondered if all the money Russ dumped into helping him was ever going to be worth it.

The work Dr. Salinas specialized in was known as EMDR and it'd appealed to Russ because it didn't consist entirely of touchy-feely emotional moments, but rather a scientifically backed method of processing memories. It was accomplished via achieving the same brain waves reached during the REM stages of sleep. Russ had talked a lot about the theory and science behind it all when Wade first began the therapy, but he'd mostly tuned the details out. He didn't know or really care what the exact phenomenon was, he just knew Russ wanted him to do it, and, drowning in numbness interspersed with pain, Wade didn't see any reason why he shouldn't.

Aside from the trauma of reliving the memories over and over, that is.

But that was something he was going to do anyway—sometimes at completely unfortunate and unexpected moments. And it was better to relive them on purpose than to find himself trapped in a crystalized horror while walking down a sidewalk or having coffee with a friend.

Dr. Salinas was a short man with dark black hair, pale skin, wire rim glasses, and a wide, handsome smile that he flashed whenever Wade arrived but rarely showed again. Not that Wade blamed him. There was little to smile about in what Wade discussed during the sessions. There were days when Wade felt guilty for having to ruin Dr. Salinas's day with his confessions.

The chair Wade sat in during the sessions was comfortable at least. At this point in his life being comfortable in a chair was praiseworthy. Along with all of his other physical injuries, his torn asshole had taken a long time to heal and for over a month sitting had been incredibly painful.

There'd even been some fear of permanent damage to his sphincter. Wade considered himself lucky beyond belief that he could control his bowels as well as he had before the kidnapping, even if taking pride in that accomplishment made him feel infantile. All in all, considering how injured he'd been when they'd found him, he'd was lucky to come out of it with a few physical scars and a metric shit ton of emotional issues.

It was the emotional issues he was in Dr. Salinas's office to deal with five days a week. Though the technical diagnosis was PTSD.

The earphones he wore for the therapy were the large, old-fashioned kind, and they felt like pleasant cushions on his head—

except when he sometimes flashed back to Owen pissing in his ears. On those days, when the earphones triggered him, Dr. Salinas used flashing lights instead, though Wade thought they were less effective.

When he'd expressed that opinion to Russ, he almost wished he hadn't.

Russ's gray eyes had taken on a hopeful gleam. "You think the therapy is becoming effective? You've had some breakthroughs?"

Wade hated to let him down.

"I don't know," Wade had answered. "Sometimes I feel a weight lift off my chest a little. Or a shifting of tension in my thighs."

Russ had nodded and given him the "I love you" look of warm encouragement he'd perfected over the last four months. Seeking comfort, Wade had leaned into him, breathing in his spicy cologne and snuggled up against his strong chest.

"Where do you want to start today, Wade?" Dr. Salinas asked. He sat in a comfortable chair, his ankles crossed, and a note pad in hand. The pad was to keep track of the moments when Wade's eyes moved a certain way, indicating that REM state was briefly achieved, and that the memory was being re-categorized or re-processed. "The beginning, the middle, the end…or the hospital?"

Wade didn't like to choose. He preferred it when Dr. Salinas said whatever they'd worked on the day before wasn't done yet and he needed to go over it again. It was never fun, always emotional and gut wrenching, but there was something to be said about the familiarity of telling the same part of the story over and over, which, he supposed, was part of the process of the therapy, desensitizing him to the experience of the memory itself.

Eventually, he'd have the option to mentally go into the

memory and imagine new, different, less horrific events, so he no longer had to remember the trauma as it had actually occurred unless he wanted. It seemed strange to imagine a time when he wouldn't be thrown full on into horror whenever his mind tripped over a reminder, but Dr. Salinas assured him that eventually he'd have a stronger grip on his mind in most circumstances.

Choosing what to work through, though, was a whole other matter. It meant a festering wound would be prodded and horrific humiliations shared with someone else besides Russ.

Wade sighed—and that was another thing that worried him, actually. He told Dr. Salinas things about his experience he was still too ashamed to share with Russ. Obviously, he'd told Russ that he'd been raped—well, his medical charts had told him that—and he'd told him he'd been forced to orgasm, and that he'd been hurt, and tortured, and demeaned.

But he hadn't told Russ that the orgasms had been astonishingly powerful. And he hadn't shared that he was ashamed, disgusted, and horrified by how strong they'd been. Nor had he told him that the idea of cumming again, ever, terrified him completely. That he felt like his sexuality had been stripped away—forced out of him in giant puddles of cum, and ripped from him in ruthless orgasms.

Dr. Salinas assured Wade that what he'd experienced was common for rape victims. He wasn't alone. "The body and brain often compensate for unsustainable fear and pain by rerouting and prioritizing pleasure. Many raped and abused people report orgasms, even extraordinarily strong orgasms, despite their pain and fear. Despite not wanting it, and doing nothing to deserve it. It's common and normal."

Wade understood and believed him.

But he still couldn't tell any of that to Russ. He wanted Russ to believe, no matter what happened between them now, that the most intense orgasm Wade ever experienced had been in his arms. For unexamined reasons, Wade needed Russ to believe that more than he needed to believe it himself.

"Well?" Dr. Salinas prodded, tapping his pencil on his pad, and giving a close-lipped smile of encouragement.

Wade closed his eyes a moment. "Yes, I'm ready."

"All right. Let's start. What are we working on today?"

"I don't know."

"Give it some thought."

Wade let it rush over him.

The beginning? Waking up bound and covered in piss, realizing Owen was his captor, first glimpsing his insanity.

The middle? His balls and penis tortured until he passed out, whippings that left his back a mess of open cuts, the pain of infections beginning in wounds, the indignity of forced piss-enemas, and the coerced orgasms that left him feeling violated and terrorized.

The end? The horror of the knives—one against his scrotum and one held to his neck—the certainty he was going to die, the intense orgasm that'd nearly swallowed him whole, and that he'd thought would be the last thing he'd ever feel, the police charging in to save him.

The hospital? The pain and humiliation of callous examinations, rough hands in tender places, and the sharp points of needles, all before Russ had been there barking legal threats angrily at the nurses and doctors who'd hurt him.

Wade had been so traumatized when he first arrived at the hospital, he hadn't known for sure if he was alive or dead. He fought nurses who wanted to sedate him, refusing to sleep for fear that he'd wake up back in Owen's room. It wasn't until Russ had climbed into the hospital bed with him, held him close, and hummed in his ear as the nurses administered the sedative, that he could fall asleep.

Wade sighed.

"It's your call," Dr. Salinas said.

Nodding slowly, Wade put the earphones on.

Today he'd start at the end.

KARI WAS WAITING for him in Dr. Salinas's lobby. Her hennaed hair swung back from her round face as he exited the therapy room. Dressed in a swirly, multicolored skirt, and a black tank top, she was a beacon of patchouli-scented love, and she hugged him like she hadn't just seen him two hours before.

"I'm okay, Kari," Wade said, bending to kiss her soft cheek. She looked so damn worried. "A little therapy never killed a guy."

She tried to laugh but her gentle brown eyes didn't sparkle. She slapped a hand on his chest, and then hugged him again. He let her. Holding Kari was good for him. She was soft and motherly, with a big bosom and some flesh on her bones. Her touch never made him remember anything he wanted to forget.

As they settled into her car, Kari passed him a take-out bag from Jink's Deli. "Russ said I had to make sure you ate something right after your session. I told him you didn't need a babysitter, and then he tried to kill me with his eyes. So, I promised."

Wade looked into the bag and pulled out a Jink's ham and swiss sandwich with special sauce. He sighed and wondered if he could choke the sandwich down. Russ would ask Kari if he ate and Wade didn't want her to lie. He also didn't want to tell Russ to back off. Sure, he was a big boy and could decide when and if he wanted to eat, but Russ was only doing what he could to relieve his own guilt and pain.

Russ tried not to let it show, but he'd suffered too. He'd agonized for weeks thinking Wade was dead. And when Wade had finally been discovered, with plenty of proof the he'd lived through torture of a brutal and sexual nature, Russ had grieved hard for what Wade had been through.

There were stages to grief. He'd heard about it growing up every time someone he loved died, or got hurt, and now he heard about it almost every day. Russ seemed stuck on anger when it came to Owen. He tried not to let it show, but Wade could see how his eyes flared with pain and hate at the mention of Owen's name. Wade couldn't blame him. If someone had done to Russ what Owen had done to him, Wade couldn't account for what he'd do.

And, in the case of Owen, there was nothing Russ *could* do.

According to the police, Owen had lost his balance when Wade passed out. He'd failed to cut Wade's jugular, leaving only a superficial wound to the side of his neck. As Owen had gone down, stumbling over the spreader bar between Wade's ankles, the police had fired. The kill shot had been clean. Straight through the head. He hadn't suffered at all.

Wade was fine with that.

Except when he wasn't.

Except when he woke at night in a blind terror and no amount of Russ's soft sounds calmed him. Then he wished Owen *had* suffered, that someone had held a knife to *Owen's* throat and terrorized him, that someone had fucked Owen until he bled. But then he felt guilty for being blood thirsty and holding on to negative emotions. His therapist said that was normal, too.

Fuck normal.

"Russ said you should eat," Kari said again, interrupting his thoughts. "But I'm not supposed to, you know, *order* you to eat or anything. So, I'm not. It's totally your choice."

Wade couldn't help but laugh a little at that. Sure, it was his choice—if he wanted Russ to give Kari a hard time later.

"I'll eat when we get home. I'll need some water with it."

"I planned ahead," Kari said, waving a hand toward the back seat. "There's water in my bag in the back."

Wade froze.

Owen's car. Lemon cookies and bottled water. Easy laughter and no idea what was coming.

A rushing sound filled Wade's ears and mind. He tried to scream, but he couldn't.

Time must have passed, because Kari had pulled the car over and was on the phone. "I don't *know*. He just stopped responding. I don't know what I said! There was water in the back seat if he wanted it? How do I know? I don't—wait, wait, he's looking at me. Wade? Are you okay? Here, it's Russ."

Wade took the phone she pressed into his hand. "Russ?"

"I let Kari do one thing, *one thing*, and this happens," Russ said. "Are you okay? I'm on my way. Just hold tight."

Wade ran a hand over his hair and blinked his eyes into the early autumn sunshine. He was parked on the side of a busy road in the Kennessaw region of Atlanta. Kari was next to him looking scared out of her mind and Russ sounded like he was running. Where? Down the halls of the law firm? Down the stairs to the parking lot? It really wasn't that big a deal.

"No," Wade said. "It's fine. I'm okay. Stay at work. It's your first full week back."

"It's too soon," Russ said. "Neither of us can handle this yet."

"We can," Wade insisted. "Your clients need you, and I'm okay. I swear."

"You're 'okay'? Kari called in a panic because you went completely non-responsive for over three minutes, Wade."

Wade took a slow breath. "I was remembering."

"I know," Russ said. "I just don't want you to have to do it alone."

"I'm not alone. Kari's here. I'm safe. I think I knew I was safe even when I was in it. I'm really okay."

Russ's breathing indicated he'd stopped running at least. "Fine. You're okay. But I'm not. I've been a wreck all day away from you. I'm not ready."

Wade sputtered. "Oh, get over yourself, Mr. Bad Ass Attorney. We're both going to be okay."

"Are we?"

"Yes. You've got a job to do. Go fix people's legal problems."

"I only want to fix *your* problems," Russ muttered.

"Well, you can't. You can't help me right now. You need to get back to work and help yourself."

"Baby, listen," Russ started, his smooth lawyer voice kicking in, preparing his argument.

"No, you listen. I'm headed out to the farm with Kari to see Nicole and Eric. Don't let me down. You need to get back to work."

Russ growled in frustration.

"I'll see you later. At home." Wade disconnected first. "I'll see him at home," he repeated, and Kari touched his hand, squeezing softly.

Home was still Russ's apartment.

The house they'd purchased together just before Wade had gone to L.A. to visit Owen sat furnished and unoccupied. After L.A., Wade didn't feel up to any big changes in his life. It was comforting living in Russ's apartment building. People were always around, coming and going, walking their dogs, playing with their kids. He wasn't alone even when Russ was out. The neighbors were right there in reach, no matter what. Hundreds of them.

In comparison, the house seemed terrifyingly isolated.

"He's crazy about you," Kari said softly.

"I know."

"You deserve that."

Wade shrugged. Maybe he did, and maybe he didn't. He wasn't going to question that now. Before he'd left for L.A. he'd known he was the real winner in their relationship. Whenever he'd wondered what a powerful, wealthy, gorgeous man saw in him, he'd remember the supernova orgasms they had together. But now he didn't know *what* he brought to the relationship anymore. Definitely not sex. Maybe not ever again.

And yet Russ didn't seem to love him any less. It was too painful to contemplate losing Russ along with everything else he'd lost to Owen. So early on in his 'recovery' with Dr. Salinas he'd decided to live in the glow of Russ's love for as long as it lasted. Maybe that'd be forever, and maybe it wouldn't. And if he eventually lost Russ? Well, he'd survived being tortured and raped, hadn't he? He'd survive that too.

Somehow.

"Here we are," Kari said several minutes later, flipping her purple-red hair over one shoulder as she pulled down a freshly paved drive. A sign featuring a painted horse and a smiling child declared the driveway led to Peach Blossom Stables and Therapeutic Riding School. "Doug will be glad you came out again. He thinks the horses will do you some good."

Kari and Doug's home and stables were out in Kennesaw, a good thirty minutes from Russ's apartment in Buckhead. Most of the area around had grown up into subdivisions and suburban sprawl, but Doug's family had owned the land surrounding the house and stable for almost ninety years. In the early 2000s, Doug had inherited it all and he'd torn down all the old, dilapidated farm buildings and rebuilt from the ground up. Now he ran a therapeutic riding school for the troubled, disadvantaged, and disabled. Wade had always admired Doug's drive and focus, as well as his kindness.

"Everything looks great," he said. "Doug's business must be doing well."

"It is! My yoga studio isn't doing half-bad either," Kari said, nudging him. "It's not far from your place."

"I know, I know. I used to be a student, remember? Maybe I'll come to a class soon."

"But you're right that the riding school is doing well." Kari nodded toward the freshly painted stable. "Doug's looking to hire, actually."

"Maybe he's got a job I can do," Wade murmured, watching one of the horses eat grass in the nearest pasture. "I'd like to stop being dead weight for Russ to carry."

Kari scoffed. "Russ likes taking care of you and you should let him."

"I need something to keep me occupied." He'd even considered going back to waiting tables. It was fast-paced and left little room for thoughts to sneak in. But part of him couldn't bring himself to do that. It felt like a step back. He'd been so proud of himself when he'd quit and started working as Kari's manny. It'd been one step closer to his dream of being a teacher. Now he had to wait until at least January, if not a full year, before he could apply to the Bagwell education program at Kennesaw State again.

Kari pulled into the garage of the fancy-pants stucco house Doug had built for her and the kids. "Wade, it's not that we don't trust you with the children anymore. It's that—"

"I know, Kari. Obviously, since I'm babysitting for them tonight."

"I mean, that's not why we couldn't take you back on as our manny. It's the zone outs…"

"I get it. I understand. I can't drive until I get a handle on them." Taking the kids to school, picking them up, getting them to all of their activities and sports had been a huge part of his job. Now another pal of Kari's was doing all of that for them. "I understand. I'm not mad."

"I know you're not, but I still feel guilty about it." She smiled sadly.

"Well, stop." Wade sighed tightly. If someone asked, he'd have to admit he was tired of managing other people's emotions around his trauma, but it didn't stop happening just because he was sick of it.

"The kids miss you." Kari reached out to muss his hair, but Wade ducked out of reach. "Nic's always saying Martina's nice 'but she's not as good as Wade, Mama.'"

"That's my sweetheart," Wade said fondly.

It'd been hard to let someone else take over his duties as Nicole and Eric's caregiver. He knew it was stupid to fear Martina might drive them straight into rape and torture, but he couldn't stop the irrational fears that sometimes overtook his mind. He'd texted Kari ten times a day when he first got back just to reassure himself that she and the kids really were safe, and everything really was fine. He'd backed off to twice a day now.

"But, if I know my husband," Kari said, smiling. "He can find something for you to do. If that's what you really want. Just ask."

Wade nodded, running a hand into his hair and considering. He probably shouldn't go out riding alone, but he could be trusted to take care of tack, brush down the animals, and help with some of the clients, so long as he was supervised. "Is he in the stables?"

"Where else?"

"I'll go talk to him now. Tell the kids I'll see them a little later."

"Okay, but Nicole's eager to show you the dance routine she's doing for the talent show."

"Wouldn't miss it."

Kari kissed his cheek and then climbed out of the car, heading into the house.

The stables were a good distance away and Wade breathed in the clean scent of fresh air as he headed toward the more odiferous region of the property. Two gentle mares pranced next to the fence as he passed them, coming over for him to rub their soft noses. Green fields rolled away to small copses of trees, some of their leaves turning yellow, a harbinger of the beautiful autumn show to come.

Peach Blossom Stables was a comforting reminder of the continuity of life. It'd been here before L.A. and it was still here now.

Wade loved the farm. It was so different from the hustle and bustle of Buckhead in Atlanta, or even the apartment complexes he'd grown up in and around Mount Paran. Besides, Kari's husband, Doug, claimed the horses were good for him, claimed animals had healing powers. And Wade didn't disagree. Though even the horses seemed to sense a change in him, snuffling against him in a gentle, respectful way that made a lump come up in his throat. Still, just being near their steady strength calmed him.

"Wade!" Doug greeted him with a wide, bearded smile and an outstretched hand. "Good to see ya, man. The horses've missed you." Shaped like a barrel, Doug was shorter than Wade, but still taller than Russ. He wore the required uniform of a man who made his living with horses: blue jeans, dirty t-shirt, and cowboy boots.

Wade took Doug's hand and let him pull him into a manly bear hug. Wade appreciated the scrape of Doug's dark beard against his cheek and the familiar tickle of his closely cut black hair. The scent of sweat and stable followed Doug everywhere until he showered after work. Then he smelled like Kari's boutique shampoo and a woodsy cologne Wade had bought him for Christmas a few years ago.

Doug's blue eyes twinkled joyfully like they had since the day Wade and Kari first met him outside a movie theater. Wade would never forget the way he'd walked right up to Kari and said, "Darlin', you're the prettiest thing I ever did see. Let me take you on a date sometime."

Kari'd wrapped her arm around Wade's waist and glared at Doug. "How do you know I'm not on a date right now? Don't you think you're being a little presumptuous?"

Doug's eyes had sparkled as he'd said without a hint of disgust or judgment, "That boy you've got your arm around is too pretty to go with girls. He needs a man to set him right. Ain't nothing wrong with that." Then he'd grinned at Kari again. "And you need a man *you* can set right. That's me. I'm ready to see what you can do with me."

"That so?" she'd asked, and when Doug smiled even wider, she'd let go of Wade's waist. "Well, you're not wrong."

They'd all three gotten coffee after that and the rest was history.

Now Doug was family and the scent of stable and horse was as familiar as a heartbeat.

"Are you sure you're up to babysitting this evening, Wade?" Doug asked, pulling out of the hug. "I mean, if we don't go to this funeral it ain't the end of the world. It's just Kari's boss's mom. He's a yoga freak. Into live and let live, and let it all go. He'd understand if we couldn't come."

"No, you should go. I'm fine. Besides, Nicole is twelve now. Between the two of us we can handle Eric."

Turning back to the tack he was cleaning up and putting on the wall, Doug said, "Yeah, well, Nic isn't always dependable. She's a kid in fits and starts these days. One second she's still a little girl, and the next she's texting her pals and flipping her hair. Gives a dad whiplash."

"She'll be dependable today," Wade said, thinking of the way Nicole was so attuned to his needs ever since L.A., and the way she mimicked Kari in mothering him.

"Oh, yeah? Why's that? Russ coming over after work?" Doug asked, smiling and moving around to where Sally had meandered back into the stable. "Whatcha doin', girl? Hoping Wade's gonna give you a treat?" He patted Sally's snout, turning back to Wade. "I know how Nic likes to get your man's attention."

Wade chuckled softly. "He might come over if he leaves work early enough. I told him I'd meet him at home, but Russ does what he wants."

"Ain't that the truth?"

Wade nodded and reached for a carrot from the bucket hanging on the back wall. Sally huffed happily and abandoned Doug. Wade fed her the carrot while patting her gently, and she nuzzled his neck when she was done.

"Here," Doug said, tossing him a brush. "She needs it."

Wade smoothed the brush over Sally's hair, and leaned against her warm body, taking comfort in her sturdy strength. "Remember when Eric named her?" he asked, thinking fondly of Kari and Doug's youngest. He was sturdy like his father but adorable like his mother. "He still said his 'L's like they were 'W's." It'd made Wade laugh to hear Eric calling for Sawwy.

"I remember."

"Got any more clients today?"

"Last one was an hour ago. It's clean up time and then the funeral. But you can take her out for a ride if you want. I mean, if that's safe and all."

"Thanks. Not today. Another time."

Silence reigned for a while as they worked together. Sally loved being brushed down and so Wade took his time with her. It became a meditation, smoothing her clean of dust and dander.

Sucking in air, at the sudden hand on his shoulder, Wade tensed, bracing himself for a moment before he met Doug's eyes and forced his muscles to relax.

"Sorry," Doug said, gripping tighter, making himself more solid for Wade. "Didn't mean to startle ya."

Wade was grateful Doug hadn't pulled away like almost everyone else did when Wade tensed up. He wondered for the millionth time how long it would take for his body to unlearn the fear that'd been trained into it. He'd been with Owen only a few weeks. How could he have learned so thoroughly that a surprise touch equals pain? It seemed unfair that a couple of weeks could overrule twenty-seven years of his body's learned expectations about human contact.

"It's okay."

"Gonna take some getting used to, I guess."

Wade nodded. Understatement of the year. Doug was good at those.

Doug's phone buzzed and with an apologetic nod he stepped out of the stable to answer it.

Wade took a deep breath and rubbed Sally's side a bit more, breathing in her scent, and steadying himself on it.

But it was too late.

The sharp rush of adrenaline took its course. Wade's stomach tensed again. He wasn't used to being alone, and while part of him craved it (and he was suddenly grateful to be trusted with his own person for even a minute), another part of him came unhinged without the grounding presence of someone who hadn't been there when Owen was hurting him.

Wade put his hands on Sally trying to stay focused on the present. He concentrated on the straw under his shoes, the soft noises Sally made, and the musty smell of the barn. Sally lifted her foot and stomped it down on the ground; the sound was muffled.

Muffled. Pain. His intestines cramping and twisting, a plug shoved in his ass to hold Owen's piss inside, and the gut-churning agony of his balls being hit with a riding crop.

Sweat broke out on his forehead and back, and he took a deep breath. It was a memory. It would pass. He was here now with the horse, and Doug, and Kari, Nic, and Eric were just a shout away in the house.

Hands over his mouth and nose, the horrible rush in his ears that signaled he might pass out. Fear, intense and consuming. If he did, he would never wake up again.

Wade gasped, pressed his forehead to Sally's side, felt her shifting uncomfortably, making worried noises, sensing his emotional instability, and he shushed her, trying to soothe himself.

As he came out of the memory, his legs shook. He was still sweaty, and tears clogged his throat.

His cock was hard, throbbing and insistent, and he desperately wanted to cum, no, he *needed* to cum. Wade shook, burning with the urge to feel the orgasm rip through him. But he fought it down, forced it to subside. The lack of release left him aching and hollow, rage bubbling with fear in his heart.

"It's over," he whispered, risking adjusting his cock so that it was tucked up and not so obvious. "You don't have to. You won't die."

"You okay?" Doug's voice asked from behind him.

Wade forced a smile. "Fine."

"Okay, well, good. That was Kari's little brother Trey."

"Yeah? How's he doing?" Wade tried to smile. "He's what? Nineteen now?"

"Sure is. He wanted to ask if I was okay with her driving up with him to look at the University of Kentucky campus. He's thinking of going to school there."

Wade followed Doug as he led Sally to her stall for dinner, his miserable erection shrinking away. He already felt more normal just having someone else around. "He's a smart kid. He probably could."

"Maybe," Doug said, shrugging. "Kari don't like it much. She'd rather he stayed close to home."

"Yeah," Wade said. He'd rather Russ stayed close to home, too. Close, like within arm's reach, but that wasn't any way to live a life. Well, that was what he'd told Russ that morning trying to convince them both his return to the law firm was a good idea. "So is she going with him? Up to UK?"

Wade fought off an odd creepy-crawly sensation at the idea of Kari traveling with anyone, even Trey. He tried to shake it off. It was ridiculous. Trey was…Trey, and her brother, and a good kid. Still, he'd learned the hard way that you can't trust anyone, really.

"Told him it ain't up to me. The woman's in charge of her own life."

Wade laughed under his breath. He suspected Kari would go with Trey, which would mean Doug and Martina would have to deal with the kids.

"Anyway, Trey said he can stop over to keep you company this afternoon, if you want. Help out with the kids." Doug glanced worriedly at Wade again.

He shoved his hands in his pockets and gave a small smile. He refrained from pointing out that in the past, he'd taken care of Nicole and Eric alone and even been paid for it. He knew things were different now. *He* was different. But he could do this.

"I'm fine. Go on. It's just a few hours. I have it covered."

"All right. Sounds good. Listen, I don't want to add to your burdens," Doug started, putting his hand on Wade's shoulder and shaking him. Wade smiled, pleased with himself that he hadn't flinched away. "But Kari's mom might show up. If she does, just let her take the kids. She's been gunning for a sleepover for awhile and she and Kari finally made up."

"That took long enough."

"Jesus, did it ever. Anyway, if she comes to get them, don't let her get under your skin, okay?"

Wade nodded.

"I gotta go round up the stragglers," Doug said, waving toward the horses dawdling down in a lower pasture. "Go on up to the house and I'll meet you there."

"Oh, Doug?"

"Yeah?"

Wade cleared his throat. It was awkward to ask, even though he knew Doug would do anything to help him. It'd be one thing if he knew Doug truly needed his help, but he suspected since he couldn't do much riding, it would just be charity. Wade was desperate to get out of his own head, though. He'd take charity. "I was thinking about a job. I need something to keep busy."

"With me? Here at the stables?"

"Yeah. I don't know. It'd have to be after my therapy appointments, but I thought I could help out doing something. Mucking stalls. Whatever you need."

Doug tilted his head, gazing at Wade for a minute, but then said, just as Kari had suspected, "You can start Monday. Wear suitable clothes. Be prepared to get dirty. I don't pay much, but you don't need much since you're Russ's kept man." Wade rolled his eyes and Doug smirked. "We have a kid with cerebral palsy and a deaf girl Monday afternoon."

"Don't they have names?" Wade chided, smiling at Doug.

"Yep. Jamie and May. I just want you to understand what you're gettin' into."

"I know what you do."

Doug nodded. "Good. It'll be nice to see you every day, buddy. And it'll make Kari happy." He winked at Wade and then headed out to call the other horses up to a closer pasture.

Wade was alone again. His heart pounded and he clenched his jaw, fighting the panic. He forced himself not to run toward the house. Walking over the flat, green grass until he was on the driveway, he repeated to himself with each step, "It's over. You're safe, you're safe."

"Wade!" Nicole called from the front porch, russet pigtails flying. "Come inside! Mom has cake!"

Wade looked around at the familiar dips and rolls of the farm one more time, and then headed inside to see his godchildren and eat cake.

Chapter Five

RUSS POURED ANOTHER cup of coffee and stared down at it for a few seconds before turning to his office sink and dumping it down the drain. He was already an anxious mess and the last thing he needed was a jolt of caffeine. He poured the rest of the freshly brewed pot out as well.

With his back to his big office, he could ignore the city sprawling outside the large, west-facing windows, and the stacks of client files on his big, mahogany desk. The same desk he'd spread Wade out over the night they'd met. The same desk he'd cried on when he thought Wade had left him. The same desk he'd sweated and fretted and been sick on when he'd realized the truth.

His office had seen a lot.

"Hey there, gorgeous. I've got an arrest record a mile long and a serious case of innocence. Wanna help me avoid jail time?" His best friend Samuel's deep voice came from the doorway along with the rattle of a paper bag.

"I'm the best at that," Russ said, turning around and playing along.

Dressed in a fashionable suit that must have cost a pretty penny, and a tie that brought out a red hue to his dark brown skin, Samuel looked about as chipper as he sounded. His white teeth shone between his wide lips, and his model handsome face reminded Russ of why they'd been lovers once. But his hyperactive smile and relentless good humor reminded him of why they were lovers no longer.

"I can't pay your fee," Samuel went on. "So it'll have to be pro-bono work, but I brought your favorite! Chili subs!"

Samuel always took the elevator up from his stockbroker job on the ground floor of the twenty-story office tower their firms shared whenever he thought Russ needed company. It was no surprise he'd shown up on Russ's first day back on the job since he'd taken a leave of absence to deal with Wade. And he was damn lucky to have brought the chili subs. Otherwise Russ would have been tempted to murder him for being obnoxiously happy on such a difficult day.

Russ sat down in his big desk chair and motioned for Samuel to join him.

Dropping in an elegant heap in the chair across, Samuel sighed. "So, I take it by the way you're hiding behind the big old Desk of Protection that asking how your first full day back has gone would be redundant?"

Russ grunted around his first bite of sandwich, but didn't bother to reply.

"Have you heard from Wade?" Samuel asked. "Is he doing okay?"

"He's with Kari," Russ said, the delicious chili tangy on his tongue. "Though why I've trusted her with him, I don't know."

"He's not breakable," Samuel said.

Russ shot him a glare. "Shows how much you know."

Samuel sighed again, grabbed the bag from Russ and prepared to devour his own chili sub. It involved a lot of fussing with the foil wrapper and then preparing napkins for the inevitable mess. "He's been through a lot, but he's strong."

"He's the strongest person I know."

"Exactly. So have some faith in him," Samuel said, taking a

bite of sub. "Mm, damn this is fine. So good. Mm-mm, yessssss."

Deciding Samuel's orgasmic response to food was another reason he'd dumped him, Russ put his own sandwich down and glared. "I have faith in him, Samuel. What I also have is a lot of fear."

Samuel slapped his hand on the desk and rolled his eyes heavenward. "Oh my God, Russ. This sandwich. Jesus. Fuck, it's good."

"I know. Now shut up about it."

Samuel popped open one of the Cokes he'd brought with him and slid a second can across to Russ. "Did you just admit you're afraid? Did I hear you right over my moaning?"

Russ snorted, grabbed a napkin from Samuel's neat stack, wiped his mouth with it and then wadded it up. "Yeah, well, you held me while I bawled my eyes out over all this shit, what's the point in playing tough now?"

Four months ago, Russ had been in court, trying to help an idiot who'd been driving a motorcycle with his girlfriend on the back. She hadn't been wearing a helmet when they'd made unexpectedly intimate friends with a deer on a back road. She'd died. Russ's client had been charged with reckless endangerment and manslaughter, and it was his job to help him get a lighter sentence. At the very moment Russ had been making a killer closing argument, Wade had woken up to find himself tied up and already violated.

That timeline was something Russ had worked out within twenty-four hours of Wade's first jumbled recounting of events in the hospital, and it'd wrecked him. All the fear, guilt, and pain that he'd felt for the prior weeks had culminated in a crushing devastation.

Knowing that while Wade had been in terror, Russ had been happily destroying the prosecutor's arguments, knowing that while Wade had been pissed on and sodomized, Russ had been crowing with success, still unraveled him. Remembering how he'd gloated to the senior attorney in his firm, Mike Zachary, "Shove *that* down Judge Cole's craw next time you talk to him, why don't you?" made him sick even now. And not for a minute that first day had Russ thought anything was wrong.

That was the worst of it. He hadn't even suspected. He hadn't known. What kind of man wouldn't *know* his lover was suffering?

It hadn't been until later that night, when he'd texted Wade, and then called, and then called again he'd had even a flash of worry. And it wasn't until the next day, when he called the hotel directly and was told Wade hadn't returned the night, that Russ's worry switched from a vague irritation to a rumble of fear-soaked anger, mixed with consuming jealousy, and a violent sinking sensation in his gut.

And, worse, it wasn't until the fourth morning when he confirmed with Kari and Doug that they hadn't heard from Wade either, that he'd known deep down that Wade was not okay. By the time Russ had wised up, Wade had been raped multiple times, his body beaten, and his mind irrevocably traumatized.

"Earth to Russ?"

"Yeah, what?"

"I was just saying that you're tough, too, lover. You're tougher than you know, and I'm proud of the way you've been there for Wade."

"What? You think I'd leave him? Walk away?"

Samuel raised his hands in surrender, gold rings glistening against his dark skin. "No, I never said that. You're a fighter, and a tenacious one at that. I've seen you in court. I've watched you defend people until you couldn't defend them anymore. You'd never leave a man you love. And you do love Wade, don't you?"

Russ bit into his sandwich again, his heart twisting. He chewed slowly, not sure if he could choke it down. He loved Wade more than he'd known possible. He couldn't explain it. It was the way Wade smelled, the way he smiled, his mussed up hair in the morning, how he played with Nicole and Eric, the tender way he treated Russ's old cat before she'd died, and the passionate way he'd given everything up to Russ in bed. But that part was gone. For now anyway. Maybe forever. Who knew? It was too soon to press it.

"Yeah, I love him," he finally said, after he swallowed.

"I know you do."

"But it's different now."

Samuel reached his hand across, offering it up, and Russ shook his head. He didn't need to cling to anyone. He was strong enough to deal with what he'd lost. He had to be.

The Wade Russ had fallen in love with was buried inside the flesh of a different person. Someone that flinched if Russ moved too fast, and cried out with fear in the night, and whose back was lined with scars from Owen's abuse. Russ had been too slow. And knowing that truth killed him. He'd spend the rest of his life making up for it if he had to, and learning to love the man Wade was now. Loving him all the better for what he'd been through.

"It's okay to admit how much this hurts you. Like you said, I've seen it already. You don't have to front now."

Russ snorted, blinking back the burning in his eyes. He wasn't going to let himself dissolve like that again. "You got to see me fall apart once. That's all you're ever going to get."

"It's not like it's a shameful thing, Russ."

With Wade, Russ had tried to stay strong. He'd mostly succeeded. It wasn't until Wade was back home, safe in Russ's apartment, that Russ had a chance to completely lose it. Their second night home, while Wade had slept sedated in their bed, he'd broken down in the living room, crying so hard he'd almost vomited.

Somehow, like he always did, Samuel had known Russ needed him. He'd come over, let himself in with the key Russ had never taken from him, and found Russ in agony on the floor. He'd held him, and Russ let himself be held.

Then, when Russ had been able to breathe again, Samuel had pulled away, handed him a tissue and said, "Here, lover. Blow your nose. You look disgusting."

And that's why they were still best friends despite Samuel's orgasms over food.

Now Samuel shoved some napkins at him, indicating his chin. "A dollop. On your chin. No, to the right. Yeah, you got it. Anyway, after what he's been through? Anyone who loves him would cry. Hell, I've cried for him. It hurts us all. Don't be ashamed of your pain," Samuel said, still trying to make him feel better for how he'd broken down that night.

"Yeah, well." Russ wiped his mouth and shook his head.

"Oh, I forgot. The great defense attorney Russ Paulson is cold as ice. He doesn't have feelings."

Russ snorted.

"The only problem is that you *do*. Especially when it comes to Wade. You have a lot of feelings. There'd be something wrong with you if this didn't hurt."

Russ frowned. The subject of his feelings made him uncomfortable, even though he was far from the emotionally detached jerk he'd tried to be before Wade came into his life. He decided to stick to the subject of Wade. "He zoned out on Kari today."

"That thing where he stares into space?"

"It's a defense mechanism," Russ said. "He remembers what happened and it hurts too much to deal with, so his mind shuts down to protect itself." He took another bite of the sandwich.

"I've seen it. He did it that day I stayed with him while you went to Costco. I brought him Rice Krispies after his nap." Samuel looked pained. "I felt like such a horrible person. I didn't know that psychopath only fed him cereal."

"When he fed him at all," Russ said, swiping a hand over his face. "How long did the zone out last?"

"A few minutes. I sat with him the whole time and when he came out of it he smiled at me and said he was sorry!" Samuel's dark fine-boned hand fluttered to his chest. "Oh, Russ, it broke my heart."

"He says he's sorry for everything. The only person who should be sorry is dead." Russ sat back, unable to eat anything else. He'd lost weight during the ordeal, too. Food just didn't taste like it should anymore.

The police had compiled enough evidence from Owen's computer, journals, and house to make a conclusive post-mortem diagnosis of paranoid schizophrenia. There had been stacks of spiral bound notebooks filled with rambling insanity about demons invading Wade's body through a portal opened by Russ's semen, and long, winding explanations about how the torture of Wade's body would make it uninhabitable by the demons.

There were also three different hour long videos, recorded without Wade's knowledge, of Owen hurting Wade, all the while ranting to his dead father, screaming at the demons, and having what appeared to be intense orgasms in response to Wade's pain.

Using every last bit of good will he'd accrued as an attorney over the years, Russ had freed the videos from police custody and taken possession of them himself. He'd watched as Chief Madison, one of Atlanta's finest, deleted all the copies from the police hard drives, leaving the only copy on a memory stick for Russ to do what he wished. He swore the police in California didn't have anything more either.

"I have the stomach for a lot of things, but not this," Chief Madison had said, shoving his thick dark hair off his sweaty forehead. "The sick shit in these videos made me puke. Like I actually heaved. I'll be honest, Paulson. Don't watch them, man. I'm telling you as a friend. You won't come back from what you see."

"Thanks for the advice."

"What do you plan to do with them?"

"Destroy them," Russ said. "We don't need them to prosecute Owen's estate for damages. We have more than enough proof. No one needs to see these videos." He'd clenched the memory stick in his hand and said, "Wade wouldn't want anyone to see him that way."

And yet Russ had watched every last minute.

Because if Wade could endure it happening to him then Russ could endure seeing it. Bearing witness. Owning his part in the horror. He owed Wade that much.

Russ had been revolted and horrified by what the videos showed him. The massive dildo shoved in past Wade's hole's ability to stretch, the agony on Wade's face as Owen had forced it further, tearing him open, inflicting the damage that had been nearly irreversible.

Wade's screams.

The horror of watching Owen shoot his load of semen on Wade's twisted, blindfolded face. The cock and ball torture that left Wade passed out for up to ten minutes at a time. The misery of seeing Wade forced to cum, watching Wade beg for mercy just as he succumbed to the orgasm. The sick pleasure on Owen's face as he watched Wade give in. The gut-wrenching madness in Owen's eyes when he looked at the camera and explained that he was closer to success now, and that his father was finally going to be proud of him.

The memory stick was wiped clean at Russ's hands by night-fall. He deleted the content and then reformatted the stick completely. Once the videos were destroyed, Russ made the decision not to tell Wade about them. They were gone now, and Wade didn't need to know. Russ could protect him from that violation at least, even though he'd failed to protect him from everything else Owen had done.

Russ pinched the bridge of his nose.

"What stupid thing are you thinking now?" Samuel asked, wiping his chili-covered fingers carefully on several napkins.

"I never should have let him go. I should have seen it coming."

"Russ—you can't blame yourself," Samuel said, scolding. "It's like you've said so many times—only one person is to blame for this, and he's dead."

"Right."

Samuel patted his arm. "You've got to get it together, lover. Keep your chin up. Wade's alive and hurting. He needs you to keep your head in the game."

"And what game is that?"

"The game where he has a chance of getting well."

Russ lifted one corner of his mouth in a small smile. Samuel didn't have a clue. Not really. He'd been around a lot since Wade got home, being there like a good friend should. But he didn't see the real damage done.

They were living day by day and Russ knew it. He was an attorney and he'd seen a lot, not to mention he was a realist. There was no guarantee that Wade would ever be well again. He'd finally found a man he loved, and he'd lost him.

WADE SAT ON Kari's porch with his bowl of ice cream, watching Nicole do her dance routine in the yard. She'd performed it five times in a row and was now working the sixth. The song played from Wade's iPhone, set to repeat, with the jangle of the guitar drifting over the grass. At twelve she was developing breasts and hips, but she was still long and lean. Her russet hair was loose now, and she flipped it to emphasize her dance moves.

Nine-year-old Eric was supposed to be taking a shower, but when Wade went back in to put the ice cream bowl in the sink, he found the boy at the kitchen table playing an anatomy game on the iPad Russ had given him for his birthday. He wore muddy jeans and a dirty shirt, and his dark brown hair, the same color as his father's, was covered in dust.

"Cor-rect! That is the—lacrimal bone! Good job!" the game chirped.

"Did you shower, buddy?" Wade asked neutrally.

"Nah," Eric said, not taking his dark eyes off the game. "Why do I have to get clean?"

"Because your grandma is coming to get you for a sleepover."

Kari's mom had called an hour after Doug's pickup had pulled out of the drive to confirm that she'd be by to pick up the kids. Wade had never gotten along with the woman, being a 'dirty faggot' and all, but ever since he'd returned from his 'ordeal' as she'd put it, he'd noticed a considerable thawing in her. He supposed that even she hadn't wanted him to be tortured in actuality, just theoretically, and in that hell she so fondly believed in.

"Then I'll bathe at Grandma Maggie's. She's got a Jacuzzi tub."

"Grandma Maggie won't let you within ten feet of her car, you're so dirty," Wade answered. "You've been out with the horses all afternoon. You know what your grandma will say about that."

"'I didn't raise your mama for all this horse poop and squalor!'" Eric grinned. "That always makes mama mad when she says that."

"I bet it does. Your mama keeps a clean house."

"Clean enough to eat off the floor!" Eric chimed, mimicking Doug.

A box of cereal emptied onto the concrete floor. Crawling on his hands and knees, shoving pieces into his mouth. Hungry. So hungry.

"You okay, Wade?" Eric asked, a hint of worry in his young voice.

Rubbing the scar at the side of his throat, Wade said, "I'm fine. It's okay. Everything's okay."

Eric put aside the iPad and stood up. "You sure?"

"I'm sure. Say, why don't you come outside with me and Nicole? You can get a bath later if you want."

"Nah," Eric said, carefully. "I'll go get my shower now, okay?" Eric looked up and smiled reassuringly, and then drew him into a hug, pressing his head against Wade's chest. "You're okay, Wade. I've got you."

"Yeah, buddy. You've got me."

When Eric had trotted upstairs to shower, Wade went back to the porch to watch Nicole go through the dance routine again. Finally, she came over to him, sweaty and exhausted, and dropped down onto the chair next to his, sighing dramatically. "That's hard work!"

"Looked it," Wade agreed, rubbing his still-sweaty hands along his jeans. He wished the memories didn't undo him so much. "Want me to get you some water?"

"No, thanks," Nicole said, lifting her braid up in the back and waving a hand at her hot neck.

After a few moments of silence, and swinging her feet back

and forth, peering intently at Wade, she finally said, "Daddy says I shouldn't ask you questions about Owen."

Of course she'd want to know about it. Wade was their godfather, but Owen had been Kari's friend, too. It'd been the three of them since high school. Owen had come to the hospital when Nicole was born, and again when Eric came into the world. He'd been at more than half of their birthday parties. He'd come to Christmas several times. Of course Nicole wanted to know.

Wade had no idea what Kari had told her, but he uncoiled inside, like he'd been poised and waiting for this moment, and now that it was here, he could relax into it. "You know what, Nic?"

"What?"

"I'd actually really like it if you'd ask me about Owen."

"Really?"

Wade nodded, looking out toward the afternoon light on the shifting green grass. "Really."

"Okay, so…" She swallowed hard. Her voice knotted up. "Why did Owen hurt you? Was he mad at you?"

Wade made a soft noise to let her know he was thinking about his answer, and he rocked back in his chair a little before saying, "You know, Nicole. I think he was. I mean, not in the regular way that someone is mad at someone else. But, yeah, I think he was mad at me."

"For what?"

"For falling in love with Russ."

"But why? Mom said you and Owen were just friends. Always just friends."

Kari knew better than that. She knew all about their blowjobs for fun and misery arrangement. But she also knew Wade had never loved Owen, and they'd both known Owen hadn't loved Wade. Not really. No matter what he'd raved on about in his madness. What he'd done wasn't love.

"This is kind of hard to understand, because I have a hard time really getting it myself," Wade pondered aloud. "But I think he was mad at me because he *didn't* love me. And I think, more than anything, Owen wanted to love me." Wade pushed his lip out and shrugged a little bit. "But he just couldn't. He resented being attracted to me and in his madness he made me into something evil that he had to cure to make it all stop."

Nicole stared at him with a slack, open mouth, mind trying to make sense of his words. Wade tried to smile, but only one half of his lips would quirk up. Maybe telling his goddaughter the truths he was figuring out wasn't such a good idea after all. Maybe Kari had asked Nicole not to talk to him about it for an entirely different reason than he'd assumed.

"So, he hurt you because he didn't love you?"

"Well, it was more than that. He was sick, Nicole. Do you understand? His brain was wrong, and it made him believe things that just weren't real. He thought I had demons inside of me. He thought Russ had put them there."

"He was *crazy?*" Nicole said, her voice full of deep wonder and horror.

"Yeah." Wade nodded. "He was."

"Did the police shoot him because he was crazy?" Nicole asked.

"No! No, of course not!" Wade touched her arm reassuringly. "They shot him because he was threatening my life, and they thought he might kill me before they could help me."

"This boy at school? His mom takes medicine and it makes her better. Why didn't they just give Owen medicine?"

"No one knew until it was too late, Nic. If I'd known...." Wade shook himself hard.

He didn't allow himself to think like that. Owen had raped

him, tortured him, torn his anus with the things he'd put inside it, ripped away his life, his safety, his health, his sexual identity, and he was *not* going to let himself think for even a moment that he could have stopped it. It was hard, he wanted to blame himself, but he wouldn't. He hoped that at least Russ would be proud of him for holding back.

"If you'd known…?" Nic prompted.

"I couldn't have known. He didn't get sick until he left Atlanta. When he was here, he would never have hurt me the way that he did. It took going away, leaving the people and places he knew… Do you know what a support system is, Nicole?"

"Um, it sounds like something that holds you up?"

"Right. A social support system is like…well, for you, it's your mom and dad, and Grandma Maggie, and Russ, and me, and people who take care of you. For me, it's you and Eric, and the rest of your family, and Russ, his best friend Samuel, and everyone who helps me when I need help. Everyone who makes sure I know I'm okay no matter what. They're the people who will never let you fall."

"There are a lot of people like that, huh?"

Wade smiled. There were, kind of. Of course, growing up, he'd felt like everyone around him had more important things to worry about than him. Between his father being in prison, his mother's fulltime job, and his stepdad's work, he'd been the last person anyone considered in the scheme of life or decisions. It wasn't until high school, when he'd met Kari that he felt like he could depend on anyone.

And then came Russ.

"I'm glad you feel that way, Nicole. And I think, when Owen lived in Atlanta with us, he felt that way, too. Like he had people to count on. But when his dad died, he went to L.A. to deal with all of that. It was scary and new, he didn't know anyone, and he had no one to help him."

"He could have called," Nicole said.

"He could have. But he didn't." Wade felt a rush of love for the little girl across from him. She didn't know how much he'd needed her to say that, to remind him of that simple truth, because no matter how hard he tried, that guilt was still there.

Wade hadn't called Owen either.

"So he went away and got sick," she said slowly. "And getting sick made him crazy?"

"Pretty much. He had…well, it's called a genetic predisposition. Do you know what that means? No? It means that his mother was sick, too." He remembered when Owen had confessed that his mom was hospitalized with schizophrenia. "And her genes made Owen more likely to get sick. And then when he didn't have a support system in L.A., he had this thing happen, it's called a psychotic break. That's when you don't know what's real anymore, and you believe things that are really scary and strange."

"Like what?"

"Like that I was full of demons and he had to hurt me to get them out of me."

"Wow," Nicole said, and her lip trembled. "Could that happen to me?"

"No," Wade said. "No, Nic. It won't happen to you." He wasn't sure if she meant the psychotic break or the torture, but, either way, no. It couldn't happen to Nicole. That was something he couldn't stand to think about.

"What was he sick with?"

Wade swallowed, turned to look toward the sound of Kari's mom's car pulling up the drive. "It's a sickness called 'paranoid schizophrenia' and he had it really bad."

"And nobody knew?"

"No one," Wade said, standing up as Maggie got out of the car. "Did that answer your questions, Nicole?"

"I don't know. I might have more."

Wade smiled down at her, and put his hand on her head. "You and me both, kiddo."

Maggie greeted him with a stiff nod and a searching look into his eyes. "How are you, Wade? Is that doctor helping you? The one with the newfangled treatments your boyfriend was so bent on?"

"I'm getting by Maggie."

Maggie narrowed her eyes at him and said, "Getting by. Okay. Well, that'll do for now, but you better keep on trying to be well. Kari loves you. And these kids do, too."

Wade remembered a time when Maggie had forbidden Kari to hang out with him, claiming that he'd turn her gay, too. Then, as time progressed and Kari hadn't given him up, Maggie sat him down and tried to convince him that he could stop being gay if he just tried, if he went to her church and confessed his sins, and if he started dating girls.

But now Maggie seemed chastened around him. Quiet horror at what he'd been through didn't allow her to add any more pain to the massive load he already carried around on his back.

Maggie went on, "Do you mind if I pray for you tonight?"

"You can pray for me if you think it'll help. Your past prayers that I'd wake up straight failed, but maybe these will be more pure of heart?" Wade said, and he smirked when she flushed, like she was ashamed.

"Just a prayer for your healing, mind you. Nothing more. If God allows you some happiness in your relationship, then who am I to judge?"

"I'll take your prayers then."

"Good. Now, where are my hugs?" she said, turning to Nicole. "And where is your brother?"

Wade watched as Nicole hugged Maggie, and they both went into the house. He heard her exclamation of distress over Eric's state and he hesitated to follow. He was curious how Eric could have failed at his shower.

Entering the house, Wade saw that Eric sat by himself at the table playing the iPad game again wearing nothing but underwear.

"Your mother really shouldn't leave you alone with him. He's not right," Wade heard Maggie say, as she and Nicole hustled Eric upstairs to dress and pack a bag.

In the past, he'd have confronted her, but now he just didn't have the energy.

He sat down at the kitchen table.

Alone again.

He breathed through it, focusing on the sounds of his godchildren and their grandmother upstairs, fighting the waves of anxiety as they began. But just as he'd known it would happen, he tumbled and tripped into the nightmare in his mind.

He was back in the ambulance riding to the small hospital they'd taken him to at first. He'd stayed in the Ojai Valley Community Hospital, the medical facility closest to the house where he'd been tortured, until it was clear he was stable enough to be moved to Cedar Sinai. The proctologist in Ojai, the one who'd originally looked at Wade's anus, declared it a lost cause, and said he'd be lucky to control his sphincter ever again.

Wade was glad every day that doctor had been wrong.

Being twenty-seven with a diaper was something he didn't want to deal with. And he thought it was only fair, given how much other crap Owen had left him to sort through, that he should be able to not shit his pants.

It only seemed right.

"Hey. Come on, Wade."

Wade jumped. Russ was kneeling in front of him, and he blinked in surprise.

"Sorry, baby. Didn't mean to startle you."

Breath coming fast, Wade asked, "What are you doing here? I thought you were at work."

"I was. I looked at case files. I ate with Samuel. I left." Russ put his hand next to Wade's cheek but didn't touch. "You were zoned out."

Wade leaned his face into Russ's palm and shrugged. He wished it wasn't a big deal. He understood it was dangerous. What if he blanked out of life while pouring his coffee and burned himself? Or worse? He was pretty sure the pain would pull him out of it, but it wasn't a theory he wanted to test.

He thought about explaining that he'd been left alone, and the memories were hard to keep away when he was by himself, but he knew that would only result in Russ being angry with Kari, and even less likely to trust Wade to anyone else's care, and it was already hard enough to get Russ to let even Samuel help out.

"How was work?" Wade asked, instead.

"Miserable," Russ said. "All my clients are guilty as sin."

"Maybe tomorrow you'll get a case you can believe in." Wade turned his head and kissed Russ's palm.

"Maybe." Russ leaned forward slowly, letting Wade see the kiss coming before pressing their lips together in a sweet, though chaste greeting.

"Gross!" Eric yelled.

Wade looked up to see the three of them file into the room with overnight bags and stuffed animals and a very worn blanket tucked under Eric's arm.

"You're going to want to kiss someone someday, Eric," Nicole said, flicking her hair over her shoulder and smiling warmly at Russ, obviously gratified when he gave her a wink.

"Will not. I'll only ever kiss Mama."

"Eww," Russ teased. "Gross!"

Eric crossed his arms and narrowed his eyes. "Fine. Maybe I'll kiss someone else *someday*, but it's gonna be a *girl*."

"Fair enough," Wade said.

"Your loss," Russ muttered.

Maggie cleared her throat. "Don't give these children wicked ideas."

"Oh, forgive me," Russ said, standing. "You must be Kari's mother. I'm Russ Paulson, Attorney-at-Law." He stuck out his hand and she declined to shake it. Russ smirked and then bowed, making Nicole giggle.

"Let's go, children," Maggie said, shoving her snoot into the air and directing Nicole and Eric to the door.

"Bye Wade," Eric said, hugging him gently again like he might break.

"See ya," Nicole said, smiling up at him, but saving her best grin for Russ. "Come see us soon, Russ? Mom will make that yummy stew you liked."

"Sold."

Wade walked them out to the car and when he got back, he found Russ shoving one of Kari's homemade snickerdoodle cookies into his mouth and scanning the refrigerator for something more.

"Hungry?"

"Samuel ruined my lunch with his orgasm noises."

Wade laughed. "Considering you've actually heard his real orgasm noises—"

Russ shook his head. "He's strangely silent in bed. Another deal breaker for me."

"I'm glad there were so many deal breakers with him or I might get jealous."

"No need. He's the opposite of what I want. Which, for the record, is you." Russ tucked a block of cheese under one arm, and turned to Wade. "Ready to go home?"

Hospital noises, nurses with squeaky shoes, and Russ looking down at Wade with eyes full of love and reassurance.

"Ready," Wade agreed, leaning in for a kiss. "And, hey, I love you."

Russ propped his arms on Wade's shoulders, still holding his stolen cheese in one hand. "I love you, too. More than you'll ever know."

Chapter Six

BACK HOME AT the apartment, they changed into pajama pants and t-shirts, and then Russ got Wade settled on the large, soft sectional sofa to watch a marathon of Black Books, a British comedy they both enjoyed. It made them laugh and took them out of their regular life in a way that comforted them both. Neither one of them had watched it before Los Angeles, and so, in the tiniest of ways, it seemed like a way forward. Each episode beckoned like a fresh, ridiculous chance at life.

The open floor plan made the kitchen, dining space, and living room visible at all angles. Wide windows along the side of the main room and the doors to the balcony opened out on Atlanta's sparkling cityscape. The décor was attractive and chosen by a decorator Russ had hired when he first moved in. The bedroom was off to the right, along with a giant closet and a nice bathroom. Again, tastefully though impersonally appointed.

He'd lived there for five years now. It was a good apartment, but he could afford better. Before Wade, he'd seen no point. The place where he'd first dropped his bags when he'd been convinced to move from the firm's satellite office in Louisville to the main one in Atlanta was the perfect distance from his work and the courthouse, and plenty nice enough to bring men home to fuck. And he'd brought home a lot of men to fuck.

After Wade, though? The apartment was a fine place to start their relationship, and he'd loved seeing Wade add personal touches to it as their relationship had grown. But, once he understood how much Wade loved kids, and he'd admitted to himself how much he personally *wanted* kids, it hadn't seemed like the right place for the future he imagined for them both.

So they'd purchased the house.

Now Russ wondered if they'd ever move into it. Would they get past sitting on the sofa hoping a TV show could take them out of their messed up heads?

Russ moved to open the balcony doors, letting in some fresh air. He winced when Wade jumped at the sound of a car backfiring on the street below.

"Okay?" he asked, crossing to the kitchen.

"Fine." Wade sounded irritable, the way he did sometimes when he was tired of being coddled. "I'll get the episode set up to go."

Taking out two cans of soda, Russ wished, not for the first time, for a beer. He honestly thought they both could use one. But Samuel had emptied the apartment of all alcohol before they even came home from L.A., at Wade's request.

"I don't need the temptation right now," he'd admitted. "My dad was an addict, snorting the shit he sold. It could be in my genes. And, yeah, I've never had a problem with drinking or drugs in the past, but I've never had so much hell in my head to block out either."

That had led to an interesting discussion where Russ had confirmed Wade was being purposely stingy with his pain meds, afraid of slipping into an addiction on one hand, and afraid of slipping into memories on the other.

"It's just that I have to work really hard to stay right here," Wade had said, motioning around him at the present moment. "The pills make it worse. And while I'd love to drink a gallon of vodka, I'm also terrified of how my mind might slip. I don't want to know where I might end up if I let go of my thoughts."

Russ understood that, and part of him was glad he didn't need to worry about Wade using pills or alcohol as a crutch to deal with his pain, but Wade's fear of letting go and reluctance to take pills to help him sleep was proving a challenge at bedtime.

Even now, four months after the initial injuries, Wade's body and mind were still healing. He needed good, strong rest, but falling asleep continued to be a struggle for him. The panic attacks usually came in that murky space between wakefulness and sleep. He felt like they were both perpetually exhausted.

"Babe?"

Russ looked up from where he'd been staring at the soda cans in his hands to see Wade approaching him, barefoot and tired-looking in his pajama pants and t-shirt, with his head cocked worriedly. "You okay?"

"Yeah. Just trying to decide which I want." He held up the Cherry Coke and then the Mountain Dew. "How about you?"

Wade wrapped his arms around Russ from behind, his tall body pressing against him warmly, and hooked his head over Russ's shoulder. "I'll take a caffeine-free Coke Zero if we have one."

Russ made the exchange, choosing the Cherry Coke for himself. "How'd you sleep last night?"

Wade shrugged. "Just the usual. I had a good dream, though. The first one I remember in a long time."

Russ turned around, gazing into Wade's hazel eyes and touching his darkly stubbled cheek. The scratch of the whiskers against his fingers was comforting. "Yeah? Care to share?"

"It was me and you out by the Peach Blossom Stables pond, and you were going on about how we couldn't go swimming there because of the leeches—which, for the record, there are no leeches—"

"So you claim."

"And we…." Wade glanced at Russ, eyes going dark and his breath tighter. "We fucked in the water. And I wasn't scared. I woke up sort of aroused, but it was okay. It was nice."

Russ touched Wade's chin, and went up on his toes to kiss his lips softly. "It sounds like a damn good dream to me."

Wade ducked his head down against Russ's neck, taking a long breath, and Russ held him close, rubbing his hands over Wade's back, feeling the soft t-shirt under his palms.

"Make a sandwich," Wade said gruffly in his ear. "You're getting too skinny."

Russ could say the same thing about Wade, but he didn't. He understood all too well how difficult it was to eat when your mind was working overtime. Instead, he said, "Only if you eat one, too."

Wade nuzzled his cheek and nodded.

Russ sent a firm message to his thickening dick to shut up and sit down. There wasn't going to be any sex any time soon, and he didn't need there to be. He just needed Wade home and safe and getting better.

"What are your plans for Saturday?" Wade asked, as Russ removed sandwich meat and mayo from the fridge, and grabbed the fresh bag of small, tasty bread rolls they used to make mini-sandwiches.

"Why? Got somewhere you'd rather be than holed up here in the apartment with me?"

Wade shrugged. "I kinda thought I'd like to go out to the farm. I've been thinking of going riding."

Russ narrowed his eyes. "Alone?" With the zone-outs that could prove dangerous.

"No, I'd take someone. That's why I was asking about your plans." His hazel eyes shifted mischievously. "*You* could go with me."

Russ shuddered, opening the fridge for the mustard he'd forgotten. "Horses. You know they don't like me."

Wade lifted his brow at Russ as he organized the sandwich fixings in the order he'd use each one. "Because you're afraid of them."

"Afraid is a strong word."

"I could set you up with Sally. She's really calm and good."

"No."

"Okay, well… Maybe Kari or Trey would go out with me." Wade shifted weirdly and his breath came in tight and strange. "Or not. Maybe only Trey if Kari goes with us, too."

Russ heart squeezed. Wade was worried about being alone with Kari's little brother? Skinny, scrawny, sweet Trey? Someone Wade could easily take in a fight? Russ's stomach went acidy at the thought Wade was so traumatized that *Trey* felt like a threat.

Grabbing a knife and a spoon from the cutlery drawer, Russ decided. If riding would cheer Wade up, he'd agree to it. It wasn't as though the horse would actually throw him, right?

"I guess I could go with you."

Wade grinned. "No way. For real?"

Russ opened the mayo jar. "The things I do for you."

"You're really gonna go *riding*? It's going to be hilarious. I should get a video for posterity."

At the words 'get a video' Russ flashed back to images he'd seen of Owen torturing Wade, and he rubbed his hand over his eyes, wiping away the sudden rush of sweat on his forehead.

"Russ? You're not chickening out already, are you?"

"Nope—we'll go."

Russ stared at the side of Wade's neck where the knife had cut. The scar was still purple and bright. He knew it would fade with time, and he hoped the memories would, too.

For both of them.

"What's new with Samuel?" Wade asked, changing the subject now that he'd gotten his way. Some things never changed.

"He and Frank are talking things over," Russ said, rolling his eyes as he sliced two rolls in half, and sat them open on blue plates.

"*Again?*" Wade asked.

"The sex has to be amazing for him to put up with Frank's bullshit. Obviously, open relationships are fine." Russ finished up making his sandwich and started on Wade's. "Before you, I was down for one. But fucking Grindr guys in Samuel's bed? That's not cool."

"Does Samuel think he can't do better?"

Russ shrugged. "I blame myself."

Wade grabbed a container of leafy greens from the fridge and added some to both sandwiches. "Why's that?"

"Samuel claims I ruined him for men with small dicks so now he's willing to accept crap behavior in exchange for a thick one."

Wade rolled his eyes. "Yeah right." Laughter burbled out beneath his attempt at scolding, and Russ felt vindicated by it. "Your dick's not that big."

"Compared to Frank's definitely not."

"When did you see Frank's dick?"

"Samuel showed me Frank's Grindr dick pics before their last break up. He's impressive."

Wade laughed and then went quiet. Russ frowned, putting the mayo and meat back in the fridge and getting out the pickles. He wished he could go back and not bring up dicks. He was just joking, trying to lighten both their moods, but what if Wade was remembering the giant dildo Owen had pushed into him? Or what if he thought Russ was pressuring him?

"I wish Samuel saw himself the way we do," Wade said

thoughtfully. "He deserves someone who puts him first."

"He does, but he's never been attracted to men like that. He was into me for God's sake, and all I did was fuck him blind a couple times a week. Until it got old." Russ sighed, a tight bubble of guilt in his gut. "I should have been better to him. I'm lucky he still wants to be friends with me. I got the best part of that deal—even if he does gross me out when he eats."

"Maybe. But you've been a good friend to him, too. You're always there for him, even if you bitch about it. And you said you were always honest with him. You didn't lead him on, or steal from him, or move into his place and sponge off him. Or fuck Grindr hookups in his bed."

"No."

"Frank does all that and worse. And then Samuel takes him back. It's like some kind of sickness with them at this point."

Relieved Wade didn't seem to be remembering his days with Owen and hadn't thought Russ was trying to push him into sex, he took his plate and motioned for Wade to follow. They collapsed on the sofa together with their snacks and sodas. Russ took a bite of his sandwich, pausing to wipe mayo from his mouth. "Yeah, well, some people just can't let go even when they should, and, in the end, everyone gets hurt."

Wade's frozen face told him that he'd finally said something deeply wrong, terribly hurtful.

"Lesson learned," Wade said, softly. "From now on, I'll be all about letting go."

"Dammit it, Wade, it wasn't you." Russ put his plate on the coffee table. "Owen was—"

"I know, Russ. Let's drop it, okay?" He rubbed his hand over his face. "I shouldn't have taken it that way. It's not a big deal. Let's watch our show."

"It's a big deal if I hurt you."

Wade's eyes softened and he reached for Russ's hand. "You didn't hurt me." Taking a final bite of his small sandwich, he placed his plate next to Russ's and reached for the remote control. "Samuel deserves better. We agree on that."

"Yes."

He nodded toward the TV screen. "And we agree that you're Bernard and I'm Manny."

"When you're not Fran."

Wade clicked play. "Then we agree on the important things. Let's forget the rest."

Russ preferred to address things head on, especially any indication from Wade that he felt 'less than' or judged for what happened with Owen. But he knew Wade was right. They'd both earned a night of peace.

The tension between them eased with their laughter at Bernard, Manny, and Fran's antics on the show, and gradually Wade relaxed, slipping down the sofa to lay with his head in Russ's lap. Gently Russ threaded his fingers into Wade's dark, thick hair and smoothed it back from his wide forehead. A light breeze fluttered in from the open balcony doors as dusk descended on the city.

"Scoot down beside me," Wade murmured, bringing Russ's fingers to his lips and kissing them. "Hold me."

Russ didn't need to be told twice.

It wasn't as though he hadn't been allowed to hold Wade since the events in L.A., but he never felt like he was allowed to initiate it now. If he did, he made sure to give Wade plenty of advance warning for his touches, and murmured reassurances that he could stop the cuddle at any time. But when Wade invited him to hold him, he didn't feel the same tension. He'd been asked and it made all the difference.

Wade was taller than Russ but preferred to be the little spoon. With the help of a pillow, he held Wade tightly to his chest as they watched two more episodes, laughing and snuggling together.

At the end of the episode, Wade rolled over to face Russ, gazing sweetly at him with a familiar expression of coy longing.

"Kiss me," Wade murmured, nuzzling Russ's cheek with his nose, and dragging his stubble along Russ's sensitive throat. "Kiss me like you mean it."

"Are you sure?"

"Yes. Please, make me feel like you want me."

"Baby, I want you." Russ's voice was sandpaper rough.

"Show me."

Unable to resist Wade when he begged, he did. Wade's lips and mouth opened for his tongue, and he kissed and sucked gently, taking his time, learning Wade's mouth all over again.

Wade trembled in his arms, but came up for more when Russ made a move to pull away. He dragged Russ's head down for a deeper kiss, a longer joining of tongues and breath.

"Cum for me," Wade grunted, when Russ broke to breathe. "I miss seeing your face when you cum."

Russ groaned, pressing his hard, aching cock against Wade's hip, and shook his head. "Baby, this is fast."

"It's been four months. I want to be your lover again, Russ. I want to make you cum."

"I know, and I want…" Russ cut himself off before he said anything he couldn't take back. Even admitting to wanting that too would be pressure, and he didn't want Wade to feel like he had to give Russ anything at all.

"What? What do you want?" Wade asked breathlessly, his pupils blown wide and his mouth swollen.

He wanted to turn Wade over and fuck him bare. He wanted to cum in his ass while sucking rough kisses on his shoulders, and marking him as his own. He wanted to eat the cum out of Wade while he writhed and begged and jerked himself off. And then he wanted to lick Wade's cum off his stomach before plunging in to fuck him again.

He didn't say any of that.

"I want you to feel ready."

"I am." Wade's brows lowered along with his voice, growling, "I'm not going to lose you because I can't be what you need."

Russ's head fell back, his cock throbbing. *Fuckity fuck*, that was exactly why he couldn't even pull his dick out right now and jerk off while Wade kissed him. Because it wasn't about what Wade needed or wanted at all, but what he was afraid of losing.

"What?" Wade asked, defensively. "Do you not want me like that now?"

"I want you, baby. Jesus, do I ever want you. But I need you to want it, too. Not just because you think I'll...what?" Russ searched Wade's eyes. "What do you think is going to happen if we don't do this tonight?"

"Tonight? Nothing." Wade sat up, his hair messy and wild as his eyes. "But next week? Next month? You and I basically met in a fuck. And you weren't exactly celibate before I came into your life. Before...*before* we had sex every single day, and maybe that wasn't going to last forever, and maybe we'd have eventually slowed down, but this isn't what you bargained for when you said you wanted to be exclusive with me."

"Holy shit, baby, all I bargained for was a life with you, and I almost lost that. I can handle my own dick for a few more..." he trailed off. Shit. He'd almost named a length of time, something Wade might use against himself as a deadline. "I can handle my own dick for as long as it takes for you to be ready for more."

Wade shook his head and stood up. "You don't get to decide this for me."

"What are you talking about?"

"I get to decide when I'm ready and I'm ready tonight." Wade paced in front of the TV.

"Baby…"

"What?"

Russ gestured at Wade's pajama pants. "You're not even hard."

"So? You are."

Russ shook his head, indicating his own pajama bottoms. "No."

"You were. I felt it. You wanted me." Wade's eyes were wild.

"I did. I do. But, listen to me. Listen carefully: we have to be so careful. We can't just dive into this."

"I know that! God!"

Russ stood up, too, reaching out a steady hand. "Take a deep breath. Talk to me. What do you think is going to happen?"

Wade covered his face with his hand, trembling.

"Just calm down and tell me what you're thinking," Russ begged softly.

Wade swallowed hard and met Russ's eye. "I'm thinking that you're gorgeous and…and have a lot to offer…" That was Wade's polite way of saying Russ was rich. "And I'm not an idiot. For all I know, you're doing Grindr hook ups when you go out to Costco. For all I know, you fucked some intern at the office today."

Russ stared up at him. What the fuck could he say to that? If Wade really thought those things? If he really believed Russ would do that? Well, what could he possibly say?

Wade scrubbed his hands through his hair and sat down on the coffee table, narrowly missing their plates. "I know that's not true. I know you didn't do those things. I know you wouldn't."

"But you're afraid I will?"

"I wouldn't blame you." Though his voice was so full of hurt just contemplating it Russ knew that wasn't true. "You deserve someone who can…who can…" he waved wildly at the dining table. "Who can bend over that table and let you fuck them mercilessly. That's what you deserve."

"Screw that. I don't care about that."

"What do you care about then?" Wade's chin wobbled.

"I care about you, baby," Russ said, getting down on his knees in front of Wade, taking his chin in his fingers. "That's all I care about anymore."

Wade sniffled. "I guess I got what I deserved, didn't I?"

"Oh, baby. No, no, baby." He took Wade into his arms, holding him as he shuddered and shook. "You never deserved any of that. None of it. No matter what you've told yourself. You only deserved love."

Wade whispered angrily, "I'm so sick of crying."

"I know."

"I wanted tonight to be different. I wanted to see you cum. Why couldn't you just give me that, Russ?"

"I'm sorry." Russ kissed Wade's sweaty neck and held him tighter. "I love you and I want to give you what you need. But you took me off guard. Now that I know you want that… Well, we'll see next time, okay? We'll discuss it first. And, listen, this is important: I'm not going to fuck around on you. You know me better than that."

"I know. I do." Wade pulled away from Russ and wiped his eyes with the bottom of his t-shirt. "Fuck. I'm sorry I said those things. I'm sorry I accused you of—"

"You didn't accuse me of anything. You said what you're afraid of and I heard you. Now you hear me: that's not going to happen."

"What if we can't ever…what if I'm not able to…ever again."

Russ shook his head and put his finger to Wade's soft lips.

"Let's take this one day at a time."

Wade's eyes filled. "I'm so pissed he took that from us."

Russ pressed his forehead to Wade's. "He didn't win. We're still here. We're still together."

"And he's dead." Wade's voice was so final and grim it sent a shiver down his spine.

Russ answered it with his own darkness, letting Wade hear it, too. "Yes, baby. He's dead."

Chapter Seven

T HAT NIGHT WADE woke up alone in their dark bedroom to the sound of a shower running. Stifling a lurch of panic, he sat up, turned on the bedside lamp, and looked around their room.

It was all the same as it was before Los Angles. He'd explored every part of it carefully when he first got back. The doctors had suggested he should do that in order to make sure their room was a safe place for him with no hidden triggers where he might stumble over them in a delicate moment and be hurtled into pain and suffering again.

That day he'd opened each drawer and checked inside. When he'd come to the one that held their sex toys he'd hesitated. Russ had stood next to him, and he'd said nothing as Wade had slowly slid the drawer open and stared at the anal plug, the vibrator, the blindfold, the thick dildo, and the soft velvet ties. He'd shut the drawer quickly, sweat breaking out over his body in a wave of fear, and turned his back on it.

"I'll get rid of it," Russ had said.

"No." Wade shook his head. "Don't. Leave them where they are."

Russ had started to argue with him, but Wade had cut him off. "The doctor said you had to do what I told you when it comes to this stuff, remember? And I want them to stay there. I want to know they're in that drawer."

Russ had licked his lips nervously, glanced up at the ceiling like he wanted to argue, but finally just nodded, and hadn't brought up the sex toys since.

At the time, Wade hadn't explained further, but he knew getting rid of the evidence of the sex he'd used to enjoy with Russ would only make it seem that much less likely he'd ever be able to enjoy sex again. With the toys safe in the bedside drawer, in the protection of their bedroom, then he could allow himself to imagine, even if it was just for a few seconds before the panic kicked in, that one day they'd use those toys again. One day, he'd cum for Russ with the same joy and greed he had before.

Wade turned onto his side, listening to the shower, and blinked at the clock. It was three in the morning. He wondered why Russ was showering. Had his beeper gone off, summoning him to meet a client at the police station? Wade hadn't heard it. He was such a light sleeper now that it would have woken him, surely.

Wade waited a few minutes, but the anxiety of being alone without another person's grounding presence started to sneak up on him. The memories edged in, like hungry predators in the shadows, and he tossed them back with his covers, getting up to investigate what was going on with Russ in the bathroom.

When he opened the door quietly, stepping into the foggy bathroom, he was greeted by a soft, wet slapping sound. Heat rushed through him hard. The shower glass was fogged up, but the movement of Russ's shadow was clear.

He was jerking off.

Wade swallowed hard, his stomach flipping.

Why was he surprised? Of course he was jerking off. It'd been four months since they'd had any kind of sex. And Wade had kissed Russ tonight. Not just kissed him! Pushed his buttons and aroused him with no pay off. Even if Russ had declined to take it farther with Wade, of course he was horny. Of course he needed satisfaction. If not by Wade's body then by his own hand.

Wade backed out the door again, but the empty bedroom taunted him. The thought of returning to the bed alone, and the added triggering stimulation of the thoughts of sex, stopped him. Instead, he took a deep breath, forced himself to walk across the cold tile of the bathroom floor and ease open the glass shower door.

Russ leaned against the wall, the water spraying down on his chest, stomach, and thighs, as his hand moved rapidly over his engorged dick. His eyes scrunched in concentration and he whispered, "Wade, Wade, Wade," over and over.

Wade's heart thumped hard, wrenching in his chest. He'd always loved Russ's body: strong, compact, muscled, and masculine. The power and control Russ exuded when naked or fucking had always blown Wade's mind from that first night on his desk to the last time they'd made love before Los Angeles.

A cascade of memories flooded him, the joy of being with Russ, the heat of their bodies moving together, and how good and safe he'd always felt with him. Even when he was cumming uncontrollably, out of his mind with pleasure, he'd been safe with Russ.

Wade steeled himself. He wanted that back. It was his and he had every right to it. He shoved down his boxer shorts and pulled off his t-shirt, tossing them aside as he stepped into the misty, warm shower with Russ. "Let me help you."

Russ jumped a mile. His fat, nicely shaped cock stood straight out from his body, and his broad chest was flushed bright red. "Wade! I didn't mean to wake you."

Wade smiled, trying to control the racing of his heart, and force the jittery sensation from his thighs. This was nothing like when Owen forced him under the shower over the drain in the room, he told himself. This was their shower, in their home, and he was in it with Russ willingly.

"Wade, what are you doing?"

"I want to help you," Wade said. "I told you earlier. I want to touch you, and watch you cum."

Cum! Cum now, Wade! I'll kill him, you bastards!

He shook his head hard, driving Owen's voice away. Dammit, he wouldn't let Owen win. He was with Russ. He wanted this.

"You don't… This is…" Russ waved at his wet, hard dick. "I just…"

"Please," Wade said softly, letting his desperation show. "Let me touch you?"

Russ's cock jerked eagerly and in the past Wade would have sank to his knees and sucked that gorgeous length down immediately. But Wade knew better than anyone how a body responded to all kinds of things a person didn't want. He waited for Russ to answer him with words.

Russ's voice was gravelly. "Do you want that?"

"I told you I did earlier and I'm telling you now. I want you. I want this. Let me have it, please." He gazed down at Russ urgently. "Please, I'm begging you."

Russ swallowed and nodded. "Okay, baby. I'm leaving it to you. You can do anything you want. But I'm trusting that you'll stop if things get bad for you. Promise me."

"Promise."

Wade's heart pounded in his chest, and he felt weird, young, like he'd never done it before, like Russ's cock was the first he'd ever touched. Which was hilarious given the number of men he'd actually been with over the years. Men he'd had no trouble sucking and fucking like sex was just a dirty, super-messy handshake. Now he was trembling at touching the man he loved.

He decided it'd be like the kiss: easier once it started. Things would happen naturally once he was touching Russ, once he had Russ's skin under his hands.

The water from the shower covered Wade in a warm wet rush—*piss streaming over his face, his neck, his arms*—and Wade moved Russ out from under it, pulling him tight, and kissing his lips. Russ's body was solid, warm, and wet. He glanced down at their bodies pressed together—his pale skin against Russ's slightly darker hue, his dark body hair against Russ's almost hairlessness, and his thin lankiness against Russ's brute force. He loved how this felt. Always had. It was still so good.

Russ's cock pressed against his hip and when Wade bent down Russ's mouth opened for him. That was right, good, a kiss so real to hold onto. Owen had never kissed him, not once through the days in the basement, and so long as Russ's lips were on his, Wade felt locked in the present.

Wade took Russ's velvet cock in hand and shoved his own hardening dick against Russ's stomach. He jerked him quickly until his wrist started to ache, and then Russ took over. Looping his arms around Wade's neck and kissing him hard, Russ shuddered and moaned until Wade felt the hot, thick spatter of cum against his thighs.

Owen's grunts of pleasure. Owen's cum on his stomach, his legs, his stomach, his face, and up his ass.

Wade's treacherous cock reacted to the memory, growing harder, not out of arousal but out of necessity and horrific training. He shifted quickly into the rushing shower water to wash the semen and the memory away. He gazed down at Russ's flushed face and glassy eyes, taking in his lover's post-orgasmic gorgeousness, and shoved the nasty memories away.

He'd done it. He'd had sex with Russ again, and he'd made Russ cum. That was good. He could be proud.

Russ's hand grazed against Wade's cock. "Sorry," he whispered urgently. "Didn't mean to touch without permission."

Wade gripped Russ's body close and buried his face in Russs neck. "I'm safe with you. Please, touch me. I want you to."

Russ's hand on his cock was so different from Owen's. It was warm and strong, more talented and sure. But even marking the differences, it didn't stop the terror from rising. He fought to keep it down, trying to keep himself in the moment, but as his orgasm built—fast, hard, and inexorable—Owen claimed his mind.

Owen's hand on him. Owen's voice in his ear telling him that it was okay, that he had him. Owen saying his name. Owen owning his pleasure and pain.

Wade broke into sobs as cum jetted out of him. Sliding down Russ's body to the floor of the tub, he wailed. Grief flooded him and he couldn't contain it. Russ knelt beside him. He heard Russ's voice and felt his hands, but he had no idea how to respond, what to say.

All he knew is that he was not okay. He'd lost more than he'd known before.

Even his orgasm had been raped from him.

"I LOVE YOU," Russ murmured. "You're okay. I've got you. You're here with me, Wade. And you're okay."

Wade was in their bed now, still naked, and wet. He struggled hard not to flash back to the shivering cold misery of being covered in piss on the mattress in Owen's basement room.

"I need to dry my hair. I want it dry. I *need* it dry," Wade said, moving quickly, getting out of the bed too fast, and wobbling on unsteady legs.

"Okay," Russ said. "We can do that. Let me help you."

Wade fought the urge to push Russ's hands away, to insist he could handle it. And then, like he'd read Wade's mind, Russ asked, "Do you want to do it yourself?"

Wade exhaled and stood up straighter as Russ moved away from him. The encroaching sensation of another person in his space went away. They both put on robes and Russ hung back as Wade got to work.

The hair dryer was loud, and Wade felt vaguely guilty that they were probably disturbing the neighbors. Though the walls were thick, it was still the middle of the night and sound traveled. But he didn't feel guilty enough to not need his hair dried as fast as possible. It was a thing for him now, every time he showered. The sensation of water dripping down his neck was enough to make him nauseous and hard, and he'd be flooded with memories of Owen's urine all over his skin, dripping as it dried.

Russ stood behind him, clearly visible in the mirror. The white robe clung to his still-damp body and he chewed on his bottom lip. Pain and guilt twisted over his face. Wade finished up quickly, moved past Russ, careful not to touch him, and climbed back into bed, turning the pillow over so the dry side was up.

Russ sat cautiously beside him, his jaw clenching and releasing with emotion. "I'm sorry. I shouldn't have…" He scrubbed at his face. "I pushed it too fast." He didn't seem able to look at Wade but then forced himself. "I want you so much. It's not a request. I don't need it. It's just a fact. And I can wait—I'll wait as long as you need. I'll wait forever."

Wade's chin wobbled. He was exhausted, sobbed out, and the anxious hum from the orgasm still thrummed in him. Weirdly, he was getting hard again. He wasn't aroused, not even close, but it was as if by cumming once his body's memories had been triggered, and he was ramping up to be forced to cum a second time. It was a scary feeling, and also good. He was tempted to slide Russ's hand beneath his robe and put it on his cock, but he didn't.

"I want you, too," Wade said. "I do. I wish I could make it all stop."

"I know, baby."

He gestured at his dick. "Russ, I'm hard again."

"It's okay."

"I need you to understand why."

Russ's brows drew together and he licked his lips anxiously. "All right."

"It's because of what happened to me. How he'd make me cum over and over."

Russ's face crumpled and Wade reached out to run his hand through Russ's still damp curls, surprised the sensation of someone else's wet hair didn't trigger him.

"Are there…" Russ cleared his throat. "Are there things he didn't do to you?"

It was the closest Russ had come to asking for more details about what'd happened. Wade had always been surprised at how much Russ seemed to understand despite how little he asked.

"Yes. There are things he didn't do," Wade said. *Things he hasn't stolen.* "But orgasm, *my* orgasm…because he made me cum so much… That's something I can't do safely now, I don't think."

"You associate that with him."

"I associate cumming with being about to die," Wade clarified.

Russ's eyes closed tight, and he started to pull Wade into his arms before remembering, pausing, and waiting for Wade to come to him.

Rocked in Russ's arms, Wade closed his eyes. His cock

thrummed harder, demanding attention, and anxiety seeped through him. "Like right now. I feel like if I don't cum, I'm going to die, but I feel like if I do, then I probably die too. Either way, I'm scared."

"God, baby, what should I do?"

"It'll pass. I can breathe through it." Wade was fairly sure it would pass anyway. He hadn't been this naked and this close to Russ when he'd dealt with it in the past.

"What does Dr. Salinas say?" Russ asked.

"I haven't talked to him about this particular problem."

Wade felt Russ swallow, his Adam's apple bobbing against the side of Wade's face where he'd buried it against Russ's neck, smelling his warm, safe scent.

"I will," Wade interrupted. "Tomorrow. I'll tell him."

"You can do it on your own terms. When you feel ready. You don't have to do it tomorrow."

"But I do. Not for you. For me." He held Russ closer and whispered, "Well, for both of us. I need to figure out if there's a way to move past this."

"Oh, baby." Russ sighed and rocked him.

It was a long time before either of them relaxed enough again to fall asleep.

Chapter Eight

D R. SALINAS RUMMAGED around in his desk, looking for a new pen. He wore a button down shirt and a green sweater vest. Wade wondered why he wasn't sweating in the still simmering September heat.

Wearing a t-shirt, jeans, and tennis shoes, Wade settled into the comfortable chair.

Dr. Salinas's dark eyes studied him kindly. "Anything we want to discuss before we get started?"

Usually, unless there was something Wade wanted to address specifically, they began the EMDR work right away.

Wade squirmed in his seat, strangely embarrassed to address the topic of sex with Dr. Salinas. After spending months reliving with him, in excruciating detail, the sensations, emotions, and events associated with his weeks of capture, it didn't make sense to be bashful now. And yet he was. This *was* different; because it was about sex he wanted with a man he loved. It was too personal and fragile to be brought out for someone else's examination.

Dr. Salinas moved to the chair next to Wade, crossed his legs, and took up his notepad. "All right. If you don't have anything to discuss, where would you like to start with our work today?"

"I want to have sex again," Wade said, abruptly. A cold, wet feeling clamped down on his heart. "I want to have sex like I used to. With Russ."

Dr. Salinas took off his glasses and leaned back in his chair.

"Are you asking my permission?"

"No," Wade scoffed. But then he caught Dr. Salinas's concerned gaze and ducked his head. "I guess?"

Dr. Salinas smiled and put his glasses back on. "Unfortunately, I'm not in the business of giving my clients permission to have sex or to do anything else they feel ready for. I'm in the business of supporting you in your healthy choices, and helping you deal with the outcome of those choices."

Wade swallowed and picked at a thread of his jeans. "So you think sex is a healthy choice?"

"I think it can be."

Wade dropped his eyes down to the side, looking at the patterned carpet. "I tried it. Last night. With Russ. It didn't go so well."

"I see," Dr. Salinas's eyes softened. "Do you want to tell me about it?"

"Russ—" He didn't want to betray Russ's trust or invade his privacy. He wasn't sure how to talk about their sex life without doing just that, though. "Russ is attractive to me. I mean, we were always highly sexual from the very start. Our sex life used to be off the charts."

Dr. Salinas nodded and made a note.

Wade remembered the way he used to ride Russ's cock with reckless abandon, laughing and kissing Russ's mouth as he'd squirmed and demanded more. That time seemed so innocent now. Sex had been simple and abundant. No hang-ups, no rules, just a lot of kisses, laughter, orgasms, and sweat. They'd taken and given pleasure, and sometimes pain, joyfully.

Looking back, he'd been so young only four months ago. Now he felt old and frail, and sex seemed dangerous and deeply scary. The way he'd fallen apart the night before after his orgasm was proof enough of that.

"He's been so patient," Wade murmured.

"Russ can wait if you're not ready," Dr. Salinas said carefully. "If you need me to talk with him—"

"He's not pressuring me!" Wade raised his hands to stop Dr. Salinas's thoughts from going farther down that path. "It's not like that. It's what I want, too. For both of us."

"So, last night?"

Wade pressed the heels of his hands against his eyes. "Why is this embarrassing? I've told you so much worse than this."

"Well, this is your future you're working on. You've had your privacy stripped from you forcibly, and you're finally getting to a place where you have something of your own again. You don't have to share it, Wade. You deserve your intimate moments, just like anyone else. But if you want me to help you, then you'll probably have to let me in just a little."

Wade swallowed and then leaned forward, running a hand into his dark hair. "Okay, look, it's like this. I wanted him. Like a lot. Almost like I used to. I really did."

Dr. Salinas smiled gently. "I believe you."

"Yeah, so I convinced him I was ready. I helped him get off. I was doing okay, dealing with the memories, staying in the moment with him, and I was so turned on watching him when he...yeah." Wade turned his gaze way, looking out the window at the shimmering heat of the parking lot. He felt an echo of it creeping up his neck. "And then it was my turn."

"Your turn?"

Wade rolled his lips in and closed his eyes. The darkness felt a little safer. "My turn to cum. And I wanted to. It felt good." He pressed his fingers to his eyelids. "But then suddenly, I couldn't push the memories aside, and it was all Owen, and I lost it."

"You were unable to achieve orgasm?"

Wade shook his head, blew out a breath. "No. I got there.

I…I couldn't stay with Russ for it. I felt like it was Owen making me cum. And I panicked. Fell apart. Hell, I cried like a little kid. Russ was miserable after. He felt really bad. I think he blamed himself."

Dr. Salinas's eyes were sad and gentle, lending comfort he didn't have to speak out loud. "I see. How did you feel?"

"Scared. Sad. Angry. Miserable. Guilty that Russ was upset." Wade put his hand up again, knowing what Dr. Salinas was going to say. "And don't tell me I shouldn't feel bad for how this affects him. I know it's not my fault, but he deserves a healthy sex life and I want to give it to him."

"And do you want a healthy sex life for yourself? Or just for Russ?"

"For myself, too, obviously," Wade said, throwing up his hands. "I loved sex before. I loved it before Russ even. I slept with tons of guys. I was a super slut and happy to be."

"I prefer the term promiscuous myself," Dr. Salinas murmured, making another note on his pad.

"I don't know. To me promiscuous sounds judgey." Wade shrugged. "Like you're indiscriminate and careless about it. But slut is hot. So is cum dumpster." He blushed and Dr. Salinas raised his brows. "I used to love when Russ called me that. His little cum dumpster. I know, it's slutty. Maybe gross. I don't care. I loved it."

"We all like what we like." Dr. Salinas didn't even blink. "So long as it's consensual it doesn't matter what that is."

"Yeah. I don't know. It was hot when he said those things to me before. Now it's all fucked up. I don't need him to call me a cum dumpster again. Not really. I just want any kind of sex life back. I want to be able to do things with the man I love and not fall apart. I want it for me. Not just for him."

"That's fair. A healthy thing. And, if you want, we can work on this together."

"I want that very much."

Relief like cold water in a drought washed through him. Was there a way to be helped? Was there a path forward? Dr. Salinas seemed to think so. Wade swallowed the lump of hope in his throat.

"I think the first thing we can do is focus on the forced orgasms aspect of your trauma during our EMDR sessions. See if we can start to put that association in the past. Once that's done, we can work on the memories to change them. Let you go into the memory to free yourself from what's happening. Reclaim it."

"Sure. That's a good idea. Also, though…." Wade paused.

"Yes?"

Wade couldn't believe he'd just told his therapist he liked to be called a cum dumpster. He couldn't believe he was telling him more about what he wanted to do with Russ.

Wade cleared his throat. "Last night, Russ asked if there were things Owen hadn't done with me. And there are some. I guess what I want to know is are those things we could try?"

"First off, those things were done *to* you," Dr. Salinas corrected. "There was absolutely nothing that you did *with* Owen, Wade. Not once you were in Los Angeles, anyway."

"Right. I know that." Wade flushed. "Sometimes it feels less horrible if I add some kind of consent to what happened. You know, with my word choices. I tone it down internally. Gaslight myself, I guess. But I know. There was no consent. I didn't want any of it."

"I'm glad you understand that."

"Back to what I was asking—there are things that Owen never did to me. Kissing, for example. Owen never really did anything with his own mouth. Never went down on me, or had me go down on him. He'd cum in *my* mouth, and on my face, but he never made me suck him off."

Which was kind of weird when Wade thought about it, since he'd given Owen all kinds of blowjobs before their Friends With Benefits thing came to an end. Maybe that would have brought back too many memories for Owen? He'd never know.

Dr. Salinas nodded, made a few more notes, and then looked up at him waiting.

"So, yeah. I want to try those things with Russ."

"It seems like a good place to start. As good as any. A way to get your feet wet. Attempt to enjoy sex on your terms again."

"I'm scared, though. Last night was hard. And Russ… He doesn't need to deal with this. He deserves so much more than a broken boyfriend who can't even cum for him."

Dr. Salinas's eyebrows went up, and he gazed at Wade for a long moment. "First, you're not broken, just wounded right now. You'll scar. Just like your body has scars now, but you'll heal. Second, let Russ decide what he can deal with and what he deserves. That's not your business, is it? Your business is to get better and focus on reclaiming your life."

Wade snorted.

"The best thing for you both right now would be to sit down and talk about it. Make a list of the things Owen didn't do to you. Go through it together and cross off any activities that don't interest Russ or don't appeal to you."

Wade had to smirk at that. Russ liked it all. If it was sex, Russ was in. Wade wasn't too worried about that. He was the wild card now. There really was no way to know for sure what position or act might trigger him. He'd need to give each item on the list a lot of serious thought.

"And then the two of you should write down a plan of action."

"A sex plan?"

Dr. Salinas nodded, and pushed his glasses up his nose. "It isn't all that uncommon for partners to agree on their sexual encounters in advance. In some sexually charged subcultures, it's expected that each encounter, or scene, will be planned in detail, often in writing with each party signing the agreement. I suggest until you're surer of yourself, you and Russ engage in this kind of advance planning. That way you'll know what's coming. And, of course, you can renegotiate during the encounter to less intense acts if it gets to be too much—or call it quits at any point."

Wade wondered if Dr. Salinas had refrained from calling the BDSM community by name out of concern that it might trigger a panic. And just like that a dozen memories of restraint and pain flooded his mind. Wade swallowed hard against his instant, unwanted erection and the simultaneous rush of adrenaline-based fear.

Dr. Salinas was still talking, "Obviously, if orgasms are a problem for you, Wade, you aren't required to have them. Many people, women especially, never orgasm with a partner, or even alone, but still enjoy the sensations of intimacy and arousal."

Wade took a calming breath and agreed. He'd never considered the idea of sex without orgasm. He tried to imagine being with Russ while holding back from that final release. His erection hadn't subsided and he shifted uncomfortably.

Dr. Salinas didn't comment on his obvious physical reaction to the conversation. He was accustomed to Wade dealing with difficult arousal and unwanted erections during their sessions. There'd even been an embarrassing incident early on when Wade had been unable to withstand the pressure he'd felt to orgasm while reliving the trauma of Owen threatening to cut off his balls. He'd filled his pants with jizz as he'd arched out of the chair in an agony of panic. That'd been an especially hard day.

Dr. Salinas went on, "Do you have any further questions or

issues you want to cover with me?"

"No. I think this is all I need to open a dialogue with Russ." He almost snorted at that. Being in therapy had him using all kinds of ridiculous phrases.

"Good. Now, with all of this in mind, would you like to start today's session with a focus on the forced orgasms?"

Wade let out a bitter laugh at Dr. Salinas's choice of words. Wade would prefer to never start the session at all. But he nodded, and lifted the headphones to his ears.

Dr. Salinas took a deep breath and Wade copied him, exhaling slowly.

"Let's begin."

RUSS WAS SURPRISED when Wade requested they go to their as yet unlived-in house that Friday evening, but he didn't push for a reason why. Ever since Wade had come back, he'd found himself complying to all kinds of requests—"Do you mind turning off that song?" or "Please don't buy the lemon-scented bathroom cleaner anymore"—without question, because if it was what Wade needed or wanted, then it was what Wade would get.

As they pulled down the long drive, under the thick shade of the maple trees lining either side, Wade gazed out the passenger window quietly at the yard stretching out in undulating waves of long grass and clumps of trees to the closest neighbor hidden behind a thicket of woods almost three acres away.

Their house stood ahead of them—two stories and handsome. Done in a Mediterranean style with a Craftsman flair, it boasted wide windows, clean stucco exterior, wood beam accents, wooden garage doors, and stone around the entrance, all in browns and creams making the house feel cozy despite its size.

Russ remembered how Wade had marveled at it when they'd first had the realtor give them a showing.

"What are we going to do with six bedrooms, five and a half baths, a study, a living room, and—"

"And a kitchen with all the best appliances?" Russ had finished for him. "We're going to make a home and see what comes along to fill it. We'll have room for guests and maybe, one day…"

Wade's eyes had gone wide at the unspoken words. *Kids, family.* "You want that with me?"

"Why are you surprised?"

Wade had stuffed his hands in his pockets, rocked back and forth on his heels, and grinned widely. He hadn't replied with words, but the happy gleam in his eyes said it all. That day Russ's fingers had itched to sign the check for the down payment just to keep that look on Wade's face a little longer.

That was four months and a lifetime ago.

They pulled up to the front but Russ didn't open the garage. Staring at their beautiful house, they were both silent.

Russ didn't offer a penny for Wade's thoughts or prod in any way. After an intense session with Dr. Salinas, Wade needed time to process. Emotions and memories could still be lingering at the surface, especially if they hadn't been able to reach a resolution during the appointment.

Besides, after the other night's emotional upheaval, Russ had no desire to push Wade in any way. He wanted to take their entire life slowly, if need be, and let everything happen on Wade's terms. Even if it meant that certain things never happened at all.

Still, after sitting in the car, parked in front of the house for nearly five minutes, he couldn't hold back, and he said, "Are we going in? Or are we just checking out the exterior today?"

Wade snorted a small laugh, climbing out of the car. "We're going in. Bring your briefcase."

Russ did as Wade instructed and joined him in the sunshine, looking over the house again.

"Well," Wade said, crossing his arms over his chest and smiling in the dimmer way that he did now. "I still think it's perfect."

"And I still think it looks like some wealthy prick lives here." Which had been a selling point for Russ, really, though he liked to pretend it wasn't. "You know, some asshole who'll shout for kids to stay off his lawn."

Wade nodded. "You'll be so cute. *Stay off my lawn!*" He mimicked Russ's voice a little too well. "I almost can't wait."

"Invite Nic and Eric over, then. I'll christen the place by yelling it from the upstairs bedroom window."

As they approached the front door, Russ fiddled with his keys, and finally found the one that fit the brass lock.

"There aren't any kids nearby," Wade said softly, turning his head from side to side, examining the size of their parcel of land. "No really close neighbors at all."

Russ hesitated, his key slotted into the lock.

When they'd bought the house, that had been a selling point for Wade. He'd wanted a place smaller than Peach Blossom Farm, but big enough they had privacy. Now, though—who knew? Maybe the distance of the neighbors was a drawback. Maybe it reminded Wade of being isolated with Owen, far from anyone who might hear or help. Maybe Wade had brought him here to have one last look before announcing they should sell the place.

Russ's gut churned at the thought.

The memories of the weeks right before Wade had left for Los Angeles, the mundane silliness of fighting over the curtains and picking out the sofa, not to mention testing out a mattress or two very thoroughly before choosing just the right one, were all special to him. He hadn't realized until that very moment how he clung to those memories as the last normal, happy times they'd had before everything had gone so horribly wrong. He'd never been a sentimental type, but selling the house, leaving that all behind for good, would be the nail in the coffin of the hopes from their past.

He stiffened his back, resolved to let it go. Sentimentality was stupid. And he was Russ Paulson. He was anything but stupid. They would build a different future somewhere Wade was more comfortable. So long as he felt safe, that was all that mattered.

"Is the lock jammed?" Wade asked, his head tilted in concern.

Russ jiggled the key in the hole, and opened the door. "It's fine." He stepped aside to let Wade go in first. He bit back the words *Home Sweet Home.* He wouldn't make Wade feel guilty about wanting to sell the place.

"It's great." Wade gazed at the long hall with wooden floors, splitting into open rooms and ending in the large kitchen. He turned to look up the long front staircase that was freshly dusted from the Merry Maids service Russ hired once a week to keep the house in tip-top shape.

Wandering into the living room and back out again, he followed the hallway down to the kitchen. Russ trailed him, his heart aching with bittersweet emotions.

Suddenly, Wade stopped in front of the stone fireplace beside the breakfast nook in the kitchen, gazing up at the painting over the mantel. Russ gulped, a rush of nerves gripping him. He'd almost forgotten. The prank had seemed silly at the time, worth the fight and the make-up sex, and even the shipping cost for a return if Wade insisted. But now…

"You are such an *asshole,*" Wade said, crossing his arms over his chest and shaking his head. "I can't believe you."

"Uh, we can send it back."

"No we can't. It's been months." Wade turned a sharp hazel

gaze on him. "You're such a jerk."

"We can take it down. Replace it. It's no big deal."

Wade's eyes narrowed. "What do you mean, it's no big deal?"

"It was...I did it...." Russ sighed. He rubbed his hand through his hair. "It was before. It doesn't matter now."

Wade stared at him, his face lined and tired. Russ reached out, but he didn't touch. He held his hand up to Wade's cheek, and waited for Wade to press into his palm. Wade finally did, but his expression didn't change.

"We can still get the painting you wanted, baby," Russ whispered. "It was so ugly I'm sure it's still there."

Wade's lips twitched a little. "No, we're keeping this one."

"I don't understand." Russ moved his hand away from Wade's cheek. "You hate this one."

"You're right, I do. But I hate even more that you're not going to even fight me for it." Wade sighed. "Look, I'm not broken, Russ. You don't have to treat me like I can't handle everything not being exactly the way I want."

"I know that."

God, every single day Wade lived with his whole life no longer being what he wanted. Russ could get rid of one lousy painting.

Wade's eyes narrowed even more, and his lips twisted in unconvinced amusement. "Right. That's why you were apologizing this morning that the only bread we had left was the fiber kind you know I don't like, instead of just telling me not to be a baby and to eat it anyway. You used to say it'd keep me regular."

Russ sighed, surprised when Wade pulled him into his arms.

"I'm so sorry, Russ," Wade whispered.

"Wade, it's not—"

"Shh. Let me finish."

"Fine, but it's not your fault."

"I know that. I really need some things to go back to the way they were. I need you to be *you*—the man I fell in love with. And I want to be me again. I want you to fight with me over that awful painting."

Russ rubbed his cheek against the soft cotton of Wade's t-shirt. "Fine. We won't send it back. Because that horrible chicken painting you wanted is ugly and makes my eyes bleed. And you got to pick the hideous meadow over our bed, when we both know that the tasteful nude I'd suggested would've been more inspiring. So now we're even-steven. Got it?"

Wade squeezed him. "Got it."

"That better?"

Wade smiled and kissed him. Russ's knees went weak as Wade sucked in Russ's bottom lip and licked along the sensitive edge of his tongue.

Russ pulled back, panting. "Baby…"

Wade nuzzled his ear, and Russ's cock hardened, trapped in his pants.

Russ forced himself out of Wade's arms. "I don't think we should head down that path again." Russ wasn't sure he could take it if Wade broke down again so soon.

Wade's face looked bombed and Russ realized what he'd said.

"No. I mean. Yes, soon. Again. Whenever you're ready. Just not this second," Russ said quickly, touching Wade's face, trailing his thumb down over his lips and chin. "I meant what I said the other night. Nothing has changed about how much I want you."

Wade closed his eyes, and took a deep breath. When he opened them, he indicated the briefcase Russ had dropped on the floor. "You're right. We need to talk first. Come on."

Russ didn't like the sound of that, but he followed Wade to sit at the never-used kitchen table anyway.

"You asked the other night if there were things Owen hadn't done to me and I realized maybe those were things we could try together. I spoke to Dr. Salinas, and he had some good suggestions."

Wade watched Russ's expression as he outlined Dr. Salinas's idea that they should have a predetermined plan for sex, relieved when he saw nothing but eager commitment. He hadn't even realized one of his concerns was that Russ might resent the lack of spontaneity required.

But as Russ's eyes took on a familiar, competitive gleam, Wade realized how short sighted he'd been. Russ loved to beat the odds. It was part of why he was a defense attorney. He was methodical, brilliant, and he excelled at wringing victory out of the letter of the law. And as Wade talked, he could see Russ was already planning to orchestrate decisive wins against Wade's PTSD, because, *of course* that was how Russ would view any pre-designed and agreed upon sexual encounter they performed together.

Wade's cock throbbed in response to Russ's expression, and he was relieved that he didn't feel like crawling out of his skin. He was safe and firmly turned-on by the idea of Russ following their sex plan to the letter, checking off each event as he went, and giving himself highest marks for every one of them. Wade knew Russ was getting hard, too. He wanted to slide to his knees and take Russ's cock in his mouth and suck him with abandon. But they had to agree to everything first.

"So, what's on the menu?" Russ asked.

An odd thrill zipped through Wade at the crass question. It was like the old Russ, the one who didn't treat Wade like he was an already cracking piece of ancient pottery in need of delicate handling. He nodded at Russ's briefcase. "We should make a list."

Russ opened the case, passing his favorite pen over to Wade along with a yellow legal pad. The heavy weight of the pen tugged at his fingers as he wrote down the first item.

"Kissing," Wade said. "Um, never. Not even before L.A. when I used to suck him off. Owen never did that."

Russ stared at the paper and waited. "And?"

"Blowjobs will be okay. But—" Wade made a dash. "I'm sorry, but I don't want you to cum in my mouth."

Russ readily agreed to the stipulation.

"And," Wade said. "Position restrictions. I'm good with being on my knees, but I'm not sure about you being over me, like in sixty-nine. We can try, but I don't know."

"We'll take it slow. We don't have to do everything all at once."

Wade's cock jerked and his lips tugged up. He could tell Russ was actually dying to do everything all at once. He'd always been greedy with Wade's body, wanting as much of him in his mouth, under his hands, and around his cock as he could get. Wade knew Russ would be patient with him now, though, but the urgency was still there, and it made him weak with love.

"I can jerk you off," Wade went on. "But no hand jobs for me. That was the main way he…I just can't."

"It's okay," Russ said. "I like you in my mouth."

Wade's heart thumped and he pushed the heel of his hand to his cock. "I'm so turned on right now." And it wasn't scary. It was good.

"Me, too." Russ licked his lips. "Is that okay?"

"Yeah. I want to try something before we go. I want you to suck me."

"Okay."

Wade almost laughed at Russ's eagerness, so familiar. The way he'd always been, and yet Wade couldn't laugh because he was too horny. It took his breath away. It'd been so long since he'd last felt like *that*. His erection and arousal problems had been persistent since he'd been rescued, but the sensation had always been tainted with fear, even the other night. This arousal was pure, organic in response to Russ and to Wade's love for him. He'd almost stopped believing that lust with that flavor could still exist for him.

"Anything else?" Russ asked, but there was no pressure for more, just desperation to get to the part where they could touch.

"Rimming. And anal sex," Wade said, and he watched as Russ's mouth dropped open, and his eyes dilated to almost black. "Me topping you."

Owen had never ridden Wade's cock before L.A. or during the torture. He'd had always been terrified of the idea of bottoming and taking Wade's cock up his ass hadn't been part of his delusion.

While Wade had always preferred to bottom, and Russ had been a nearly exclusive top, there'd been four or five times when Wade had held Russ down and fucked him. Usually as part of a fight that turned into make-up sex in the middle. Russ had always gone primal, shooting his load and howling like a crazy man when Wade took control.

If Russ was up for it, Wade thought fucking was something he could handle. Though he wasn't sure he'd be able to let himself cum.

Wade looked down at the list. It was short and specific. He supposed they could work out entire scenarios from this list, once he'd tried the basic parts of it a few times with some success. Even if he never progressed or moved forward, it was a list a sex life could be salvaged from if necessary. He hoped.

"Well, I guess that's everything. If we take it slow, depending on how I react, maybe I'll be able to try more."

"But for now, we stick to this list. No deviations," Russ said firmly.

"Right," Wade agreed.

Russ nodded. He licked his lips and looked around at their house's kitchen. "So why are we here, Wade? Why did you want to talk about this here?"

Wade took a deep breath. "I know this is weird, but hear me out. I wanted some place fresh. The apartment is safe, familiar, but it's got all kinds of memories there now. Memories of the kind of sex we used to have. Memories of the last few months. Even the memory of the other night. I want us to start our work here, in our home."

Russ's eyes brightened even more. "You want to move in?"

"No," Wade said, shaking his head. "I'm not ready to leave our routines yet. But I want to only have sex here for now. Nothing at our apartment. This place can be a blank slate to put these experiences on."

Russ frowned a little.

"What?" Wade asked.

"Nothing. It's not important."

"If this is gonna work, I have to know everything and feel safe. I need to trust you. And you need to trust me, too."

Russ looked down at his hands and then back up at Wade again. "You're talking about 'having sex'. After we said we loved each other, you stopped calling it that and started saying we were 'making love'."

Wade stared at Russ, his heart flopping painfully in his chest. *Now I'm going to make love to you, Wade. I'll kill the demons with my love.* He held tight to the edge of the kitchen table, trying to keep from tumbling into bad memories. Owen didn't get to be here right now. Not in his new home. Not writing on his blank slate.

"It's not important," Russ said again.

Wade swallowed. "What we do together? It's making love. It's just things got rewired for me. I don't know how to explain it."

But he did know. He'd been rewired and now sex wasn't about giving and getting love and pleasure from Russ anymore. It was about performing acts in defiance of rape, of claiming his body for himself. Russ was the safe space, the lover who made it possible, as well as being the man he loved; but what they'd be doing together would be as much about bringing Wade back to himself as it would be about expressing their love for each other. Maybe more so.

"It's okay," Russ said.

"You always hated it when I called it that."

"I pretended to hate it," Russ admitted, looking at Wade from under his lashes with a vulnerability in his eyes that struck Wade to the quick.

"I know."

Russ sighed. "Well, that killed the mood."

"It's okay," Wade said. "I want to go upstairs to our room." He glanced over to the kitchen fireplace and the horrible painting Russ had gone behind his back and purchased. "Unless the meadow isn't really up there?"

"Nope. It's up there. You're not gonna be traumatized by a surprise nude."

"Good. Because I've been traumatized enough and have the diagnosis to prove it." Wade forced a chuckle and waved toward the painting over the fireplace. "And now this damn thing is going to take up a whole session with Dr. Salinas."

"Oh, please, the one you wanted could cause a brain hemorrhage just by looking at it."

They sat in silence for a few moments and Wade stared at the list of sex acts. They seemed funny and stark in his handwriting. The mood had changed. His throat was dry and his hands clammy. He felt clumsy. He didn't know how to go from sitting at the kitchen table to being upstairs with his cock in Russ's mouth. From the looks of things, Russ wasn't sure how to bridge that gap either.

Finally, Russ stood up, put out his hand, and said, "I believe you promised me I could suck your cock. I'd like to collect, if that's all right with you."

Wade took Russ's hand, knitting their fingers together, and nodded his head. It sounded ridiculous, like he was heading onto the football field against a tough opponent, but all he could think of to say was, "Bring it."

WADE SAT ON the edge of their bed, and Russ held both of Wade's hands tightly, kneeling between Wade's jean-clad thighs, slurping gently on the head of Wade's cock.

Russ tried to keep his eyes on Wade's face, measuring his responses. Wade stared down at him with a hot, intense expression, and Russ alternated between sucking him fast, and taking it very slow.

They were both still clothed. Wade said it felt safer that way, and Russ didn't push the issue. His fingers tightened on Wade's as he bobbed his head up and down, sucking and twisting his tongue over the head of Wade's cock, delicately and then roughly flicking at the frenulum before dipping into his urethra.

Wade squirmed but held on tight, his hips flexing up when something Russ did felt especially good. His noises came in short and sweet bursts of breath.

"Nng, feels good, Russ. So good."

Russ pulled off with a pop and Wade's cock bounced against his t-shirt clad stomach. Wade leaned down to kiss Russ, groaning into his mouth.

"Please," he whispered against Russ's lips. "More."

Russ ducked his head, his hands still twined with Wade's, and nosed Wade's hard cock, finally getting his mouth around the head again. His blood raced to smell his skin again, taste his musk, and feel him react to every touch.

He'd missed sex with Wade so fucking much. He hadn't even known, hadn't realized the full extent of the loss until now. Tears pricked his eyes. He wanted to push Wade back on the bed, crawl over him, and rut against him until they both came, but that was off limits. The blowjob Russ was giving might end up being the only thing they did, but it was enough. It was something.

Wade moaned, twisted his hips up, and then stilled. Russ worked harder, tasting the pre-cum leaking onto his tongue, feeling Wade's cock quiver and flex in his mouth.

Pulling his hands free, Wade grabbed Russ's head, and pulled him off his cock. He took a few calming breaths, and then twisted his fingers into Russ's hair to guide him back, whispering, "Take it slow, okay?"

Russ carefully slid down Wade's shaft, feeling the head butt up against his soft palate, and then he began a slow, slick, up and down. His own cock throbbed, and gripped it one-handed through his pants and used the other to cradle Wade's balls.

Rubbing them gently with the palm of his hand, he felt the scar where they'd operated to save Wade's testicles after they'd ruptured from Owen's abuse. He trembled with overwhelming tenderness for the delicate skin and the contents of Wade's sac. They'd been damaged enough that there was still concern about fertility, but, from the way Wade responded to Russ's gentle handling, there was no loss of sensation. He concentrated on making Wade's cock and balls feel as good as possible.

Wade crooned soft aching sounds, and guided Russ's head off again, taking long, slow breaths.

Russ gazed into Wade's hot eyes, the pupils blown wide and dark. "You okay, baby?"

"Yeah—" Wade gasped, his breath coming in short and shuddery. "Just—ugh." He squeezed his eyes closed and seemed to struggle with himself.

"Stay here with me."

Wade met Russ's eyes, present and focused. "I'm still here. I just got really close…and I can't. I'm sorry."

Russ released his hold on the base of Wade's straining cock. "Shh, don't be sorry." He leaned up and Wade's mouth was urgent, wet and slick against his own.

"You now," Wade said, pulling at Russ to move up the bed. "Let me help you."

Russ fell down against the mattress, resting on his back, while Wade knelt beside him, looking flushed and unbelievably fuckable. Russ held himself still and let Wade push his pants and underwear down enough for his eager cock to spring free.

Wade licked his lips, and reached down to touch his own dick, still hard and wet with Russ's spit. He released a painful noise of frustration, before bending to take Russ into his mouth.

Russ groaned, his hips coming up, desire he'd pushed aside and ignored for months tempting him to fuck into Wade's beautiful mouth wrapped so deliciously around his cockhead now. But he held back, making himself let Wade take the lead. Wade flicked at Russ's frenulum, the heat and slick of his mouth and tongue almost taking Russ too far, too fast. "Pull off. I might cum."

Wade pulled away, his hand moving rapidly up and down Russ's cock.

Russ bit his lip, shocked that he was so close already; they'd only just begun, but it'd been so long. He put his hand on Wade's wrist, but didn't still his movements, and he gasped, "Cumming."

Wade let go, diving for Russ's mouth and kissing him urgently as Russ grabbed his own cock to jerk himself through the orgasm. Hot cum splattered his fingers and wrist. Wade kissed him until he stopped shaking through aftershocks, and then pulled away, his eyes glowing and warm.

Russ huffed. "Damn. I feel fifteen again. No stamina."

Wade smiled at him, dopey, and still flushed. "Good to know I've still got it." He swallowed awkwardly, looked down at his own still-hard cock, and settled next to Russ with his head on Russ's chest. "Can we just rest here until my hard-on goes away?"

Russ wrapped his clean hand around Wade's shoulders, holding him close. He held up his other hand, covered with sticky cum. There was nothing else for it, unless he wanted to wipe it on the bed and deal with laundry, so he brought it up to his mouth and licked it clean. He noted his cum tasted saltier than Wade's usually did.

Wade watched him intensely.

"Okay?" Russ asked.

Wade nodded, and then hitched up, leaning just over Russ's face, hesitating. And then he kissed him, tentative and slowly, and then with a languid, urgent, happiness that it took Russ a moment to understand.

Russ smiled into the kiss, whispering against Wade's tongue and lips, "I love you."

Wade's redoubled passion in the kiss told Russ he loved him back.

Chapter Nine

WADE STOOD BY Moira's desk watching her type up a memo about changes in weekly reports. He felt warm and tingly, because as soon as Russ was done with his client, they were heading over to their house, where Wade was going to try being naked while they had sex.

They'd worked out the agreed upon scenario that morning over coffee, before Kari had shown up to drive Wade to his appointment with Dr. Salinas and then out to his new job with Doug on the farm. Then she'd dropped him off by Russ's office on her way to the grocery store, after the new nanny had shown up with the kids.

The folded up sheet of paper with their sex plan burned a hole in his back pocket. He tapped his feet, jingled his keys, and paced back and forth.

"I'd offer you coffee," Moira said, glancing up from under her black bangs with a lopsided smile. "But I think you've already had too much."

"Yeah, sorry," Wade said. "Just a little jittery today."

"Anything I can do to help?" Moira asked, giving him her full attention. "There are some doughnuts in the staff lounge. I could grab you one. They say carbs are good for anxiety."

"And bad for my waistline."

Moira rolled her eyes. "You sound like my mother. She died on a diet, you know."

"Like the diet killed her?" Wade asked, eyes going wide. "Jesus, I'm sorry."

"No, like she dieted her whole life trying to be thin, and on her deathbed she was still insisting on low-calorie and low-fat. No one should die without enjoying their food, Wade."

"I enjoy food."

"Let me get you a doughnut." As she stood up, Wade was reminded of how tall and thin she was, like a lamppost—all lines and no curves. She didn't wait for him to refuse again, walking with her long, masculine strides toward the break room.

Wade shrugged. A doughnut wouldn't hurt anything. He'd eat it if it'd make Moria feel like she'd helped.

He patted his front pocket again to make sure the pack of gum was still there. He'd purchased it at the gas station earlier while Kari was filling up. A dizzy swoop filled him when he thought of their plans for the evening. Twice now he'd sucked Russ's cock and it'd been a-okay. Tonight he was going to up the ante even more. He was going to stay the course to the end and let Russ cum in his mouth.

Wade accepted the doughnut and napkin from Moira when she returned. It was sweet against his tongue and he smiled, glad she'd insisted. "So," he asked. "How's your son doing?"

Moira's son had been in an automobile accident last spring while on vacation with his non-custodial father. He'd ended up needing some stitches on his head, and surgery for a ruptured spleen. The week after that, she'd made a few mistakes on the job, for which she'd thoroughly expected Russ to skewer her alive. Instead, Russ had sighed heavily, put his fingertips to his eyes, refrained from castigating her, and suggested she take a few personal days to get things under control.

Wade remembered her telling him about it with wide eyes and surprised laughter in her voice just a few days before his trip to California. "You've really changed him," she'd said. "I never would have guessed when you were his afternoon hookup that I'd be standing here saying this, but you've made him a better man."

"Nah," he'd told her. "He's always been like this. It's just before, he didn't want anyone to know."

Moira had rolled her eyes. "Take the compliment. You've thawed Russ Paulson's cold, cold heart."

Now she smiled up at Wade and pointed at a recent photo of her son on her desk. "Henry's doing great. Thanks for asking. And his father feels so guilty about what happened that he hasn't been late on his child support once. I can't believe you remembered that."

Wade cocked his head. "Why wouldn't I remember? You were pretty worried about him."

Moira's black eyes went weird and emotional, the way people's did lately when talking to him, like they just couldn't keep themselves from imagining all over again what he'd been through, and hurting for him.

Strangely, Wade found it comforting. It reminded him that people in general were good. Not everyone was dangerous. Not everyone was Owen.

"So much has happened since then. I thought…." she cleared her throat. "Never mind." She checked her email and just as Wade swallowed the last bite of doughnut, she groaned.

"I need to finish this," she said, nodding toward her computer screen. "Or Russ will have my head. According to the email he sent two minutes ago…" Her eyeroll was amusing. "He wants it done before he leaves."

Wade went to sit on a chair in the waiting area. Normally, he'd go into Russ's office and wait there, but there was a client inside. His leg shook up and down as he mentally swung back and forth between imagining in detail what he and Russ were going to do, and then skittering away from those thoughts. He was equally afraid of getting a hard-on or hitting a snag where he panicked. Either response wouldn't be good right now.

Dr. Salinas had been impressed with what they'd accomplished over the weekend, and their EMDR work had focused on the forced orgasms. Each time he relived one, he felt it receding into the distance. Dying by fading away. Dr. Salinas was proud of his work that day and he looked forward to telling Russ about it.

He was excited to have something to look forward to, even if it was scary and hard. It felt like the first time in forever. It felt like a quivery approximation of what he'd felt when he first fell in love with Russ. A rush of something new.

Putting a piece of gum into his mouth, he thought about the weekend. They'd gone riding out on the farm like they'd planned. Russ had been adorable and fussy on Sally but eventually gotten into the ride, enjoying the fresh air. Then they'd returned to the apartment together, hands entwined, and Russ had plopped down on the sofa with a satisfied grin. And Wade had felt satisfied, too. An optimistic, sweet sensation he'd nearly forgotten.

They'd driven out to the house on Sunday to practice sex again. Wade had let Russ blow him and, though orgasm still seemed far too dangerous and completely unattainable, he was thrilled with his progress. At least Owen hadn't ruined him entirely.

Wade bounced his foot up and down. He popped a second piece of gum in his mouth and shoved stray thoughts of Owen away.

"Wade," Russ's voice next to him made him jump. "You okay?"

Wade took a calming breath, stood, and smiled. "Yeah. Are we ready?"

Russ glared toward Moira. "You got that finished yet?"

"I just started it a few minutes ago. Get a grip," she replied, sending him a dark glance beneath her straight bangs.

He huffed, crossed his arms over his chest, and said, "Not a miracle worker, are you?"

"Never claimed to be."

"Well, I am, and I expect you to keep up."

Moira snorted.

Wade's mind flashed to the day before and the almost unbearable goodness of Russ's mouth pulling at his cock. He'd seemed like a miracle worker, all right, down on his knees and his talented tongue doing all the things Wade had always liked best. Heat raced up his neck and Russ's eyebrows rose as he noticed. "I'm ready to go, babe," he whispered.

Russ glanced back to Moira clacking away on the keyboard and frowned. Then he gripped Wade's arm and squeezed, sending him a hot smirk, before turning to say to Moira, "Have that on my desk first thing in the morning."

"Aye-aye, Cap'n," she said, not even looking up.

Russ reached out to Wade. "Let's go."

Wade's stomach fluttered as he twined their fingers together. "Lead the way, Counsellor. I'm all yours."

WADE STOOD, AS their agreement had spelled out, in the middle of their bedroom in their new house. He dug his toes into the warm, thick Aubusson rug under his bare feet, and, with shaking fingers, he pulled his green Henley over his head, throwing it to the floor. He almost wanted to call the whole thing off, but he focused on the plan and decided to stick it out.

It wasn't as though he hadn't been naked with Russ before.

Most recently in the bathroom that morning as they'd traded out the shower. But it'd been perfunctory nakedness. And while Russ had been privy to his body during his stay in the hospital, this was the first time Wade had invited him to take a good long look—and to touch.

The scars weren't as bad as they could've been. Given how infected several of the wounds had become, they'd all healed very nicely. Wade had bought a hand mirror and spent some time looking at them in the bathroom a few weeks ago. There were a few that looked like big raised Xs and one that looked like a long Y from where the whip had laid him open. Wade shuddered. That had been a very hard day with Owen. He squeezed his eyes shut. They'd all been very hard days.

"Wade, look at me," Russ said, his voice commanding but loving.

"Sorry," Wade mumbled, obeying.

"Don't be. I'm going to touch you now." He stepped closer, putting a soothing hand on Wade's arm. "Are we good?"

Wade nodded; his fingers tingled a little, and his toes felt strangely numb. Russ's hand slid up to his chest, and rested over his heart, fingering through his dark chest hair lightly.

"Shh," Russ hushed him. "You're hyperventilating. Do we need to take a break?"

Please, Owen. It hurts. Just a little break. For God's sake, Owen, please.

Wade shook his head. "No."

They were just getting started. He could do this, he *wanted* to. He reached out and grabbed a fistful of Russ's shirt, tugging him close. He turned his face into Russ's neck, breathing him in, and whispered, "I want you."

"I know, but we don't have to push things. You can dress again at any time, baby. In fact, it's a rule that you'll put your clothes on if you feel overwhelmed. We wrote that down together, remember?"

Wade released Russ's shirt and reached into his back pocket to pull out the paper. He unfolded it, and studied the words he'd written so optimistically that morning.

He peered into the shadows of the room. The bed was a comfortable king-size. They'd pulled the big duvet off and folded it onto the chair when they first came in, leaving the white, soft sheets exposed. The blinds were drawn on the windows against the afternoon sun, and the room was the perfect temperature. After the fluorescent lights that had accompanied Owen's abuse, like the lights of a hospital or school, allowing Owen to see every detail of Wade's pain, the shadows were comforting. There'd been nothing comforting with Owen—it'd been all sharpness and edges and hurt.

Their room, though, originally designed for maximum relaxation, was sheltered and welcoming. Russ's expression, so open and tender, let Wade sank into a sense of confined safety. Cushioned by the shadows, held in place by the plan on the paper in his hand. There would be no surprises, no edges to bite into him. He was here by his own choice, and it was good, with warm colors, and a soft rug, an even softer bed, and gentle Russ.

Wade let the plan drop to the floor, unbuttoned his jeans, unzipped them, and pushed them down to his feet. Steadying himself with Russ's arm, he kicked them off, and then lifted his arms a little and let them fall. His cock was flaccid, but he was safe so it was okay.

Russ asked gently. "Do you want my clothes off, too?"

Wade took in Russ's suit pants, button up shirt rolled up to his forearms, and leather belt. He wasn't sure. He wanted to see Russ, to feel his skin under his hands, but he wanted to save a little space between them for a minute, until he got used to being naked this way again. Somehow, Russ's clothes remaining on made him feel safe, despite his own nudity. He shook his head.

Russ's thumb ran the length of Wade's jawline, soothing. "Okay. Let's get on the bed."

The sheets slid under Wade's back as he pushed himself back to the pillows. Russ's long fingers trailed up Wade's body to his face. There were scars on his front side, too. Wade squirmed as Russ's tickling fingers moved over places where the whip had gone too deep and left a permanent reminder.

Wade didn't know if they were ugly. He hadn't let himself think of them much at all, keeping his body as separate from his mind as possible, registering himself mostly as 'safe' or 'not safe' at any given point in time. Here, now, though, it crossed his mind that Russ might not like them.

But Russ's expression was hot, intense, burning with lust for Wade. His eyes glowed with an angry affection, protective and yet already thwarted. He'd been unable to spare Wade the violation, but Wade had no doubt, looking at Russ's face, that he was capable of preventing something like it from ever happening again. He was sure, as Russ gazed down at him, touching the slashing scar across his chest, just below his nipple, that Russ would kill someone who tried to hurt Wade.

"Shove your fingers in like that again, and you'll go to your grave screaming for your mommy."

That'd been when Wade was still in the hospital and Russ had nearly eviscerated a male nurse who'd been too rough testing the damage to Wade's anus.

"Oh," Wade sighed, and relaxed into the bed. "I'm okay. I can do this."

Russ smiled softly. "You sound pretty sure."

"I am."

Russ slid down over Wade's hips, giving him a scorching

glance, and then he opened his mouth. All Wade could register was a hot, wet, so-damn-good that brought his dick up to a shocking hardness immediately.

Wade stared at the ceiling, the shadows bled in from the corners, and he gave up to the delirious, hot feeling that swelled in him. Russ's saliva dripped down his shaft and flowed over his balls in wet rushes. Suction made his eyes roll up and his toes curl hard. He reached down and pulled Russ off.

He yanked Russ up to kiss and moaned against his lips. He wanted it to last a little longer, but his body was trained to cum. He could feel the overwhelming push for it in his system, like an addiction, like the need for breath. But orgasm rang with terror, and he couldn't dive in, couldn't indulge, even though his body wanted it, ached for it. His mind would shatter.

"Dammit," he cursed softly, pulling out of Russ's kiss, panting into the air between them. Russ's clothes rubbed against his naked body, and he clutched at Russ's shirt for some safety.

"Hey, it's okay. We'll slow it down."

"It's not that," Wade said, panting. "It's that I want to cum so damn much, but I'm scared."

"It's okay. You don't have to. You're here with me, and you don't have to do that."

Wade shuddered against Russ, breathing slowly, feeling himself edge away from the drop over into panic. "Will you hold my balls down?" he asked. "I want it to last longer. I want to enjoy it more. Please, Russ?"

"You don't have to beg, Wade," Russ said. "It's your terms, remember?"

Russ slid his hand down and wrapped around Wade's balls—poised and ready to unload—and he gently tugged them down. The pull was good, a sweet stretch, and Wade grunted as the threat of orgasm backed away.

Russ kissed him again, and then slid down to suck Wade's aching cock again. Wade pushed his heels down against the bed to keep from shoving up into Russ's throat. He held himself as still as possible, wanting to lay back and enjoy, and not just jizz hard in screaming agony.

Russ's mouth was so talented. Wade remembered the first time Russ sucked him. He'd been in Russ's big leather office chair and Russ had been under the desk on his knees in his suit. Wade had lasted almost no time at all under the onslaught of Russ's technique, and he'd been shaky and shocked after, left speechless while Russ had licked his lips with a sexy smirk, so damn arrogant and pleased with himself.

Wade squirmed his hips up, rolling his cock over Russ's tongue and into the back of his throat. Russ took him *in*, swallowing around his cock with unbelievable control. Wade's hands went to Russ's hair to tug him off, when Russ yanked his balls hard, ripping him back from the edge of orgasm again.

"Oh, *God*," Wade gasped, his hands flying up, grasping at the air in an attempt to hold on, and then he yelled, his cock jerking slightly, and Russ squeezed and pulled, keeping him from cumming but edging him hard.

It was so good, and the soft mattress beneath his back, and the darkness of the room kept him safe, even as he was near tears from how damn good his cock and balls felt, sucked and spit on, and sucked some more.

"Wanna, God, I wanna...so much," Wade muttered, but Russ pulled his balls again, and moved away, leaving Wade's cock thumping with each beat of his heart, slick with spit against his stomach.

"Not today," Russ said. "It's not on the list."

Wade nearly cursed. They'd agreed not to renegotiate anything that upped the ante during sex itself. They'd only negotiate down. And now Wade was so turned on, his nipples tight, tingling, and aching, and his balls drawn up despite Russ's last tug, he wanted so badly to test it. He could handle it. He knew he could.

Russ pulled his balls back down again, and whispered, "I want it, too, baby, but not today."

Wade hadn't realized he'd begged, until Russ was kissing him, saying into his mouth, between passionate licks and nips, "Please don't beg me. I can't let you today. You have to be able to trust me."

Wade groaned, and rolled Russ onto his back, jerked his suit pants down and got his hands on Russ's hard, thudding cock. Swirled into the darkness of the room, the light from the blinds was diffuse and warm, and his brain melted with lust and want as he sucked Russ's cock in so fast that Russ arched, pushing against Wade's shoulders.

"Jesus, Wade, *fuck*," Russ said, scrabbling at Wade's hair. "Off, off, I'm going to cum."

But Wade didn't budge; he wanted it. He had the gum for this reason, and he wanted it, dammit. He sucked at Russ's cock like a greedy, starved thing.

Russ shook under his hands and his cock swelled in Wade's mouth.

"Last. Chance," Russ gritted out, and then it was too late.

Wade swallowed and swallowed as a load of cum filled his mouth. Russ cried out as he hunched in ecstasy.

Suddenly, Wade gagged, pulled away, and had to cover his mouth with his hands. Russ's cum was different from Owen's, but it was still cum, and the slick of it against the inside of his cheeks, and the slime of it on his tongue made him heave. He scrambled to the ground, trying to reach the pocket of his jeans before he threw up, and Russ was beside him, helping him get the gum in his mouth. Chewing with his eyes shut, grateful for the burst of cinnamon, Wade hunched to the ground, trying to get the swirling nausea to subside.

Russ rubbed his back and Wade covered his face, working hard not to cry.

"I'm sorry," he choked out, his hard cock still aching.

Russ sighed and held him close, rocking him back and forth.

WHEN RUSS AND Wade crawled back to the bed together, they curled up with their heads at the foot and their feet propped on the pillows. Staring up at the painting of the meadow that Wade had picked out, Russ made a mental note to strip the bed and put on new sheets before they left for home.

After he'd calmed down, Wade had pushed Russ's suit pants off and unbuttoned Russ's shirt, so Russ was just in his boxer briefs, twined up with Wade who was still naked. He rubbed Wade's shoulder in silence, and listened to the sound of Wade chewing the three pieces of gum he'd shoved into his mouth to keep from throwing up.

Russ's emotions swayed between gratefulness that Wade still wanted him close, and guilt for having let things go that far. Even though they'd agreed to it to begin with, it had been too much, too soon. Taste and smell were such visceral things—the strongest memories were attached to them, and despite his attempt to eat healthily so his cum would be more palatable than Owen's, there was no way it didn't still just taste a hell of a lot like *cum*. He'd been an idiot. A greedy idiot who'd wanted Wade too much.

"Hey, Russ? Stop it," Wade said from where his head rested on Russ's chest.

"Stop what?" Russ asked, knowing full well what Wade was

talking about, but hoping to deflect it.

"Stop feeling guilty. I'm the one who pushed it. It's my fault."

Russ groaned. "You're right." He felt Wade stiffen. "I'll stop if you do. It's not your fault, and it's not mine. It's Owen's and he's dead. We've got to clean up his mess, and I don't care how long it takes, Wade. I'm not going anywhere."

"What if I can never—"

"So, you're giving up? One botched attempt at a blowjob and you're just done? That's absurd. Blowjobs are hard work. They take practice. Ask any seventeen-year-old girl and she'll tell you."

Wade laughed softly, which was Russ's goal, aside from making his point.

"I believe in you, baby. I'm just sorry today ended badly."

Wade brought his fingers to Russ's mouth, and Russ noticed they were still trembling a little as he traced Russ's lips. "Me, too." He pushed his index finger against Russ's lower lip, and then dropped his hand to Russ's chest, resting it over his heart. "I got excited after our success this weekend and pushed too hard."

"Maybe," Russ said. "But we can look at it another way, too."

"Oh, yeah?"

"It wasn't a failure. You were engaged right up until you weren't. You were turned on, hard as a rock, into it, and it felt good for you."

"That's huge," Wade agreed.

"Yep. I'd call this venture a success."

Wade snuggled up closer, and Russ let his fingers run over the scars on Wade's back. He felt a shift in his body tension.

"Do they bother you?" Wade asked.

"No," Russ said. "Should they?"

Aside from the obvious, that they were a reminder of what'd happened, Russ didn't see any point in dwelling on them as anything more than part of Wade now. They weren't going anywhere. He wanted the right to grow to love them as evidence of Wade's strength.

"Well, they're not exactly attractive," Wade said, lifting up to get a better look at Russ's face.

Russ shrugged, brought his hand up to Wade's cheek, and said, "Depends on what you like in a man. I like bad-asses, myself. You know, hot guys who can withstand going to hell and back, and confidently sport the scars to prove it."

Wade narrowed his eyes at him, a small almost-annoyed smirk on his lips, obviously trying to decide how seriously to take Russ's comments. Finally he put his head back to Russ's chest, and then reached for his hand, bringing it up to his back again. "Feel how bad-ass I am, then. I suspect you'll be impressed."

Russ ran his index finger over the X making Wade break out in goosebumps. "More than you'll ever know, baby."

Wade kissed Russ's chest.

"You're fucking tough," Russ said.

"I'm fucking scary," Wade agreed, pressing a kiss to Russ's nipple.

"Terrifying."

And he meant it. For Wade to have survived what he had showed the kind of strength Russ couldn't even imagine. He wasn't sure there was anything Wade wouldn't be able to do or endure after his ordeal. At his deepest core, Wade was made of something unbreakable and pure—like a diamond under his skin.

Russ kissed the top of Wade's head, wondering if he even knew how much Russ relied on his strength. Russ didn't think he'd have been able to come back from that kind of torture, not even for Wade. And Russ knew he'd at least *try* to do anything for Wade.

Anything at all.

Chapter Ten

FOR VARIOUS REASONS, it'd been almost three days since their last sexual encounter. The time elapsed seemed to make it both scarier and more thrilling to contemplate trying again.

Sitting alone, across from Samuel and Kari in the crowded, deliciously-scented Flying Biscuit, Wade listened to his best friend bicker with Russ's best friend. It was a familiar scene, one that had taken place many times before over the last year, even if Russ wasn't there with them yet. He'd texted to say he was stuck in court but he'd join them later.

"Samuel, you can't be serious," Kari scolded, leaning forward over the remains of her meatloaf. Her face glowed with the warmth of the overcrowded restaurant and her red hair was piled up on her head in a messy bun. "The last man you 'fell for' from Grindr turned out to be a complete jerk. Maybe start looking elsewhere."

"You liked Frank," Samuel said, rolling his eyes. "You said he was charming."

"When did I ever say that? He was constantly scoping out any room he was in for someone to screw. He even hit on Doug."

Samuel took a bite of turkey pot roast, groaned and slapped his hand on the table again. "Damn, this is good."

"We know," Kari said. "You've come in your pants twenty times already over it."

Samuel ignored her moaning and stuffing in a few more bites.

His shirtsleeves were rolled up, exposing his fine boned wrists, and his white shirt stood out against his skin. "Goddamn, this is delicious. Babies, you're missing out."

"I think the entire restaurant is sharing in your bliss," Wade said.

"Enough about your food! Seriously, Samuel, you have to stop doing the Grindr thing. Every man you meet from there is an asshole."

"Darling, you have no idea how many men I've met from that app. And only a few of them have been assholes. Most of them have been big, hard dicks."

Wade snorted.

"Oh, please," Kari said, rolling her eyes. "You know you've never topped for anyone."

Samuel giggled and took another bite. "We're trying to have a nice meal with Wade. Why squabble over my lovers?"

"Who's squabbling?" Kari asked. "Not me. I'm just stating the facts. And history shows that your taste in Grindr hook-ups can't be trusted."

"Pierre is a true gentleman." Samuel referenced the man he'd had sex with twice since Monday. "Russ liked him," Samuel said, like that was proof of anything, and Wade coughed into his napkin again.

"When did Russ meet this guy?"

"I brought him by the office yesterday."

"Before paying for this Pierre dude's Uber home," Wade murmured.

Russ had not, in fact, liked Pierre, but unlike Kari, Russ didn't really give a shit if Samuel blew off some steam with a hot new piece of ass from Grindr. Russ wasn't interested in getting his friends to fall in love. Hell, Wade knew Russ had never meant to fall in love himself.

Wade sighed. Pierre was a stranger, and Wade wasn't even comfortable with people he was familiar with now, like Trey, being alone with the ones he cared about most. He hoped before long he'd be able to get a sense of safety back, but the first thing he'd thought when he heard about Samuel and Pierre was, "What kind of hell will you bring my friend?"

Samuel was a grown man and he could do what he wanted. Wade had often enough before…

"Oh, *really?*" Kari drawled. "Russ liked him? Somehow I doubt that. We all know Russ has good taste." She smiled at Wade and reached across to pat his cheek like he was five.

"Russ has great taste," Russ himself said, dropping into the chair beside Wade. He kissed Wade's cheek. "Hi, baby, enjoying din-din with the women in our life?"

Samuel squawked. Kari just laughed.

"It's a blast listening to them poke at each other," Wade said, smiling and indicated his chicken potpie. "I'm done if you want the rest of mine."

Russ took him up on it, digging in eagerly. "Did I miss anything good?"

"Oh, no," Kari said. "Samuel and I were just warming up. You're in time for the main event."

Samuel's phone buzzed and he glanced at the message before putting his napkin on the table, shaking his head. "That's my booty call." He kissed Kari's cheek, stood and then came around to kiss Russ's cheek too. "I'll see you tomorrow at lunch, lover."

Russ nodded.

Samuel mock-glared at Kari before she could protest, saying pointedly, "Who I hook up with is my business."

Kari put her hands up in the 'surrender' pose and Wade sighed as Samuel walked away.

"Did you have to needle him so much?" Wade asked, sitting

down again.

Kari chortled and lifted her glass to toast the air. "Oh, but harassing Samuel about his poor life choices is so *fun*."

"Don't look at me," Russ said. "I wasn't even here."

Wade sighed.

Russ had nearly devoured Wade's leftover chicken potpie.

"Why do you let him date jerk? Kari asked Russ, kicking him under the table.

Russ shrugged. "Pierre is all smarm and big dick. Nothing to write home about, but nothing to give a guy grief over either."

"But from that app? For all we know he could be a serial…" Kari stiffened in her seat.

Russ rubbed Wade's back soothingly between bites, and said, "Let's not go there."

They spent a few minutes talking about Wade's work with Doug and then it was time to go. Russ paid for everyone's dinner over Kari's protests, muttering, "At least your best friend pretends like she's going to pony up. Mine just leaves it to me."

"Okay, I need to hit the powder room," Kari said, grabbing her purse. "I'll be back. Don't talk about anything fun without me."

Wade watched her walk across the room, maneuvering through the crowd, and then turned back to Russ who finished devouring what was left of Wade's meal.

"If you're still hungry, we can order take out, you know. This is a restaurant. They have more food."

Russ shot a brief smile Wade's way, and then said, "Actually, I was hoping to get to the next course." He waggled his eyebrows, and Wade's stomach knotted in anxiety. He couldn't talk about it here. It wasn't their safe place. He felt much too vulnerable with all of these strangers around.

Russ frowned, wiped his mouth with Wade's napkin and

leaned in closer. "You okay? We can skip tonight. Go back to the apartment, finish up that episode of *Black Books*."

Wade looked around to see if anyone was looking at them, or listening to their conversation. "I'm just nervous," he conceded.

"You still want to go to the house?"

Wade put his napkin beside his plate, and summoning courage, he smiled. "I do. When Kari gets back, let's get out of here. I'm ready."

"So am I."

After kissing Kari's cheek and leaving a good tip on the table, Wade took Russ's hand and they left the restaurant, exiting into the warm evening. As they climbed into Russ's car, Wade took the paper with their plan on it from his back pocket, and smoothed it out.

Russ kissed the back of Wade's hand. "Are you ready?"

Wade took a deep breath. "Yes."

They drove toward their house in silence.

Twenty minutes later, Wade, rested comfortably on his side, naked and flushed. Russ sat beside him, one hand on Wade's hip, making gentle circles on his skin, and holding the plan they'd drawn up that morning in his other.

Russ scanned his eyes over it, lingering on the last item. He wasn't entirely sure Wade would be able to handle it. They were already introducing one new item, rimming, and while he knew Wade had always loved that in the past, this was a whole new ballgame.

Russ met Wade's eyes, and examined his face. "You're sure about wanting me to let you cum if you ask to?"

Wade's gaze didn't waver from his, but Russ saw a spark of fear. "I'm sure," Wade said, sounding determined.

Russ nodded slowly. They'd already agreed to it this morning. Rimming had been Wade's *thing* before everything had happened, and he'd used to cum without even touching his cock when Russ did it hard and fast.

Asking Wade to hold back from cumming, if he was able to get to that level of enjoyment would be almost impossible, and it was, after all, part of what they were working toward, anyway: Wade freely enjoying sex and the natural outcome of his pleasure. The real question was whether Russ could handle the fall-out if Wade went into a panic reaction. He steeled himself. If it came down to it, he could. It wouldn't be fun, but he could handle anything Wade threw at him.

"All right," Russ said, unbuttoning his shirt, and putting the list on the bedside table. "Let's start."

He shucked his clothes, and was hard before he even got his boxer-briefs off. Wade was hard, too, watching Russ with avid eyes and lying on his back on the blue sheets Russ had put on the bed before they left three days before.

It was remarkable how Wade was changing with their encounters, becoming more and more relaxed at the onset, more sure of himself, giving up to the sensations and enjoying being edged. He still panicked sometimes if he got too close to cumming, but Russ was good at pulling him back from the brink in a way that calmed him down emotionally.

That was important to Russ, that he be able to bring Wade back to a state of equilibrium quickly, while still maintaining Wade's lustful wanting. It turned out it was usually as easy as tugging on Wade's balls hard enough to hurt a little, while talking to him in a warm, commanding tone. "Wade, you're with me. Relax. Breathe." He'd catch Wade's eye and watch as he melted into the mattress, breathing deeply, relaxing, and then Wade would guide Russ's mouth back to his cock to bring him up to the edge again.

Wade had explained that Dr. Salinas said it was good for

them to perform these activities as close to daily as they could manage. So long as Wade was able to maintain positive outcomes, and handle any poor ones with grace, then the practice of engaging in pleasant sex acts together every day would help to rewire Wade's brain.

And the fixed setting was good, too, Dr. Salinas had said, because they could control the stimuli introduced. Later, after things were once again in full swing between them, they could try introducing different locations, always understanding that even three years from now there could be a surprise trigger for Wade when doing something new or when in an unfamiliar place.

For now, their room was a safe haven for them both. Even when Wade arrived at their house stiff or short with anxiety, Russ could see the tension release from his shoulders as he came into the room and looked around. He often stared up at the picture of the meadow while he took off his clothes. Russ might have thought it was a dumb painting when they bought it, but it seemed to be Wade's focal point for peaceful feelings when he wasn't looking at Russ, and for that reason the painting was now a favorite.

"What do you think about when you look at it?" Russ had asked several days before, head at the foot of the bed again, staring up at the painting. He was curled up with Wade, limp from orgasm, and waiting for Wade's hard-on to calm before they left the room to go home.

"Mm," Wade had mumbled against his chest, and then he'd shrugged. "I don't think about anything. I go there."

Russ had stroked his hair and said nothing. He wasn't sure what Wade's words meant exactly, but then again, he wasn't the fanciful type. If it worked for Wade, that was all that mattered.

"Here," Russ said now, positioning himself on his back with his head at the foot. "You'll be able to see the...." he waved at the painting. "Get over me."

They'd practiced this a little the prior week, the sixty-nine position, with Wade on top, fucking down into Russ's throat, and Russ's cock alternating between Wade's hot mouth and spit-sloppy hand. Wade had done well, almost cumming in that position, and then Russ *had* cum, and Wade had jerked him through the spurts, only moving aside to wipe the cum off his hand quickly when Russ was fully done shuddering through aftershocks. It was a huge success in both of their minds, and they'd decided that it would be best to rim in that position, too.

Wade passed a pillow to Russ to prop his head up, making it easier to get his mouth on Wade's hole, and Russ grinned as Wade slid in beside him, hot, wet mouth on his neck and then moving up to his lips.

"Evening stubble," Wade said, in a breathy voice.

Russ smirked into the kiss. "You love it."

"I do," Wade agreed. "Remember that time you didn't shave for a few days?" He shuddered in Russ's arms. "That was amazing."

Russ did remember. He'd been so busy with preparing for court and then collapsing in exhaustion that he hadn't had time to shave. He'd woken from a seriously needed sixteen hours of sleep to a sandwich, a shower, and a very horny Wade. He'd rimmed him for an hour with his beard scratching at his anus. Wade had cum so hard he'd actually bitten a hole in the pillow, which they'd both laughed about for days.

Wade kissed his way down Russ's torso, and then moved back up for a quick kiss and to stare down into Russ's eyes. Finally, he turned around and settled himself on top of Russ, his face buried between Russ's legs, wedged in there, and taking deep, obviously steadying breaths.

While Wade took slow breaths in the space between Russ's

thighs, Russ took his time, massaging Wade's ass-cheeks and rubbing his hands up and down Wade's haunches. Wade's hard cock thudded gently where it rested against Russ's neck and collarbone, and he moved his hands gently in place to pull Wade's ass open wider.

Wade's hole squeezed and released in anticipation. It looked tight, with hair swirling around the edge, and there were two thick scars at two o'clock and six o'clock, where Wade's asshole had ripped from Owen's torture. The scars were raised and red. Russ wasn't sure how the sensation would be for Wade now. He'd read that many scars were numb and others could be incredibly sensitive, especially if located on top of a muscle. Which was, of course, what Wade's anus was.

He kissed where Wade's thigh joined his buttocks, and then he kissed the hole, close-lipped and gentle. Wade sighed, and pushed back. Russ did it again, feeling the soft, responsive muscle twitch against his lips. He let out a hot breath and Wade squirmed in his arms. Then he licked.

Wade groaned, lifted his head, and gazed up at the painting before ducking his face between Russ's thighs again. His hole squeezed tight and then opened, gripping at Russ's tongue.

As Russ tickled the tip of his tongue along the edges of the scars, Wade wrapped his arms around Russ's hips, and brought two of his own spit-slick fingers to Russ's anus. Russ bore down on them and moaned against Wade's hole as the sudden stretch burned up his spine. Wade hooked his fingers, and Russ grunted as his prostate was pressed.

"You're pushing the envelope," Russ gritted out. "That wasn't on the list."

Wade twisted his fingers in Russ's asshole, and prodded at his prostate. Pressurized pleasure radiated through him. He didn't care if it wasn't on the list. It was his body, not Wade's, and the list covered what Russ would do to *Wade*. Russ was certain that Owen had never insisted that Wade finger him during the ordeal. It felt safe—so he let it go, diving into Wade's ass instead, mouthing at Wade's hole with his lips, tongue, and lightly with his teeth.

Wade bucked and wriggled until Russ had to grab his hips to keep from being smashed. He drilled his tongue against Wade's hole, listening to his rising wail of pleasure, as Wade bucked and jerked, fingers twisting distractingly in Russ's ass.

Russ's tongue slid into the tight, clamping heat of Wade's anus.

"Oh God!" Wade clutched at Russ's thigh with his free hand, and screwed his fingers into Russ with the other, crying out and trembling all over.

"Russ, Russ, Russ," he chanted as Russ ate his ass. He pulled his fingers free, clambered up to his hands, and made small yelping noises every time Russ pushed his tongue in deeper.

Russ pulled back. "Okay?" he asked.

"Don't you dare stop," Wade ordered, backing his ass toward Russ's face.

Russ had to push up on Wade's ass cheeks to keep from being smothered as he licked at Wade's spasming hole. Then he shoved Wade forward again, feeling his hard, leaking cock smear pre-cum all over his chest.

He spit on Wade's asshole, drove his tongue in and wormed it around. Wade cried out and bucked against him. "Oh, fuck!" Hot, wet cum pulsed all over Russ's neck, chest, and stomach, as Wade's hole squeezed hard on Russ's tongue. "Oh, babe! I'm cumming! Fuck, fuck!"

Russ had to work to keep his tongue shoved in against the working muscles.

As the spasms faded, and Wade stopped calling out, Russ

pulled the tip of his tongue from Wade's still quivering ass. He licked at his hole sweetly, gently, soothing it and, hopefully, Wade at the same time.

Wade shook over him, his cock jerking, and his ass twitching under Russ's ministrations. Finally, he collapsed, smashing Russ's still hard cock up against his chest, his breath coming in deep heaves. He buried his face between Russ's thighs again.

Russ continued to lick softly at Wade's asshole, rubbing his hands up and down Wade's lower back and over his ass cheeks and thighs. He expected Wade to turn around, kiss him, or begin to panic. But to his amazement Wade just hunched back and pushed his ass at Russ's face some more. He then took Russ's cock into his mouth, sucking lazily, slowly, and clearly wanting to be rimmed more.

Russ's own anxiety released. He gave his mind over to the sensation of hot, wet suction on his cock, and the taste of Wade's sweet ass on his tongue. He sucked at Wade's hole, drilled it, and pulled Wade's cheeks apart to push in deeper, while Wade's cock fattened up again and he squirmed in Russ's arms.

Part of him was amazed, and another part thought he should have known. They should have started with rimming right away. Wade loved it. He always had. Russ grinned against Wade's ass cheek.

Wade pulled off Russ's cock, spit on it, and jerked it sloppily while he moaned, open-mouthed against Russ's hipbone, too overwhelmed to keep sucking. "So good, babe. Don't stop. Don't stop, please," he babbled.

Russ had no intention of stopping. He'd rim Wade forever.

WADE COULDN'T BELIEVE how sensitive his asshole was now.

The scars that'd been oversensitive to the point of sometimes causing him discomfort when performing necessities were crazy sensitive now, too, but in a good way.

Russ's tongue running over them was pure pleasure, and when Russ breached him, stretching the scarred sphincter muscle, Wade nearly flew off the bed in shock. It was such a sharp bliss, drawing up through his core like a good kind of knife.

Rimming had always been his favorite thing, aside from a dick in his ass. It felt so damn dirty and hot, and the sensation had always driven him wild. Now, it was three-fold as intense, and he felt himself entering a space he hadn't let himself go in a long time—the place where pleasure ruled him. It was scary as hell, because it was close to the way he'd felt when he was forced to cum with Owen, but what Russ was doing to his hole was so good it was worth the risk. So Wade let go of his mind and fell into a raw and primal place inside.

He didn't know when he started eating Russ's ass, too, but he was. Curled on their sides, legs wrapped around each other's torsos, with their mouths latched to the other's asshole, licking, slurping, biting, they brought each other pleasure. Russ groaned loudly; the vibration of his noises and the scrape of his stubble mixed into the madness of the sensations.

Russ tasted good, familiar, and smelled like Wade's best memories of sex. As he drove his tongue into Russ's tightness, his cock jerked at the memory of the times he'd fucked Russ, usually while Russ had struggled against him, still pissed off from some stupid fight over wallpaper or bed sheets. He bit down on the edge of Russ's twitching hole, remembering how Russ's anger would eventually turn to a shaking orgasm as Wade had plowed him.

It was too long ago. He wanted his cock in Russ again, but not like that—this time he wanted in with slow, steady thrusts.

So he did it with his tongue, pushing it in and out as Russ groaned, licking and shoving his own tongue inside Wade, too. They were connected, curled together, pressed into each other's most private place, intimate and deep.

Wade pulled his mouth away to kiss Russ's thigh, and then he froze—*needles, pain, gloved fingers shoved in, a voice saying to him "We need to sew you up", a whisper he shouldn't have heard "His anus is a lost cause", agony as more fingers pushed inside*—Russ's finger had grazed against his hole, and he didn't want that. He rolled away from Russ, panting, and Russ was already there.

"Shh, Wade. I'm not putting it in. It just got in the way. It's okay. I'm here. It's me. Relax."

Wade's cock was achingly hard, and his asshole still quivered, but the beautiful moment was broken. He let out a soft, choked sound as he collapsed back on the bed, shaking and staring up at the painting of the meadow. The green and purple, the blue and the dark red, flowers and trees, sky, white and golden clouds.

"I'm sorry, baby."

"S'okay," Wade whispered.

"It's been an intense session. We should have stopped sooner." Russ's voice sounded shaken, though, and Wade looked over at him.

Russ's cock, bright and thundering with his pulse, quivered against his belly. And Wade realized that while he'd cum, and handled it really well—a thought that shot him through with joy that almost overrode his panic—Russ was still waiting.

"Let me jerk you," Wade said, rolling onto his side.

"If you can deal with your balls being blue most of the time, I can, too," Russ said.

Wade frowned. He didn't want that. It wasn't a competition, and, besides, he *wanted* Russ to cum. He loved it when Russ's legs went straight and stiff, and his belly tightened with pleasure.

He adored it when Russ clenched all over, shooting his load, and straining. It was hot, and Wade loved the way Russ shook during it, and trembled after it, and how he kissed Wade when it was over, all lazy and stunned with pleasure.

He wasn't sure what compelled him. It wasn't his new style. Maybe it was the memories of fucking Russ when they'd fought, maybe it was just a resurgence of his old sexual confidence. But if Russ was going to be a martyr about his mistake of touching Wade's hole, then Wade was going to show him how stupid that was.

"Russ," Wade said. "Get on your knees. Hands behind your back."

Russ chuckled, wiped at his eye, and said, "What?"

"Do it. You supposed to do what I say in here, right? For my mental health." Wade's heart still beat a little fast from the shock of unwanted memories, but he focused on Russ. "On your knees. Hands behind your back."

Russ blinked at him, but slowly complied, gazing warily at Wade. "This isn't on the list," he said, crossing his hands behind him.

"No, it isn't," Wade agreed.

Kneeling next to Russ, he grabbed both Russ's strong wrists in one hand and spit into his other. He gripped Russ's cock, stroking hard and fast, the way he knew Russ liked. "You're going to cum for me, babe. You're gonna shoot your load all over this bed and I'm gonna be the one to make you do it."

Russ moaned, his hips jutting forward.

Strength and power pulsed in Wade. He was in control. He was in charge. He was safe.

His own cock was still hard, and he pushed it against Russ's hip. Gazing into Russ's eyes, he smiled when the tell-tale signs began: dilated pupils, stuttering breaths, and harsh, strangled sounds.

"That's it. Let me see you cum."

Wade jerked faster, until Russ said, "Wade, I'm going to—"

And then he let go of Russ's wrists, ducked his head down, and sucked Russ's cock down.

"Oh fuck!" Russ shouted, his hips cocking forward, shoving the head of his dick into Wade's throat, even as his hands shoved on Wade's shoulders, trying to push him back.

Wade gripped on tight, though, swallowing all the cum from Russ's helplessly spurting cock, feeling the man he loved tremble and quiver above him. It took everything to hold on through it, but he did. He wasn't going to give up until he'd taken every bit of Russ's load.

When Wade pulled off, Russ fell over onto his side, still quivering with aftershocks. Scrambling to the bedside table to shove in the pieces of gum he'd placed there when they first arrived, Wade held back his urge to retch. Cum churned in his gut, but he kept it down. He wiped the back of his hand over his mouth and turned back to Russ. "I did it."

Russ's mouth hung open, sucking in air, and his eyes were wide. Wade stared at him—Russ's chest had dried cum on it from Wade's orgasm, and his still hard cock shone all slick with Wade's spit. His heart pounded, the cum settling strangely in his stomach, and he waited, surprised at himself, shocked that he'd pushed again, and a little scared of Russ's reaction.

Russ finally reached out a hand, and Wade took it, collapsing against his side.

"Was that okay?" Wade asked.

"Mm," Russ said stroking his hair, and Wade clung to him. "You?"

"I think I'm okay," Wade said. "But I guess I'm not ready to have your finger in me yet."

"My finger can wait." His voice was rough, like he was exhausted and shocked.

"I know you weren't going to…."

"I would never violate our agreement. It just got too close. You were squirming a lot and I was trying to hold on."

Wade sighed and cuddled in closer. Russ's strong body was warm and sweaty against him. He nuzzled Russ's neck and wanted to cry with relief and a weird let-down he couldn't explain. "It was great. Rimming is just as good. It might even be better."

Russ made a rumbling noise that stood in for a question.

"The scars are sensitive," Wade whispered. "Not numb at all. They're really sensitive. Like *fuck*." He laughed in a short huff.

"You're getting hard again," Russ said, looking down at Wade's cock, disbelief in his voice and eyes.

Wade ran his hands over Russ's chest, picking at the dried cum there. "I came." He could hear the wonder in his own voice. "I came pretty hard."

"And you didn't freak out."

"Well…" Wade said. "Not because of that."

Russ was quiet or a long time and Wade knew he was trying to decide if he should scold Wade for trying too much, too fast. But he finally said, "You've earned a reward with that panic-free orgasm. Tell me what you want. Anything at all."

Wade sat up on his elbow. "I want to stay here tonight. All night. You and me, and our room."

"Fine by me."

"I want to stay naked with you. I want you to suck me."

"You got it, baby." Russ's cock twitched and started to fill again. "Anything you want."

"And I want you to rim me some more." He knew he sounded shy. He felt weirdly greedy asking for so much.

Russ's smile, though, was easy. "I can't wait to eat your ass again."

"Speaking of eating…"

"I'll order a pizza."

Wade nodded. "And one last thing?"

"I already told you, baby. Anything."

"Let's play corrupt attorney and innocent client."

Russ's eyebrows shot up. "That's not on the list."

"But it could be. There's no reason we can't play it." He'd used to love to pretend he was a client of Russ's and that he couldn't afford to pay Russ's fees.

"Hmm, well, I guess I'll need to text Moira that I'll be late tomorrow since I'm going to be up all night interviewing a very special client."

Wade grinned and rolled away from Russ onto his stomach. Pulling his legs up under him, he shoved his ass in the air. "Mr. Paulson, I know personal injury isn't your specialty, but if you'd take my case on, you won't be sorry. See my asshole was injured a while ago. I might need to sue the hospital. Why don't you have a look to see how it's healed?"

Russ's eyebrows stayed raised but he said, gamely, "Well, Mr. Maguire, even though personal injury suits aren't something I handle, I suppose I could take a quick look to see if you have a case."

"I'd appreciate that."

"Is that position going to be okay for you?"

Wade wasn't sure, but he wanted it to be. It was a good position for Russ to get his tongue in deep. He used to love to prop himself up like this and let Russ eat and finger him until he begged to be fucked.

"Yeah."

Russ studied his face and nodded, before moving behind him.

"Okay, well, Mr. Maguire, let's have a look at that hole, shall we?"

Wade closed his eyes and moaned as Russ's hot breath and slick tongue slid down his crack. It felt so good that he bit down on the pillow, and held very still. It was all too soon that he was dragging Russ up to kiss him through the aftershocks of another orgasm, holding the threatening roll of panic at bay.

Chapter Twelve

"Things are moving pretty fast now," Wade said to Dr. Salinas. "I guess that hasn't changed."

Dr. Salinas made a motion with his hand to let Wade know he should elaborate if he wanted.

"I just mean, when we started out—you know, before L.A.—things were always really intense between us. We did just about everything two people can do. Nonstop." He laughed. "It was, uh, pretty out of control."

Dr. Salinas said, "That's often how it is in the beginning of relationships."

Wade nodded. "Yeah, it eventually cooled down enough to be manageable. It had to. But the other night it felt like we were headed in that direction. I really didn't want him to stop. I wanted more than we'd agreed to. It was only because Russ stayed focused that we didn't."

"What do you think would have happened had he agreed?"

Wade sucked air through his teeth and looked off to the side. "I'm not sure. I think, though, that I might be ready to see."

"And the zone-outs? They're still improving?"

"Yeah, it's been over a week, and I still get kind of anxious, but I'm doing a lot better. I spent an hour alone yesterday during my job on the farm, and I was all right. I mean, I almost threw up a few times, but I was all right." Wade laughed.

The relative difference between 'all right' before Los Angeles and after were huge, and some part of him couldn't help but find it funny.

"And the experience of your memories. How would you describe them."

Wade groaned, rubbed his eyes with the heel of his hands. "For the most part, I try to avoid them, but if they come, I think they're better. I'm seeing them from the outside, like we talked about. But, I don't know. I feel like there's a lot still unresolved."

"We'll keep working on it. But this is promising. The time that you're spending working on having sex with Russ seems to be paying dividends in your treatment as a whole. Your mind seems to be taking the sensations and re-categorizing them well. It says a lot about how safe you feel with him."

"I trust Russ completely."

"He seems worthy of that trust."

Tension released in his lower back. "He is."

"Good. Let's start where we left off last time. You were working on the memories of the forced orgasms. Is there one you want to focus on today?"

Wade swallowed and nodded, thinking of the time he'd had his hands tied together and his feet fettered, and then Owen had held his head in the deep sink full of water. It'd been terrifying. Wade remembered struggling and fighting while Owen fucked him from behind, and how Wade had thought for sure he would drown, but just as he nearly passed out, he'd cum so hard he'd screamed his last breath into the water and Owen had pulled him up. Wade remembered gasping for air and shaking, shooting a second load against the floor, as Owen plowed into him again and again.

"I have it," Wade said, putting the earphones on.

And so they began again, just as they did every day.

RUSS ATE A sandwich alone in the kitchen with his phone pressed to his ear, listening to Samuel gush about the orgasms he'd endured the night before at the end of his new lover's battering ram of a cock.

"I shot myself dry, Russ. Which I haven't done in *years*."

"Not since me, huh?" Russ couldn't help but laugh a little under his breath as he put his sandwich together.

"Oh, please. You have such a high opinion of your prowess, and I hate to let you down, but you weren't that good."

Russ shrugged and grinned. "If you say so."

"I do. But you know who *is* that good? Sweet Baby Jesus, Pierre had me screeching so loud the neighbors left a note this morning."

"Screeching? Ouch."

"In the good way, lover." He sighed. Russ could imagine his well-manicured hand fluttering to his chest. "It was bliss. Sheer bliss. I can't be embarrassed because the orgasms were so out of this world. I can't remember the last time I felt so physically sated. So sexy. So *happy*."

There was something contagious about Samuel's erotic joy. It was almost enough to make him want to share some of his own sexual escapades of late—but what he and Wade did was too personal, too private. Strange how love did that to sex, making it more than it had to be, making it better, special, and secret.

As Samuel babbled on, Russ ate his sandwich. He cocked his head to listen for Wade, to make sure he was okay. He was alone in the bedroom, and Russ was letting him test the limits of his nerves. He'd noticed there'd been a redoubled effort on Wade's part in terms of making strides toward returning to normal modes of day-to-day behaviors.

"It's all fun and games, until coffee tables attack," Samuel said. "That bruise isn't going to fade anytime soon. But it was worth it."

"Sex injuries always are," Russ said around the final bite of his sandwich.

That set Samuel off on a 'remember when' round of rehashing sex injuries past, including a few instances with Russ. He laughed fondly at the old days. It was good to still be friends with a man who knew him so well.

"How's Wade doing?" Samuel asked quietly.

Russ looked at his watch. It'd been ten minutes since he'd left Wade in the bathroom shaving to take Samuel's call and make a sandwich, and while nothing seemed amiss, he decided to go check it out. "He's okay, but I should go before long."

"I understand. Any progress?"

"A little."

"Do you know when I knew he was more than a hook up for you?" Samuel asked.

"When?"

"When you stopped telling me much about him. Then I knew. He's too dear for you to share."

"I love him."

"I know." Samuel sighed. "I wonder if I'll ever love someone like that."

"Maybe Pierre."

"Ha! He's an idiot. An idiot who makes me cum until I think I'm dying, but an idiot all the same. No. I'll never love Pierre."

"But you're happy for now."

"I am. And I know even with everything awful that happened, you are too. With Wade, I mean."

Russ nodded and made his excuses to end the call. It didn't

take much. Samuel had told him everything and probably needed to call someone else who'd be a lot more enthusiastic about Pierre's power cock. After saying goodbye, he put his plate in the dishwasher before heading back to the bedroom.

Wade sat in a chair by the window, a book open in his hands, and a look of concentration on his face. Russ hesitated in the doorway, not sure if he should go in, or leave again. He hadn't seen Wade sit alone like that since *before*. He fought the urge to ask if he was all right.

"It's okay," Wade said, looking up. "I'm sort of reading. I was trying to, anyway, but I guess it was more of an exercise in will power. You know, how long could I sit here without tripping into memories."

"Seems a worthy experiment," Russ said, drumming his fingers on his thigh. Wade's voice was calm. He seemed all right.

"Samuel's okay?"

"Aside from a sex injury obtained by being rammed over the edge of a coffee table," Russ said. "He's fine."

"Oh yeah? Pierre still?"

"Yep. He gives Samuel the sex squeals. Apparently he was loud enough to piss off his neighbors."

"Wow. That's crazy."

"I'm surprised they didn't just think he was eating a really great steak."

Wade laughed quietly and then looked back down at his book before holding it up so that Russ could see the cover.

It was the book on trauma survivors, PTSD, and EMDR. Russ remembered when Dr. Salinas had sent it home with Wade. After Wade had tossed it aside in disinterest, he'd read it in forty-five minutes. Gobbling it up in hopes of finding something to help the man he loved. Due to his near photographic memory, he could still spout off the gist of what was on any random page if asked.

All in all, though, it hadn't been very helpful. He'd found when it came to trauma and Wade, it was best to just focus on whatever Wade tossed at him. He took it one day at a time.

"Some people choose not to have kids after surviving serious trauma," Wade said softly. "They don't have the constitution for it anymore. It takes too much energy just to be alive and be themselves."

"Page ninety-three," Russ replied, stepping deeper into the room.

Wade gave him a 'puh-lease, shut it' look, and shrugged. "I don't want that to be me. I want a family. I don't want to be too broken to have what I've always dreamed about. What you've always dreamed about too. I don't want to be Jack Maples—"

"Page ninety-five."

"—who lives alone with three cats because he can't handle human interaction."

Russ almost laughed then, covering it quickly with a cough. Wade was so far from Jack Maples on page ninety-five already, and he was only a few months out from the horror he'd lived through.

Wade filled his days with human beings—Doug, Kari, Samuel, Nicole and Eric, the kids at the riding school, and Moira. Sure, they were familiar people to him, for the most part, but Wade had nothing to worry about. He'd never be truly alone.

"Me. Three cats. Same difference," Russ said. "I see why you're concerned."

Wade's mouth twitched in a lop-sided smile.

Russ went on, "But, hey, I use a toilet. So you're already beating the pants off Jack Maples in the housemate department."

"Russ," Wade chided.

"Baby," Russ chided back, kneeling down in front of him. He

took the book from Wade's hands and tossed it on the bed. "You have every right to have the longest, biggest pity party ever, and I don't want to piss on it. But maybe it should be about something a little more realistic than the idea that you, Wade Maguire, beloved best friend of Kari and Doug, godfather to Nicole and Eric, friend to flaming Samuel, and lover to me, could ever end up living alone with three cats."

Wade's lips twitched again in an almost laugh. That was good enough for Russ.

"If you're going to worry about something, worry about something that could happen. Like that you'll be smothered to death in a group hug, baby."

Wade did chuckle at that. He pushed his forehead against Russ's. "I just want to get back on track for the life I planned to have before."

"You are. You're doing good work. Be patient."

"I never thought I'd hear you advocating patience, Mr. Bend-Him-Over-The-Desk-And-Fuck-Him-Blind, Mr. Let's-Move-In-Together, Mr. Let's-Buy-A-House."

"Then you haven't been in most of my meetings with clients and their families. Sometimes, things take time. Especially the law. And even more especially? Healing. And some things take as much time as they take."

"I know."

"We'll have that family, baby. I have it on good authority."

"Oh, yeah? Whose?"

Russ smiled, running his thumb over Wade's lower lip. "Yours. Because I never give up and you never give up. We'll both get what we want."

"I want you," Wade said, quietly.

"Of course you do," Russ said, kissing Wade's cheek. "I'm a hell of a lot better than three cats and a litter box."

Wade laughed and shoved at Russ playfully. "You are such a jerk."

"And you love me."

Wade's eyes were soft and warm. "You know I do."

Chapter Thirteen

"I JUST NEED to stop in here for a few minutes," Kari said, as they pulled into the parking lot of her yoga studio in a shopping center in Mount Paran. She'd picked him up from Salinas's office and was going to take him out to the house to meet Russ after work. Her red hair hung loose around her shoulders and her swirly hippie skirt smelled of patchouli. She unbuckled her seat belt. "I'm so sorry, Wade, but Sharon asked if I could make sure that all the yoga blocks were in the back room for Tuesday's class. I know it's a little thing, but if they aren't there, Sharon will never trust me again. She's weird like that."

Wade glanced into the backseat at Eric, busy eating some fruit snacks and playing a video game on his iPad.

"I'll just stay out here with Eric."

Kari looked skeptical, and Wade tried to not feel hurt by her expression. "I don't know, Wade. If the blocks aren't there or I run into anyone chatty, it could be a while. Why don't you both come in? People will be happy to see you. Everyone remembers when you used to attend classes."

First she'd said a few minutes, but now she was saying 'a while'. Wade didn't like the ambiguity, but he didn't know what else to do, so he unbuckled his seat belt and climbed out of the car. His palms went clammy as they all three started into the studio. Swallowing hard, he forced a smile as he held the door for Kari and Eric, and then followed them inside.

The studio was just the same. It even smelled the same, like a mix of stale, air-conditioned air, lavender air freshener, and new carpet. The door opened on a spacious reception area with flowers and inspiring posters hanging around a flat, wide sofa and several chairs. The glass walls to the studio rooms themselves were being wiped free of handprints and nose smudges from small hands by a young, unfamiliar receptionist type. All around people milled about in tight or barely-there clothing, the scent of sweat slipping into the air.

Hands clapped Wade's shoulder over and over, all attached to yoga students and teachers he recognized and had known moderately well enough once upon a time. But now dizziness spun in his head along with an urge to run away from the constant contact. Eric's fingers tightened on his own, and he looked into the boy's eyes, so like Kari's, wide and full of worry.

Wade smiled, taking a deep breath.

"I'll be right back. Just hang out here and I'll just be a minute," Kari said, breaking away from the people greeting them and hustling toward a door to a back storage room.

"Right," Wade said, nodding and swallowing. He turned a shaky smile on the group of teachers and students around him.

"Good to see you, Wade," a husky voice said.

Wade's heart tightened hard as he turned to see Hunter Simon, a local police officer who'd been assigned to deal with aspects of the investigation into Owen's life in Atlanta. He'd interviewed Wade twice, specifically seeking any information tying Owen to local missing persons and bodies. They'd found nothing, but Wade knew Hunter had seen his entire file.

Hunter was a handsome man in a florid way. Red face, dark hair, and a paunchy stomach that came along with the stereotypical doughnuts he probably ate. But his eyes were a kind, gentle brown, and his chin was good. Still, the man in front of him knew more than anyone in Atlanta except Dr. Salinas and Russ about what he'd been through. What were the chances he'd be here today?

Speechless, Wade stared at Hunter and his throat and tongue went dry. Hunter sensed his discomfort and gripped his arm encouragingly. "I've been taking classes here for a few months now. Stressful job, you know," he said, almost as an apology.

Wade grunted. Eric squeezed Wade's fingers even harder, like he knew how much he needed to stay tethered to someone familiar.

"I've been meaning to contact your…" Hunter frowned. "Your attorney."

"You mean Russ?" Wade asked.

"Paulson, yeah. He asked me to let him know if anything new came to our attention in your case. Well, the case involving you."

Blue and green spots swirled in Wade's vision. Could Hunter see his effect on Wade? The violation? The pain? A slick, sliding sensation dripped down Wade's face, and he wiped at it, even though he knew it was all in his mind. Owen's cum was long washed away. His heart thumped hard, sucked in a breath, and Eric clenched his hand.

"I'll get in touch with him this week. Or you can let him know he can contact me if he's still interested in…knowing more."

"Sure." Wade squeezed a weird smile out for Hunter, and said, "Thanks. I…uh…just—" He waved toward the bathroom and Hunter nodded. Wade darted away into the restroom.

It'd been remodeled since Wade had last been there, but it didn't seem to matter. As he leaned against the wall, holding Eric at arm's length, Wade was bombarded with memories—a jumble of things that had ruined his life: Owen holding a hand over Wade's nose and mouth, cutting off his breath, until he forced

Wade to orgasm. Owen raping him, hurting him, clipping his body with clothes pins, pouring hot wax on Wade's cock and balls, hitting him, whipping him, the insanity of true belief in Owen's eyes. It all hurtled through him and he rocked on his heels, focusing on the soothing noises coming from Eric's throat.

"You're all right," Eric said, over and over. "Wade, you're all right."

Yes. He was safe. He was all right. And not zoning. Still present. Wade took deep breaths. That was good. Progress. Dr. Salinas would be pleased. He'd be pleased with himself, too, if he wasn't clinging to a nine-year-old's hand for sanity.

"Wade?" Kari's voice came from outside the door. "Eric? Are you all right in there?"

"Yes," Wade said, swinging it open and stepping out, Eric on his heels. "I just…I'm sorry, Kari. I have to get out of here."

Kari's eyes widened and she nodded, grabbed Wade's arm at the elbow, and led him out of the studio. "Let's go then. Let's get you home."

Back in Kari's car again, Wade covered his face.

"Is Wade okay, Mom?" Eric asked, buckling his seat belt in the backseat.

"Yes, sweetie," Kari said. "He'll be fine."

Wade huffed softly and then cleared his throat. He wished he felt as confident as Kari sounded. "Did you find the yoga blocks?"

"Yes," she said. "They were all just where I told her they'd be." She started the car and pulled into traffic.

Later, sitting at the small garden table on the concrete patio behind Wade and Russ's house, Eric showed Kari the Minecraft amusement park he was designing on his iPad. Wade ignored them, staring at the bed of purple and russet mums set against a background of beautyberry shrubs.

Birds chirped and flocked above. Dark clouds of swooping

crows arrived from northern climes in readiness for winter. Eric's dark brown head ducked low over the screen, and he gathered his jacket around his shoulders, a sharp cool undertone to the breeze. Kari's henna-red hair floated around her shoulders and her twirly, long hippie skirt was tucked up close to her legs and gooseflesh pricked her arms.

They'd barely spoken two words since they'd pulled out of the yoga studio parking lot. Wade knew Kari was waiting for him to be ready to talk it over and, also, probably hoping he didn't say anything at all. Eric would have awkward questions later. No doubt about that. He knew Kari was already trying to figure out how to explain to Eric what kept happening to his godfather.

"Russ will be here soon," Wade said, studying the murder of crows lighting in a tree at the back of the property.

Kari sighed, rubbing her eyes and looking away from Eric's game. "So, are you going to give us the tour while we wait?"

He hesitated. Kari had been inside the house before, back when they first bought it, but she'd never been inside since the furniture was delivered. She'd been hinting for a while now that she'd like to see how the place had shaped up. But the house was his and Russ's safe space; taking Kari inside would put her on Wade's mental map of it—her reactions, her comments. He wasn't sure if he was ready to give up any of the house to other people just yet. It was part of why they hadn't moved in.

"Russ should be here soon," Wade repeated, gazing down the long drive, wishing Russ's car would turn up right at that moment. He didn't want to explain his uncertainty about asking Kari into the house, especially with Eric listening.

"Oh, wait, is this a trauma thing? Like earlier?" Kari asked, putting her hand over her mouth. "I'm sorry. I had no idea the studio might trigger you."

"It wasn't the studio," he started to explain that it had been

Hunter Simon, but then he shook his head. "Honestly, there's no way to know what might do it. Dr. Salinas says five years from now, ten even, I might see or hear something that sends me back."

"God, Wade." Kari's eyes filled with tears. She darted a glance at Eric who was still staring at his iPad but obviously listening.

"It's fine, Kari, really."

"No, it's not. And I get it. I mean, it's okay that it's not fine. I'm just sorry that I'm the one who did something to bring it on."

"Don't blame yourself."

"Russ will blame me."

Wade snorted. "Maybe, but he shouldn't. It's got nothing to do with you or the studio. It was Hunter Simon. He's the cop handling the investigation on the Atlanta end, and you couldn't have known he'd be there, or that he'd talk to me."

"Hunter Simon? He's a sweetheart. I'm sure he didn't mean to—"

"Let's just stop talking about it now."

"Of course. Whatever you need," Kari said, reaching out to touch his arm, and then stopping short like she used to when he first got home from the hospital. "I get it."

"Come on," Wade said, decisively. "I'll show you the house."

He'd keep them downstairs. He and Russ didn't do anything downstairs anyway, except eat pizza or take-out in the kitchen. They hadn't ever even watched the giant flatscreen Wade had insisted on, or cuddled on their couch they'd made sure was deep enough for two grown men to lie on together. No, they pretty much just stuck to their bedroom, and the work they did up there to heal Wade's psyche.

"You don't have to prove anything to me, Wade," Kari said, shoving a hank of hair behind her ear. She wrapped her arms around herself and tried to conceal her shiver. "We're fine out here."

"Don't be silly," Wade said, tapping Eric's shoulder and heading toward the door at the back of the house. It led directly to the kitchen. "Buddy, are you hungry?"

"A little," Eric agreed, uncertainly, shooting his mom a look like he wasn't sure if he'd given the right answer.

"Well, we don't have a lot, but let's see what we have in the fridge. I think Russ keeps some sodas and yogurts in there."

Eric smiled anxiously. "Got chips?"

"In the cabinet," Wade said, keying open the door and leading them inside. He glanced up at the hideous painting over the kitchen fireplace, gratitude slamming into him. The awful thing was like Russ's presence in the room: insistent, comforting, and compelling.

"You let him buy that?" Kari asked.

Wade grinned. "Let him? No. But I'm glad he did anyway."

RUSS DROVE RECKLESSLY, eager to get to Wade and their house. Even after over a month of being back at work, Russ still felt a panic at the end of the day, an odd fear that he'd get home and Wade would be gone.

Today, though, he was even more anxious. They were meeting at the house, and Kari had texted earlier that Wade had had an 'episode'. Russ wanted to get his hands on Wade to make sure he was all right.

Walking through the front door of the house, Chinese take-out bag in hand, Russ paused. Music came from the kitchen along with the sound of Eric's voice and some of Wade's laughter. The anxiety coiled in his stomach relaxed in a whoosh, and he smiled as he walked into the kitchen, sunset light pouring in the back windows.

Tinny music came from an iPad and Wade sat at the kitchen table with Kari, his head tilted onto his fist, and a big smile on his face. Whatever had spooked Wade earlier seemed to be over and done with.

Eric, in his socks, slid across the wood floor, demonstrating some wacky dance move. "See," he said, a bit out of breath. "First you kick out and *then* you slide."

"Uh-huh," Wade said, his eyes crinkled in laughter. "But why's it called the Cubbadown?"

"I don't know. What's a nae-nae and a whip? Or a Macarena?" Eric rolled his eyes and then repeated his silly dance. Wade laughed, his head tilting back.

Relief and a sweetness that felt a lot like joy slipped into Russ's pulse. He knocked on the door lightly and asked, "House party?"

Wade grinned and stood up, moving toward Russ quickly. He wrapped his arms around Russ tight, ducking his head to breathe deeply at Russ's neck.

*So...**not** over it.*

Russ tilted his head back to let Wade nuzzle in close. He kissed the top of Wade's head, and then mouthed at Kari, "Okay?"

Kari shrugged, lips twisting anxiously. "Well, Eric and I should get going." She nodded at Russ's take-out bag and said, "We need to get dinner and you boys need to eat."

"I brought enough to share."

"Doug and Nic will be waiting at home," Kari said, smiling sweetly.

Wade straightened up and went to her, giving her a hug. He whispered something in her ear. Kari pulled back, patted Wade's cheek, and then took Eric by the elbow. She slapped Russ's stomach as she passed by on the way to the front door. "See ya later, big guy. Take care of him, okay? It's been a rough day."

Wade chuckled a little and shook his head. "I've had a lot worse. Don't worry about it, Kari. I'm fine."

She smiled sadly, and waved over her shoulder. Eric called out, "Bye Wade! Don't forget to kick and then slide."

"I'll remember, buddy," Wade agreed.

Russ followed them to lock the door and then returned to the kitchen. He waited as Wade got plates and serving spoons to divvy out the Kung Pao Shrimp and potstickers. "So?" he finally asked.

Wade groaned and collapsed to the kitchen table, head in his hands. "I don't know if it's worth talking about."

"If it caused a zone out, it's always worth discussing."

"That's just it," Wade said, sounding tired. "I didn't zone out."

Russ frowned when Wade told him about seeing Hunter Simon at the yoga studio and the message that he had some more information for Russ if he wanted it. "Anyway, it was just too much. I had to get away from him. But I didn't zone out. I started to remember, but I didn't get lost in it." Wade looked up, his hazel eyes looking bruised and tired. "It was like Dr. Salinas said it should be. It was almost like I was watching the memory happen to someone who looked like me, instead of being there, having it actually happen *to* me."

"That's good. Right?" Russ said, sitting down beside Wade, and rubbing his hand through his soft hair.

Wade sighed and leaned into Russ's touch like a cat, before sliding to the floor to bury his head in Russ's lap, wrapping his arms around his waist. Russ filed his fingers through Wade's hair and waited.

"It sucked, though," Wade said, softly, and Russ could feel

the heat of Wade's breath hit his stomach underneath his shirt. "Eric knew I wasn't okay, and he took care of me. But he's just a kid. It's too much for him."

"He's fine. You're fine, too. It just means he's a good kid, and that he loves you."

"But I was his manny, and I'm his godfather. I don't want him to take care of me."

Russ sighed. "There was this really smart person once, and you know what they said?"

"Who was it? You?"

Russ smirked. "No. It was a person I happen to admire and respect a whole lot. And they said family takes care of each other. Love isn't always fun or easy, but you do what you have to do. You bury bodies if you must. You never stop being there for family. Eric's not too young to learn that lesson. Well, maybe he's not ready for the part about the bodies."

"I never said that," Wade said.

"I didn't say you did."

Wade looked up. "You said it was someone you admire and respect, that's…like me, and maybe Samuel."

"And Kari."

"Oh," Wade said, and his mouth twisted into a smile. "Right. Well, now, *that* makes sense, coming from her."

"Yup."

Wade shook his head. "You and Kari. You both really love me."

"We do." Russ bent over Wade, burying his nose in his hair and taking deep breaths of his scent. "You have no idea how much."

"I kind of think I do," Wade said, his voice muffled against Russ's abdomen but audible all the same.

Russ didn't know what kind of information Hunter Simon

might have for him, but whatever news the man had about Owen, he wasn't going to let it hurt Wade. He'd do anything in his power to prevent that. No one was going to hurt Wade ever again.

WADE SAT ON the side of the bed, and watched Russ open the small package he'd brought in and tucked away so that Kari and Eric wouldn't see it. They were both naked and Wade was hard, but he waited patiently, heart thumping, to see what was in the box before they began.

"It's not my birthday and Christmas is over a month away," he joked, trying to lighten the mood.

Russ pulled out a thick circle of leather, about two and half inches wide, with two buckles on the front.

"If you don't want to do this, say you don't. I won't mind. Don't feel obligated. I bought this thinking it might help you. It's a ball stretcher."

Wade reached out to take the leather from Russ's hand. It was soft, and the inside of the circle was even softer. "What's it for?" Wade asked, confused. He didn't need a cock ring—he had no problem getting hard. It was cumming too soon—or cumming *at all*—he struggled with.

"It's designed to hold your testicles away from your body. It makes it a lot harder to orgasm. Though, fair warning, if you do cum, it's usually much more intense."

"Why?"

"The muscles which contract your balls toward your penis for ejaculation work extra hard to get them up even though they're blocked by the leather. The resulting sensation during orgasm can be extreme. But the point of it, like I said, is to keep you from cumming at all. I thought it might help you feel more secure. So you can enjoy blowjobs or other activities without worrying so much."

Wade studied the leather ring in his hand. A memory of Owen binding his gripped him. He gritted his teeth to keep from falling too hard into the memory. He fingered the leather. Owen had used a ratty shoestring, and later lengths of cotton fabric that Owen had torn from Wade's t-shirt. This was a soft, rich strip of leather. It was different.

"After the damage done to your testicles," Russ said, steadily, putting his hand on Wade's knee and holding firmly, anchoring him to the bed. "We wouldn't want to put too much pressure on them. The fit should be loose enough for your balls to not be overly restricted, and tight enough that they won't move up, making orgasm and ejaculation more difficult. Maybe delaying it indefinitely or entirely."

Wade nodded, fingered the soft inside of the leather cuff, and then handed it back to Russ. "Put it on me."

Russ hesitated. "You can take it off anytime. Or just say no."

"Let's try it," Wade said.

He wanted to add something new to the list for the weekend. He wanted to ask Russ to stay at the house with him for two full days and he wanted to work on getting to a place where he could fuck Russ. He'd been mulling it over for several days, and his main concern had been cumming as soon as he got into Russ's ass. That idea had terrified him—he knew how vulnerable they'd both would be if he lost it with his cock buried in Russ's body.

If this ball stretcher worked to hold him off, then he felt he might be able to actually accomplish his goal. He was willing to try it and see.

"Okay," Russ said, dropping to his knees between Wade's thighs. "Say the word and it comes off."

The sensation of Russ tugging his balls down low, in order to fit the leather cuff around the top of Wade's scrotum felt oddly good, like a deep stretch through his lower abdomen and into his groin. He shifted and watched as Russ pulled the cuff closed, using the buckles to make it snug.

Wade licked his lips, gazing down at his hard cock and the black, thick band that pulled his balls down and out from his body. It almost looked pretty. The scar from the surgery on his testicles didn't mar the sweetness of the package.

Wade moved a little, tested how his balls reacted, and was surprised to find that he felt *safe*. His scrotum was locked away, keeping that part of him tight and confined, but leaving his cock available for pleasure.

Russ's fingers skimmed over the cuff and under it, testing the strength and tightness, and found it satisfactory. "Good?" he asked, looking up to search Wade's face.

Wade didn't know what he saw there, but Russ swallowed hard. Other memories fought at the back of his mind, shoving like kids on a playground, trying to get his attention, but he stayed focused on Russ's eyes.

He wanted to make a silly joke to break the tension, but he couldn't think of one. He buried his hand in Russ's curly hair, and pulled Russ's head forward, wanting his mouth on his cock now, wanting to get a sensation that had nothing to do with Owen or L.A. or being hurt so badly he'd wanted to die.

Russ sucked the head of Wade's cock in going down until his soft palate gave way and Wade's cock pushed into his throat. Throwing his head back, Wade groaned, knees drawing up, as he hunched over Russ's bobbing head. His stomach tightened as he hurtled toward the edge of an orgasm.

And then he felt it. The orgasm that'd been screaming ahead too quickly broke away, like a plane pulling back up to soar into the sky. Sweat broke over him and he moaned as Russ kept fucking his own mouth with Wade's throbbing cock. The ball stretcher had held him off.

Wade's legs shook, and he fell back onto the bed, panting. "It worked."

Popping Wade's dick out of his mouth, Russ crawled up beside him and flopped onto his back, chest heaving with effort. "Get over me. Fuck my mouth."

Wade held onto the headboard and rutted into Russ's open mouth, shocked and awed at how Russ's throat constricted around him. He murmured soothing sounds when Russ gagged and when he felt on the verge of cumming, he pulled out of Russ's throat and plopped his balls, held low by the stretcher, into Russ's mouth instead.

Russ sucked and licked them as Wade rested his head against the headboard, breathing through the urge to cum. The stretcher eased the urge to shoot away entirely. It was easier to fight orgasm off with his balls held down by the cuff. Wade relaxed and closed his eyes. He was safe.

Angling his cock back to Russ's lips, Wade fucked his throat again. He was soaked in sweat, his head back, and his eyes rolled up. Russ took him in deeper and harder, gagging sometimes, but never pulling back. Gazing down at Russ's earnest face, Wade started to cry. He didn't know why. Joy and pleasure coursed through him so hard it was agony. His cock and balls felt too good. His body was burning up with pleasure. It was beautiful and he'd been afraid he'd never be able to feel this good again.

Russ stroked Wade's thighs and ass, comforting and sure, but didn't force Wade to stop fucking his throat. Wade closed his eyes, let the tears fall, and let himself *feel*.

Later, with Russ's cum drying on his stomach, and Wade's balls uncuffed and his cock finally soft again, Wade listened to

Russ's soft snores and felt grateful. He hadn't allowed himself to orgasm and he'd refused to be rimmed. He'd wanted to rely completely on the ball stretcher to keep from cumming. It'd been a test, and it'd worked. Now he knew he could rely on it to deal with his anxiety during sex and only cum if he wanted to.

He knew there would always be times when he'd choose not to cum. Maybe even more often than he chose to let himself do it. Orgasm was too much of a loss of control, all physical, emotional, and mental barriers dropped. After Owen, Wade found pleasure and strength in keeping them erect—even with Russ. Wade wasn't sure when, or if, that would change. He was only grateful that Russ seemed all right with it. That he looked for ways to make that easier for him.

Wade looked down at his soft cock, enjoying the feel of it resting against Russ's warm thigh. He wrapped his arms around Russ's torso, holding on tight. Closing his eyes, he took a deep breath. There in the quiet of their room, in the afterglow of wonderful, loving sex, he admitted to himself another reason why having an orgasm still scared him: they weren't even close to being as intense as what he'd experienced during the torture from Owen.

No, the orgasms he'd had recently from being rimmed by Russ, while being just as good as any he'd had before his ordeal, were pale shadows of that all-consuming ecstasy that'd convulsed him during Owen's brutality. He knew it was only that his body had attempted to wash away the agony of torment, but it was still horrifying to know the most obliterating orgasms of his life had been at the hands of his torturer.

Wade opened his eyes, leaned up to look down at Russ's sleep-slack face. His heart clenched with love for him. Russ, who was so good to him, and who held him through his panics. Russ, who took him as far into pleasure as Wade would let them go.

Russ, who made Wade laugh and who was so damn brilliant he made the sun look less bright.

It was Russ for him, in every way.

And yet the orgasms he'd had in those moment of incredible fear had been so massively intense, like the weight of a star imploding and exploding inside of him. He'd never felt anything like them before or since. And as Wade allowed himself that thought, shame snaked through him, sickening him, making the warmth in his chest wither away.

It wasn't just memories of pain and violation that hurt him. It was the knowledge that some part of him, deep down inside, wanted to feel that horrible glory again.

Not with Owen. With Russ.

Chapter Fourteen

HUNTER SIMON'S OFFICE was a desk shoved into the corner of the busy precinct main room. Russ would have preferred more privacy for their discussion, but the endless bustle, ringing of phones, and hearty conversations around him covered their words for the most part.

Hunter wore khaki pants and a white button-up shirt. His dark hair swirled around his head like he needed a haircut, and his coffee-colored eyes looked tired. "Have a seat," he said, waving a round Dum-Dum lollipop toward a hard, Heywoodite chair from the nineteen-sixties beside his desk.

Russ remembered the chair's design from his elementary school years. It'd dug into his back and ass even then. As an adult, it wasn't much better. He cleared his throat and loosened his tie. It'd been a long day in the office and his evening was still ahead of him. Those used to be a time of play or rest, but now they were another kind of work with Wade.

"So, I've got something for you."

The box Hunter tapped with his foot was marked Retired Evidence and cleared up any confusion about the reason Hunter thought he might want to come by. Framed photographs and scribbled notebooks stuck out of the sides of the box, along with old VHS tapes of slasher films.

Some wackjob psychologist in California had claimed Owen was inspired by the movies or, rather, was demented by them.

But Russ had his doubts about that. He'd seen plenty of slasher movies growing up and he'd never kidnapped, raped, and tried to kill anyone. In fact, he'd only tried to help people. Though, seeing as how he was a defense attorney, some people might protest that description.

"I'm glad you stopped by, Paulson," Hunter said, sucking on his lollipop. "I wasn't sure Wade would give you the message. I was going to call, but it's been busy."

"Always is," Russ said, smiling grimly.

"Same in your line of work," Hunter agreed. "Always plenty of criminals to go around."

"Hey, my clients are innocent."

Hunter laughed, rattled the sucker against his teeth, and pulled it free. "So I hear. Every damn day." He rolled his eyes good naturedly, and then sobered, his gaze falling to the box beside them. "Well, I guess you know what you're here for and why I contacted you. I thought about telling Wade he could stop by and take a look, but well... It's nasty, this business, and he signed a power of attorney for you. I figured you'd handle it best."

"Thanks for not putting that on Wade. He's struggling."

Hunter grimaced and kicked at the box again. "Can't blame him. Anyway, I've been going through the dregs of the Owen Sanders crap they sent my way. And, of course, I found something."

A chill touched Russ's spine. "More recordings?"

"Yep." Hunter frowned and thrust the sucker into his mouth again. His thick lips puckered around it. "Nothing new. Just repeats of the original recordings, but he burned them to a DVD. Backing up his computer files, I guess," Hunter said, with a sarcastic twist to his mouth. "Sick fucker."

Russ swallowed hard as Hunter rummaged in the box, retrieved the silver disc, and held it out to him. "That's it. It's all yours."

Russ's fingers trembled as he took hold of it. "You're not going to need it?"

"Like we talked about before, this case is over. Video evidence isn't needed. He was caught mid-rape. The fucker is dead. No family members are arguing our conclusions. It's all paperwork at this point. Take it." Hunter met his eyes firmly. "Do what you need to do. Take care of Wade. You know what's best in that department."

"Thanks." Russ hoped he did. His gaze fell to the disc and the black words scribbled on the front of it: *FOR WADE, WITH LOVE.* Was this Owen's demented idea of a gift? Had he planned to share the videos with Wade one day?

Sick fucker, indeed.

Hunter popped the sucker out of his mouth, leaving his lips shiny. "Speaking of, I saw Wade at the yoga studio the other day." He rolled his eyes. "Which you know already, since that's why you're here."

Russ nodded. His voice had fled, his heart pounding with old rage. The disc in his hand shook and he put it into his suit coat pocket.

"He seemed…" Hunter groaned and shoved a hand into his hair. "Well, I never knew the guy before, but the other day he was jumpy. Made my heart hurt. I hate it for him."

"Me too."

Hunter darted his eyes away, gazing over Russ's shoulder at some of the other cops chatting. Then he leaned forward and confessed, "I felt guilty. I shouldn't have said hello. Would that've been better? If I'd just ignored him? Pretended we'd never met?"

"It's hard to say. Wade takes it a day at a time."

Sometimes a moment at a time. Russ's chest ached. What he wouldn't do to wipe that caution away, to have the old Wade back—the man who'd been into impromptu fucking and surprise dates. The man who'd loved to be called a cum dumpster and had taken PrEP to offset the risk of his previous promiscuity. The man who'd somehow settled for Russ and monogamy. The man who'd jumped on Russ's cock whenever he could and ridden him gleefully with a wild grin.

That Wade was never coming back. So what?

Russ was going to love the hell out of the Wade who had.

"Such a damn shame. This country's mental health system is for shit." Hunter clicked the sucker against his teeth again as he jammed it back in. "All right, not to be rude, but take that damn thing and go. It's been eating me alive knowing it's here. Like it's haunted or something."

"I appreciate you getting in touch with me."

"No problem." Hunter motioned at the paperwork on his desk.

"If there's ever a way I can help you, just let me know." Russ spoke through a cloud of horror and simmering rage. He'd thought he'd destroyed the recordings months ago. Who else had watched this disc? Who else had witnessed Wade at his most stripped down and vulnerable? In pain and hurting?

"I sure wish you could help me now," he said, chuckling darkly. "I've got two heroin ODs to deal with this afternoon and I've still got to type up a few more notes before I can close the Sanders case again. Hopefully it'll stay closed this time. No more boxes of shit sent my way from California. They keep pawning their work off on me, I'm telling you."

Russ stood and shook Hunter's hand, his knees weak and trembling. "Just one thing, before I go…"

"Sure."

"Did you watch it?" He held up the DVD.

Hunter shuddered. "Not the whole thing. Just double-checked that the inventory from California was right and that it matched the description of the original videos. I never want to think about those videos again. I definitely didn't want to watch it twice."

Russ nodded. "Thanks. I just know Wade wouldn't want people to see him like that."

"My lips are sealed." Hunter said solemnly. "Wouldn't breath a word of what I saw for anything in the world. Neither would Chief Madison."

Russ didn't stick around after that. He made it through the precinct with only a few stops to distractedly greet police officers who'd helped his clients out with key testimonies in the past, and then he was out in his car, alone with a piece of hell.

He stared at the disc, unsure of what to do with it.

It'd been almost six months since the kidnapping and he didn't want to do anything to hinder Wade's progress. Still, a small voice told him the disc wasn't his to keep. Before, he'd had no doubts about destroying the videos. But the universe had coughed another copy up again, and it felt wrong to get rid of it without telling Wade, without asking what Wade wanted to do.

The disc trembled in his fingers. It was too much.

Quickly, he shoved it in the glove compartment. He'd deal with it later. For now, he still had to pick up take-out, get Wade from the farm, and then there was the evening's work ahead of him. Wade, and what they were working on together, was going to take all of his focus.

He didn't have room for more.

RUSS ENJOYED GETTING fucked as much as most not-uptight guys with a prostate, but, even so, he preferred to top.

When Wade had asked him about it once, he'd had a hard time explaining why. In the end, he'd simply said he liked being the one acting on the object of his lust. Even if the guy he was fucking was in charge of telling him how fast and how hard, Russ enjoyed being the one to thrust and penetrate. And while Russ wasn't going to complain about lying on his back while a hot man rode his cock, his favorite positions always included climbing on top and giving it to the guy until they both shot their loads.

With Wade, his feelings on the matter went even further than that. Not that Russ hadn't liked it when Wade fucked him in the past, but he never felt as intimate, or as hot for Wade, as he did when he was topping. He loved it when Wade lost control and came apart under him. Russ felt right, perfect, driving his man delirious with his cock. He felt most like he was making love to Wade, not just having sex, when he was on top. But Russ knew that had to change. It was possible he'd never get to fuck Wade again.

Next to him on the bed, Wade fiddled with the fastenings of his ball stretcher, making them a little tighter. Wade's hands shook, and Russ reached out to still them, checking the restraint around Wade's scrotum himself, making sure it was just right.

"Get up here," Wade said, gruffly.

Russ smirked. He wanted to make a joke, say something about Wade being eager, but it stuck in his throat. They'd already both sucked and licked and touched and fondled. His ass was lubed and ready to be penetrated, but his heart was trip-hammering with nerves, not lust.

"Ready?" Wade asked, resting back against the pillow, as Russ positioned himself over where Wade held his cock up for Russ to ride.

Russ nodded once, and then closed his eyes, took a deep breath, and opened them to keep a close watch on Wade's face. The burn of entry was difficult, and he lifted back up before the thick head of Wade's cock had pushed all the way in. Wade's eyes glowed hot. He blinked at Russ and licked his lips, and then his face scrunched with pleasure as Russ lowered himself again, pushed down and forced the mushroom tip of Wade's dick past his sphincter. The agony of his ass clamping down was too much, and he took shallow breaths, pulled off, and then forced himself onto Wade's cock again. Deeper this time, taking in a good half of Wade's length.

"Fuck," Wade breathed softly, and his fingers flexed on Russ's hips hard enough that Russ thought he might bruise.

Russ moved then, shallow dips up and down Wade's shaft, dragging his spasming anus over Wade's cock in a rhythm that soon overpowered his anxiety. He let himself relax, concentrating on working Wade's dick in his ass. Wade squirmed under him, holding back from thrusting up, clearly savoring the sensations, and Russ smirked as Wade cursed softly again.

Wade's legs skidded restlessly over the bed below, hands clenching and unclenching on Russ's hips, and his face twisted up as sweat beaded on his forehead. Russ's ass burned from the stretch of Wade's fat cock, and he felt it up and down his spine, felt it deep in his gut, and when he slid lower, taking in Wade's full length, and felt the brush of Wade's pubes against his ass, he was full.

Wade moaned beneath him, brought his feet up to plant on the bed, and flipped them. Russ grunted as the change in position pushed Wade even deeper. Russ's cock slid against the hairs below Wade's navel, and he moved to rub and get some friction where he needed it. Wade fucked him hard then, his elbows planted on either side of Russ's head, and his hips beating a double-time beat, as he gazed down at Russ's eyes.

"So hot," Wade murmured. "Your face, all open for me."

Russ groaned softly, not at all sure what Wade saw, but knowing it must echo the way he was feeling—full, fucking *full* of cock. And there was no feeling quite like that in the world. It blew his defenses, he knew. Another reason he liked to top.

"Gonna cum," Wade said, a trace of sudden panic in his voice, but then the flash of fear faded as the ball stretcher did its job. "Oh, God, oh, God," Wade said, pumping even faster, the jamming pull and thrust of his cock rocking Russ deep into the mattress. "So good. So tight."

"Come on, Wade," Russ muttered. "Fuck me harder."

He didn't know why he'd said it. His brain was mush already, and he was sweating, desperately rutting up to meet Wade's thrusts, and his cock was dripping so much pre-cum between them that it was a smooth, slick tunnel between his and Wade's stomachs.

"Harder," he said again.

Wade leaned down, kissed him, and then the fuck became so wild that Russ's eyes couldn't stay open. His body was fucked so hard into the mattress that the bed creaked ominously, and Wade's hips hit Russ's ass cheeks with resounding, staccato slaps. The stretching burn in Russ's anus rushed over him in waves that made him twist and turn, struggling a little against the intensity he'd requested, and then Wade grabbed his wrists, forced his hands over his head and fucked him with a wild focus that pummeled Russ's prostate.

He yelled, squirmed, and tried to get away but Wade gripped his arms tighter, using his body weight to hold Russ in place. They arched and fought against each other like animals, crying out in full rut, out of control in their coupling. Russ kicked his feet against Wade's ass, and reached between their bodies to pump his own cock wildly. He threw his head back as Wade bit his neck, and yelled.

The orgasm was like a riptide over him, and he lost all sense of time and place as he shot and shot into the slick, hard channel his dick was caught in, and when he fumbled out of the trembling goodness that made his entire body quake, he was still being fucked. His eyes rolled back, and he jerked, shook, and clung to Wade's sweaty, undulating back. Swells of aftershocks made him stiffen and curse, until finally, finally, Wade pulled out, sitting back on his heels.

Russ panted and looked between his own cum and sweat slick stomach to Wade's cock, so red and painfully hard. Wade shook with want. Russ could see how much he was struggling to gain control, how desperately he wanted to cum, but his balls were held back from letting him reach orgasm by the ball stretcher. It was doing its job very well.

Wade stared down at Russ, and then he pulled the fasteners of the ball stretcher free, tossed it aside, shoved Russ's knees back, and plunged his cock back into Russ's smarting ass. He pumped hard and fast, threw his head back and yelled at the ceiling as his cock convulsed inside of Russ in huge, jerking spasms. Russ stared up at Wade's face, his heaving chest, and the scars that shimmered in the darkness. Wade thrust again, shuddered, and then collapsed down onto Russ, breathing hard and already crying.

Russ, still jittery from his own orgasm, tried to put himself back together so that he could be there for Wade—but it was hard after being so thoroughly screwed. He felt completely undone. He shuddered through another small shock of pleasure and kissed the top of Wade's head. Damn, he really preferred to top. Taking it was just too intense.

WADE DIDN'T MOVE off Russ for a long time, letting himself drink in his man's scent and feel comforted by Russ's hands on his back. He could feel his cock softening and slipping out of Russ's ass, and he was conflicted about that. He wanted it to be stuck deep in Russ forever, because it felt amazing, and nothing like anything Owen had ever done with or to him, sane or not.

The sex they'd just had was the most free that Wade had felt during all of their activities, the most like his old self, and yet… He wanted to be fucked again. He'd always liked that best, and even though he was terrified of it, it was still what he craved the most.

As the cum slid out of Russ's ass, Wade put a finger down to touch where his cock was still inside, feeling where they joined, and then he sighed.

"Are you sure we didn't need a condom?" he asked. Although, it was a little late now if Russ had changed his mind on the matter.

"I'm sure."

Post-mortem examination indicated that Owen hadn't had any active diseases, and Wade's HIV tests continued to be negative, so the doctors all agreed that it was safe. Still Wade worried. If he gave something to Russ…

"Shh," Russ said, obviously reading his thoughts. "We're fine."

Wade kissed Russ's neck and then snuggled in closer as his cock slipped all the way out. Russ made a soft sound, and Wade kissed his neck again.

"I love you," Wade said, thinking of how Russ had lost control.

He knew Russ had always said he liked topping best, but Wade wondered if that was because Russ felt too vulnerable when he was being fucked. From Wade's perspective, Russ *lost his mind* whenever he was screwed, and Wade had a hard time understanding why he didn't want to feel that way every time. But Russ was a control freak. Wade knew that. And he didn't enjoy losing control. And given that bottoming was the position Wade usually preferred, it had been a perfect match. Before.

"Love you, too," Russ murmured. "But you deviated from the plan, baby."

Wade smiled against Russ's sweaty skin. "I know."

He hadn't planned to cum, but, in the end, he hadn't been able to hold back. Russ had been so wide-eyed, so blown apart, and Wade had felt like he wasn't going to survive if he didn't put his load as far up Russ's ass as he could. And, yeah, the orgasm had slammed him into tears, but it wasn't for the same reasons as in the past. It was because he finally *had it back*. The orgasm had felt like *his* for the first time since Los Angeles. It wasn't something he snuck up on from behind like with rimming, it was something he took for himself, and he'd felt so *good* he'd burst into tears.

"You all right?" Russ asked.

"I'm great," Wade said. He shivered a little, and then held himself up for Russ to see his face. "I really am. I loved fucking you. I loved cumming inside you. I want to do it again."

Just thinking of doing it again made him feel tingly and excited. His cock started to fatten up. He kissed Russ's mouth, and then rolled them onto their sides, a smirk on his face.

"What? Now?" Russ said.

"Yep." He pushed Russ's leg forward and positioned. "Let me in."

"Seriously?"

Russ moaned as Wade pushed inside.

"Jesus," Russ whispered, and he reached back to twine his fingers into Wade's hair.

Wade's eyes fluttered at the sensation of sinking in. It was tight, hot, and so damn sloppy with his leaking seed. He reached around to play with Russ's cock, and found it still hard, too. He kissed Russ's shoulder, then his neck, and whispered, "Still so open for me, babe."

"Fuck," Russ said.

"Mmm," Wade agreed, and he started a slow roll. This time he'd make it last.

Chapter Fifteen

I N THEIR BED at the house, Russ watched Wade sleep. His eyes darting back and forth beneath his lids, and his lips and face slack in a peaceful, warm way that Russ loved. Russ shifted in the bed, his cock achingly hard, even though he'd gotten off earlier with Wade.

He couldn't stop thinking of it. The way Wade had looked and sounded after he'd cum in Russ. The way he'd shuddered all over, his nipples raised in tight peaks, his cheeks flushed from exertion, and how his eyes had reflected something new, something Russ wasn't sure he'd ever seen before, not even before L.A. when things between them had been normal and good. It was something Russ wasn't sure he could categorize, a kind of peace or satisfaction that seemed born of transcendence.

Words failed to encompass the sense determination Wade had exhibited, muttering as he'd fallen back the second time, still shaking with aftershocks, "Russ, promise me that you'll fuck me."

"When you're ready."

"Now," Wade had said. "Fuck me now."

Russ had refused, and Wade had laughed, wrung out, and shaking still. "Okay. Stick to the rules. But, tomorrow, you'll fuck me. That's the plan. Got it?"

He'd sounded so sure. Russ had nearly rolled him over and fucked him on the spot just to prove him wrong, but he had to be the strong one. He needed to make sure Wade always felt safe.

It was five in the morning now. Technically, the next day. He could make that plan real.

Russ's cock jumped and ached. "Dammit," he whispered. He had more control over himself than this.

In the morning, Wade would wake up and the endorphins from the orgasm would be gone. He'd be in his right mind again, his terrified mind. And Russ would be patient and agree to whatever Wade wanted to put on the plan for the night. That had to be the new normal.

The disc Hunter Simon had given him was still in his glove compartment. He hadn't decided what to do with it. He didn't want to make the wrong choice but the idea of it being in the world made him sick. Tomorrow, he'd put it somewhere safer, like in his locked office desk, until he could make up his mind whether or not to tell Wade or destroy it on his own.

"Russ?" Wade's voice was sleepy.

"Shh," Russ said, bringing his hand up to Wade's cheek. "Go back to sleep. It's early."

"Yeah?" Wade whispered.

"Yeah."

"Do you have to go to work?"

"No. Got a text in the night. This morning's client is switching to another attorney."

"I'm sorry."

Russ smiled softly, and rubbed the line of Wade's stubble with his fingers. "Just means he's an idiot and soon to be convicted felon. And it means I get to sleep in with you."

"Then why aren't you sleeping?" Wade asked, his eyes dark with concern.

Russ shrugged. "Insomnia, I guess."

Wade's eyes shadowed even more. "Are you... You know, never mind. Maybe I don't want to know."

Russ sat up and snicked on the bedside lamp to get a better look at Wade. "Nope. Now we have to talk."

Wade rubbed at his eyes and then sat up, too. "Are you mad at me?"

"For what?"

"For trying to get you to deviate from the plan?"

Russ snorted. "Hardly."

"Then…what?"

Russ was stumped. "*What* what? I'm not mad at you."

"Then why are you awake?"

Russ blew out a rush of air. "I told you. I got a text and couldn't go back to sleep."

Wade frowned. "You're not being honest. There's something you're not telling me. I don't want there to be secrets between us."

Russ opened his mouth and closed it again. Before dawn was not the time to confess about Owen and the recorded videos. But was there really going to be a better time? He sighed and said, "Fine. You've found me out. I've been keeping something kind of big from you."

Wade's eyes filled with fear. A hook of guilt snatched at Russ's heart. He couldn't do it. He couldn't tell him. Wade wasn't ready to deal with that kind of information yet.

"I was referring to my dick, baby," Russ said, gesturing at his crotch. "Nothing else."

"Your dick?" Wade hiccupped a laugh. "You *are* a dick."

"Yeah, well, what can I say?" Russ turned and snicked off the lamp. "Go back to sleep."

Wade snuggled up next to him in the darkness, his breath a warm, damp rush against Russ's throat.

"Russ," he said. "I meant it earlier. I want you to fuck me. Make love to me. I want that. I do."

"Me, too, baby." His cock responded like Wade had just delivered a printed invitation for it to visit his ass. He swallowed. He wasn't sure it was the right time. Wade was eager and he always had been. It just used to be easier.

"I want it right now," Wade said. "It's tomorrow. And that's all I want. Right now."

Russ didn't actually *choose* to roll Wade onto his back and start kissing his mouth like it was all he needed to live, but he did it, responding to the need in Wade's voice. Wade grabbed Russ's cock, jerking it fast and wild, making Russ dizzy with need, aching through and through with want. It'd been so long. And he'd wanted Wade so badly. And he missed sinking into Wade's sweet, tight ass so damn much.

"Are you sure?" he managed to get out, reaching for the lube in the bedside drawer.

"All I need is your fingers to get me open and then your dick in my ass. That's all I need. Right now.

"Christ," Russ muttered, smearing lube on his fingers quickly. That was all that Russ wanted, too. Screw a plan, screw caution, or taking things slow. It'd been a long time. And Russ wanted, and Wade needed, and, damn it, he'd make it good for them both.

RUSS'S EYES WERE wide, his face red, and his body completely still beneath Wade, as Wade whispered over and over, "I'm sorry, I love you, shh, let me just…" like a mantra that could keep them both steady and okay, as though the words would explain away the fact that Wade had just freaked out, rolled Russ over, and started riding him hard in a full-on panic state, and that Russ was desperately trying to talk him down from it.

"Wade, calm down, ease up. You're fine. You can stop this. You're in control here."

Wade knew that somewhere outside of what he was feeling—the fear, the pain, the sweet rush of intense pleasure, and, most of all, the terrifying vulnerability that was only held at bay by the hand he had placed firmly on Russ's throat, and the tight grip Wade had on Russ's wrists, pressed down into the bed over his head—he truly was safe. He was with Russ, in their bedroom, and these emotions didn't fit in here. They didn't go with this life. But he didn't care. The entire fuck was beyond him.

It had started out good and right. The pain of Russ's thick cock straining past the scars at Wade's anus had been so intense he'd felt pinned into the present by it, safe between the ball stretcher and the pain.

When Russ had made it inside, his cock thudding in Wade's tight ass, Wade had pulled Russ down on top of him, kissed him long and hard, reveling in the sensations that seemed to tear him in so many directions. His heart pounded as he wrapped his legs around Russ's waist, and held him inside. Intimate, tight, trembling, proud, he took the man he loved inside for the first time in so long that it felt almost like he'd never had Russ before.

"I love you," Russ had whispered, and then he'd thrust, and everything changed.

Wade suddenly felt bigger than his skin, a weird expansion that blew his awareness out to the size of the whole room, and then slammed back again to focus every particle of his body, every bit of his awareness, on the cock moving slowly, firmly in and out of his ass. And then something really fucked up had happened, something Wade hadn't realized was even a possibility—

He'd gone feral, wild, his fight instinct had welled inside of him, and he'd used his legs and arms still wrapped around Russ to roll them over. Russ's cock jammed painfully into him as he jerked Russ's arms over his head in one hand, and put his hand on Russ's throat with the other, squeezing Russ's hips into place with his knees.

"Don't move," he'd barked. "Just...don't—"

That was what seemed forever ago and only seconds, as Wade rode Russ's cock hard and fast, aching for release from panic's grip, his cock slapped down on Russ's stomach and then back up against his own with the insane pace he was setting. He couldn't feel pain anymore, just desperation and fear and vulnerability and an even more unsettling terror that he was okay, he was all right, and it was up to him to stop this madness now.

"Shh, just let me. Please," Wade said again, throwing his head back, and squeezing Russ's wrists tighter. Orgasm and release from the pain and fear seemed only seconds away, if he could just reach it, he'd be okay. He wouldn't die. Owen—

No! Owen wasn't here.

"Russ," Wade panted, a weird sobbing noise exploding from his chest. "Russ, please, just let me! Just let me!"

"You're hurting me." Russ's voice was steady, calm, and dead certain.

Wade froze with Russ's cock half-out of his ass. He stared down at Russ's face, and when he saw that Russ was looking at him, *really* looking at him, without any haze or confusion or fear, he crumbled. He released Russ's throat and wrists, collapsing down onto his chest.

Long moments passed. Russ stroked his back and made soft sounds. Wade didn't cry. He thought he'd probably forgotten how, but he did whisper over and over, "I'm sorry, Russ. So sorry."

"Shh, now," Russ said. "It's okay. I've got you. And I'm okay, too. We're both okay, Wade." He shifted, and it was only then that Wade realized that Russ was still hard, still inside his body, and still subtly fucking him with slow, sweet, soft rolls of the hips, a soothing fuck that had Wade rocking back onto Russ's cock in response.

Wade shuddered and unclenched his muscles, taking deep breaths, calming himself as Russ hushed him.

Russ's love was palpable, feeding into him by way of Russ's hands on his back, and his breath in his ear. This was what Wade wanted, what he'd wanted from the day he met Russ. He wanted him everywhere, as deep and hard as he could go. He could let Russ in.

Wade turned his face toward Russ's neck, burying it in the sweaty crevice, and kissing him softly there. "Don't stop?"

"I wasn't planning on it," Russ said. "Do you remember the safe word?"

Wade nodded.

"You tell me when this ends, baby. Until then, I'm going to keep making love to you."

"Don't stop now."

Wade wrapped his arms underneath Russ, which changed the angle of the fuck a little, putting more pressure on Wade's prostate. He held on for dear life. Russ was balls deep and he pulled back with a slow drag that made Wade shift and squeeze Russ's torso to hang on.

"I'm not going to last," Russ said. "You need to decide if you're going to stick with the plan or if we need to downgrade it."

"Plan," Wade said, hoping that whatever had taken him over before didn't grab him again when Russ came in his ass.

"Let me see your face," Russ demanded.

Wade sat up a little, the shift of angles making him gasp, and the twinge from his ass bringing him front and center of his own mind.

Russ smiled at him, touched his cheek, and said, "I love you, Wade. Throttle me, and fuck me, and do whatever you need to do, but that won't change, and I won't leave. Do you understand me?"

Wade felt his throat closing up. His balls drew up hard on the ball-stretcher, and the discomfort of it was perfect, fucking perfect. He could ride that hurt-pleasure as long as Russ's mouth was there on his and his cock buried deep inside. Wade's scarred hole pulled. And he huddled against Russ, turning his head to bite down hard on his forearm. The pain shot into him.

Ride it, ride it, his mind flew—

and he broke free. A moment in flight, and a descending, horrific terror that this was when he would land back in the basement with Owen, and then a swerve—

a flinging sensation—

a chair, earphones, and a snap in his brain—

reprocessing—

recatorgorizing—

waking mid-flight toward something golden and bright and screaming. Pain and *full of Russ*—

and, *fuck!*

Semen pushed up from his balls in a stinging rush. Orgasm slammed through him, pulsing, aching, hard pleasure, burning through the fat of his fears, and leaving him shivering as he pumped load after load of cum against Russ's stomach.

Russ touched his cheek. "Kiss me."

Wade groaned. It was right that they should end as they began. Only this time Wade was on top, taking Russ's thrusts, his mouth on Russ's, his hands tangled in his hair, as he felt Russ's telltale tension. Kissing Russ through his orgasm, he shook and moaned, collapsing against the bed, exhausted to the core.

Russ cuddled him close and Wade closed his eyes, feeling his asshole burn and ache. He was safe. He was home. There was no one in the room but the two of them.

He'd wanted this.

"You're my sweet cum dumpster," Russ whispered, and a lump formed in Wade's throat.

"Thank you," he murmured, pressing against the bruise forming on his forearm. He let Russ soothe him to sleep.

Chapter Sixteen

WADE KNEW IT was ridiculous to be so proud of getting screwed. He shouldn't feel like he'd done something amazing just by taking a cock up his ass. But he couldn't help the massive, cheesy grin of pride that kept spreading over his face at the worst times. Like now, when he was sitting with Nicole and Kari in a booth having breakfast at Early Risers.

"Well, don't you look like the cat who got the cream," Kari commented.

Wade shrugged and took a sip of his orange juice. "I'm just glad to be here." He put an arm around Nicole's shoulders and went on, "I've got Nic and you and a good breakfast. The sun is shining, and it's a beautiful fall day."

"Mm-hmm," Kari said, narrowing her eyes. "Does Russ have anything to do with this cheerful, optimistic outlook?" Wade felt the heat rise to his cheeks and Kari went on before he could say anything. "Uh-huh. Of course he does." She patted his hand, and Wade pulled it away.

"Russ's great," Nicole said, popping a piece of French toast into her mouth. "He picked up a dozen cookies from Zanni's Sugar Shack the other day when he was dropping me off at gymnastics for Mom. And he even let me have one!"

"Just one?" Wade asked, laughing softly.

"Well, he was just going to give me half of one, but then he said, 'Spare me the puppy eyes' and he gave me an entire cookie!"

Wade shook his head, marveling that Russ had somehow so charmed his goddaughter that he could give her one cookie and keep the other eleven for himself, and Nicole still proclaimed him 'great'. Russ was handsome, but he wasn't *that* handsome. And surely Nicole was too young to be swayed by sex appeal. He hoped. He wasn't ready for her to grow up.

"So what's the plan for today?" Wade asked.

"Well, first we need to get you to Dr. Salinas's and then Nic and I have a dentist appointment. Once our teeth are shiny, I'll pick you up and take you to the farm. The vet should be gone by then."

"I'm worried about Sally. I hope the vet says she's going to be okay." The day before Sally had been off her feed and acting like she was in pain.

"She better be. Doug will lose his shit if we lose her."

"Language, Mom," Nicole corrected.

They finished the rest of their meal in relative quiet, enjoying each other's company. Wade had never been part of a family growing up—not one that was functional anyway. But he was part of Kari and Doug's family now. A burdensome part of it, but he felt they loved him all the same.

At Dr. Salinas's office, Wade was welcomed into the therapy room with a wide smile, and asked to have a seat.

"Give me just a few moments here and we'll get on with it."

As Dr. Salinas's pen scratched across his pad of paper, Wade slipped a hand into his shirt sleeve to finger the tender place on his forearm. Biting himself while being fucked was something he'd never done before. It'd been grounding. Strangely good.

He pressed down on the bruise. The bloom of pain traveled out to a wider margin than the bruise itself, feeling bigger the harder Wade pressed. He concentrated on it and his cock stirred. His nipples tightened. Biting his lower lip, he squeezed his anus, remembering the thrust of Russ's cock. He'd loved it.

"So," Dr. Salinas said, placing his pen down carefully. "Where do we stand today, Wade? You look conflicted."

Wade released the pressure against the bruise, and felt the pain ebb away along with his momentary arousal. "I think there might be something wrong with me."

Dr. Salinas lifted his eyebrows and waited. Wade almost wished he was more like Russ and would have snarked, "That's why you're here, right?" But Dr. Salinas wasn't that kind of guy. He was too professional for that.

"I…well, let me explain. I'm pretty happy because we did it. Russ and I…we…had intercourse. Well, we had before, but this time he was on top, and… You know what I'm talking about." Wade chuckled a little, stupidly embarrassed. "But there's more. And, you know what? I don't know how to say this."

"There's nothing you can say that will shock me."

"Right." Wade swallowed, looked off to the side, and said in a rush, "I got off. It was great. But I had to hurt myself to really enjoy it." He pushed his shirtsleeve up and showed Dr. Salinas his arm. "It helped. And I think that's probably really screwed up, isn't it? I'm totally screwed up."

Wade sat and waited for Dr. Salinas's judgment, wondering at his own lack of emotional investment in his screwed-up-ness. Instead of really beating himself up over it, his mind flashed with memories of how *good* it had been to have Russ fucking him, how hot, how incredibly right, and so much closer to what he wanted. Closer to what he'd lost.

The orgasm he'd had with the ball stretcher on had been so intense, so beyond the normal pleasure that he'd felt one step away from the terrible glory he'd experienced at Owen's hands. He felt a kind of hope that he could actually go there with Russ—if the stars aligned, and everything was right. And he wanted that. So much. He wanted to share the biggest, most elemental sensation he'd ever experienced with the man he most loved in the world. If it took pain to get there, he wasn't sure he wanted to fix that part of himself.

"A lot of people will tell you that self-injuring is always wrong. I think it depends on the injury."

Wade tilted his head, interested.

Dr. Salinas went on, "Injury to the point of damaging yourself in some permanent way, leaving scars or threatening your health *is* potentially problematic, obviously. But pain is also an excellent way to stay focused on the present. Many people find pain keeps their mind from wandering."

Wade nodded. "It kept me focused. I didn't think about Owen at all."

"Some people experience pain like a seat belt. It keeps them buckled into the present, instead of getting flung into the past or into thinking about the future." Dr. Salinas went on, "That's one reason pain has been an intricate part of the sexual experience for many people since the dawn of time—biting, hair tugging, scratching—are all nearly universally part and parcel of an intensely passionate sex act."

Wade leaned forward, elbows on his knees, and listened intently.

"If you and Russ have no problem with adding pain to your activities, and so long as that pain is not triggering negative memories and associations for you, then it's not necessarily something to be avoided in your sexual repertoire." Dr. Salinas cleaned his glasses and smiled. "In other words, Wade, no, you're not screwed up."

Wade felt a burble of relieved laughter pressing to escape, and he scratched at the hair behind his left ear, grinning a little.

Dr. Salinas wasn't through yet. "However, always use safety

precautions, safe words, and research your activities if you escalate things into dangerous territories. Things like breath play, knife play, and gun play are truly dangerous and shouldn't be entered into lightly, if at all. Just make sure it doesn't escalate into something you can't control."

"Russ is never out of control," Wade said in reassurance.

Dr. Salinas's eyes narrowed a little and he said, "Hmm. When it comes to you? I'd vehemently disagree with that sentiment. Now where do you want to start today? The beginning?"

Wade cleared his throat, wondering whether or not successfully proper processing of that final stunning orgasm that he'd thought would be his last moments on earth would help him forget how intense it'd been and to let go of the longing to feel that with Russ instead.

Wade picked up the headphones and said, "The end."

DOUG PULLED INTO Russ's office parking lot and smiled at Wade. "Here you go. Delivered to your prince in a pumpkin."

Doug's beat up pick-up truck stood out like a sore thumb among the posh Porsches, BMWs, and Mercedes Benz. Wade didn't mind, though. Doug and Kari's lives were real, and messy, and honest. They were the earth and Russ was his sky. It was fine for Russ to drive a Porsche and wear shoes that cost more than Wade's entire wardrobe had before they met. That's what sky did: shine bright.

God, he was swooning over Russ today like a little kid with a hero crush. Like Nicole swooned over Russ. Heck, he could probably give him half a cookie and Wade would think it was amazing. Seemed like a night of having a consensual cock up his ass was key to unlocking his glowing, gooey affection.

"Thanks for driving me."

"No problem. You did a real good job helping me out with May today. That girl likes you, if you couldn't tell by all her signin' in your direction."

"She's a good kid. I just wish I knew how to sign too."

"That's why she has her interpreter. But, ya know, why not? We should watch some YouTube videos and learn a few things."

"Deal. Hey, I know I don't say it enough, but thank you," Wade said as he gathered his things together to climb out of the car.

"Like I said, it ain't a problem. I was heading this way anyway."

"Not for the ride. For everything." Doug tried to wave it off, but Wade pressed on. "You've helped me more than you needed to, given me a job, and been my family."

"Whoa now, back up. You've been family forever. We didn't make you the kids godfather just for fun." Doug's eyes twinkled. "But you've earned your keep in the stables. I'm proud of you. I know working as my stable hand ain't your dream job. I know you wanted to go back to school to be a teacher, and maybe one day you can. But, hell, Wade, you've been a true help to me. Worth every dime I've paid ya."

"Anyone could do the work I do for you."

"Nah," Doug said, gripping Wade's shoulder warmly. "Not everyone would charm May, or convince Todd, that surly little delinquent, that smiling ain't the end of the world."

"He's not a delinquent!"

"He will be soon. And then Russ can try to keep him out of prison."

Wade shook his head, laughing softly. Todd was a handful and ungrateful, but he'd been partially paralyzed by a mini-stroke and he had a lot to deal with. Wade could relate.

Doug was always patient with Todd, though. He just rolled his eyes and sighed in relief once the boy was buckled into his folks' car and on his way down Peach Blossom Farm's drive.

"Speaking of Russ, you better get in there," Doug said, looking up at the glittering high rise. "If he's expecting you, he'll get to worryin' if you're late."

"Pretty sure he's got clients he has to see before we can leave."

Doug cocked his head. "Oh? In that case, want to head to the tack store with me? I could swing ya back by on the way home?"

"Thanks, but I like to hang out in his office sometimes." Wade didn't mention that it was a game he played with himself: how long could he be comfortable alone in there before he scurried back out to bother Moira?

"Oh, yeah?"

"Good memories."

Doug huffed a laugh. "I remember. Back when you were his boy toy."

Wade shrugged. "Every beloved partner has to start somewhere."

"And you started out bent over his desk," Doug said, laughing. "Okay, if ya ain't coming with me, scram."

"Aye, aye." Wade opened the door.

Doug scrubbed a hand into his bushy black hair. "Hey, one last thing. Don't be telling yourself lies like I don't need ya, because I do. But also don't be thinking I can't live without ya, because I can. If you go back to school, I'll understand."

"I'm not ready for that yet," Wade said, climbing out and hitching his bag over his shoulder. "You've got some time with me still."

"Good. It broadens my horizons having my queer bestie around. Makes me look all liberal and shit to my clients."

"You *are* liberal and shit."

Doug shrugged. "I'm a redneck, but there are a lot of things I don't give a crap about. Like who a person loves and who they screw. Besides I've always loved ya, dude. You and Kari've been my people since I met that girl. That'll never change. See you tomorrow."

Shutting the truck door, Wade blew Doug a kiss as he pulled away.

Inside the elevator up to Russ's office, a man got on at the second floor. Wade scooted to the far side and held very still, waiting for him to get off. When Wade reached Russ's office floor first, he bolted off the elevator quickly.

"Hey, Moira," he said, smiling down at her crammed in at her desk behind a stack of files. "How's it going?"

Her severe expression softened and she glanced away from her computer screen. "We've been tagged for an internal audit. No big deal. The usual. But a pain in my ass. How about you?"

"It was a good day at the farm. Horses, fresh air, no computers or files to speak of."

"But a lot of manure, I bet."

"Of course."

"Can't win for losing," Moira said with a smirk. "He's in the conference room with a client. Do you want to wait out here or in his office?"

"Office."

She nodded as her fingers clicked over the keys and she doubled checked something in a file. "You know the way."

The door to Russ's office creaked open and the scent of spicy cologne and furniture polish greeted him. The wood desk and credenza behind it gleamed in the afternoon sunlight that poured in from the wide windows. The city views were fantastic, and Wade walked over to look out for a minute, pondering the people on the sidewalk below and the cars moving on the streets.

Turning back, he sat down in Russ's chair at his desk. The leather creaked as Wade rolled the chair forward over the plastic floor mat. The same one his cum had landed on dozens of times during their lunch hook-ups. Russ's laptop was turned on and a note was stuck to it in Russ's spiked handwriting.

You can browse the internet, but be careful not to delete or touch open files.

Wade leaned back. He wasn't eager to distract himself with mindless Facebook scrolling or, worse, getting pissed off by political posts and tweets. He rested with his eyes closed for a few minutes, his fingers drifting up under his Henley shirtsleeve to press at the bruise on his arm. A smile crept across his face.

He squeezed his thighs together, remembering Russ holding him as they'd fucked. He'd done it. He'd managed the thing he'd thought he'd never be able to do, and he'd enjoyed it. A lot. Of course, he'd had issues at first, but that was to be expected. He'd work through it with Dr. Salinas some more and he'd be back to being Russ's cum dumpster before long.

He sighed as his eyes popped open. Dust motes circled in the air around him. No, he'd probably always struggle to some degree. But they were getting somewhere at least.

A chalky taste settled in his mouth and he slid open Russ's desk drawer to see if he had any mints or gum. Popping a stick of Juicy Fruit into his mouth, a disc with his name on it caught his eye. The writing wasn't Russ's, but it said *FOR WADE, WITH LOVE.* Was it a gift? Something Russ had made for him? A video montage of all the photos they'd ever made together? Their anniversary was coming up, after all. If you could call a fuck over this very desk at the Christmas Eve party he'd attended with Ow—

Nope.

He shut off that thought and brought his mind back to the disc. Maybe it was a present for him. Or what if it was something Russ had made before L.A. and had never given him because it seemed meaningless afterward? Well, it wouldn't be meaningless to Wade.

He hesitated. If Russ hadn't given it to him, then clearly he didn't want him to see it. Or he was saving it. But still, it wasn't like Russ to do something sweet like that. To put his name on something and say 'with love'. It wasn't his handwriting. Maybe it was Moira's. Or maybe he'd hired someone to put together something nice.

What if it was a video proposal?

Wade's heart leaped and a dizzy wave crashed over him. His fingers shook as he reached for the external disc drive Russ kept by the computer. He'd just have a peek to satisfy his curiosity. Then he'd put it back in the desk drawer and act like he'd never seen it.

And if it was a proposal? And Russ had chosen not to give it to him after L.A.? Well, he couldn't blame him, could he? After all, he was a changed man, no matter how devoted Russ seemed to be.

The disc whirred in the machine and started to play.

A cold sweat broke over Wade's body. Owen's voice came from the computer's tinny speakers. On the laptop screen, Wade writhed in pain, then he arched up and shot cum in an arc as Owen skewered him on a massive dildo. "Please!" his own voice begged.

Wade grabbed the trashcan and vomited up what felt like his whole heart.

Chapter Seventeen

R USS WATCHED WADE pace the length of their apartment's floor from the kitchen to the balcony door and back.

"And you just thought I didn't need to know," Wade said, his arms crossed in front of his chest, and his hair a mess from running his hands through it. He shook all over and yet whenever Russ approached with a hand outreached to soothe, Wade knocked it away. "So, you get to decide what's best for me? Like I'm a child? I'm *not* a child, Russ. And I had the *right* to know!"

Russ swallowed and nodded. "I realize that—"

"Oh, you do? You realize that? Because if I hadn't snooped and discovered you've been keeping information about *my life* from *me*, I'm willing to bet I still wouldn't know. Would I?"

"I wanted—"

Wade interrupted. "You wanted? *You* wanted? Well, gee, Russ, I guess I didn't realize that *my* rape, that what happened to *me*, had anything to do with what *you* want! But I guess I was wrong. I mean, Russ Paulson, Attorney Extraordinaire knows best doesn't he? You're the brilliant, wealthy, powerful man and I'm the screwed up waiter-slash-bartender you've been slumming it with, right?"

Russ rubbed his fingers at his temples, and tried to get a handle on the conversation. "Wade—"

"So you watched it?" Wade pressed his lips together in a harsh line, his eyes bright and wild with anger. "You saw what he did to me?"

Russ made a stammering sound that he wished he could take back as soon as it'd come out of his mouth, because Wade's eyes grew hard and cold as ice.

"You watched it. How much did you see? Everything?"

Russ shook his head, trying to come up with words. The kitchen counter dug into his hip where he leaned against it, backing away from Wade's fury. It was surreal, how they'd gone from the naked, intimate, tender trust of the night before, to this tension-filled, rattling rage now. Everything, all that they'd built and earned, could, at any moment, fall to pieces.

"Tell me!" Wade demanded. "I have a right to know. That was *mine*, Russ. Mine! And you stole it. At least Owen had the guts to look me in the face when he raped me!"

"Owen was insane," Russ snapped, a thread of anger twisting through him. "Nothing he did took any guts. Psychosis removed the need for bravery. But, you know what does take some fucking guts, baby?"

Wade's eyebrows shot up challengingly.

"Surviving this."

Wade sputtered, and turned on his heel. "Don't give me your bullshit about 'brave, strong Wade'. You didn't even trust me enough to tell me the truth."

"I wasn't talking about you," Russ whispered.

Wade froze and his shoulders inched up. "You're talking about you?"

"Yes."

Wade's voice could have frozen hell. "Well, if it's so fucking hard for you, babe, you're off the hook. You won't have to coddle me anymore. I can take care of myself."

Russ snorted, and regretted it when he saw Wade's back stiffen even more. He pushed off the counter. "Fine. You want to know what I saw? I saw him piss on you and jerk you off. I saw him fuck you with dildos that made you bleed. I saw you scream and cum for him. I saw him hurt you until he forced another orgasm out of you. I saw him burn you and cut you. And I hated him. And it made me sick and broke my heart. I want to kill him but he's dead. I want to go back in time to the night we met and, instead of fucking you, I want to snap that bastard's neck. That's what I want."

Wade's lips trembled.

Russ's dropped his voice down. "And I wish to God it had been me instead of you, because I love you that much. I'd have taken every single bit of it if it meant you didn't have to. And if you don't get that, baby, then I don't know what to say."

Wade's eyes, still wild and riveted to Russ's face, filled with tears as he fought something inside of himself.

Russ went on, "I didn't want you to know about the recordings because you lived it all once. I didn't want you to have to live it again. I'd do anything, Wade, *anything at all* to take some of what happened away, to bear that burden for you, and I thought that was what I was doing."

"You were wrong," Wade said, jabbing his finger in the air between them.

Russ nodded solemnly. "I understand that now."

Before he'd met Wade, if he'd been told that this would be his life, he'd have laughed and declared it a ridiculous impossibility. But now, having loved Wade with everything he had to give, he didn't want a future without him in it. He'd had plenty of time to imagine that clearly while Wade had been missing.

But maybe it had come to that anyway.

Keeping the videos from Wade might be so heinous a crime they couldn't move past it.

Wade was an impulsive, warm, and unfathomable man. Russ

never completely got a grip on him before Wade managed to surprise him again. That was always why they'd had such heat. But what if this time Wade's surprise included calling it all quits?

His heart cracked painfully. "Listen, don't be impulsive. Don't overre—"

"Stop. Just stop," Wade said, both hands out in front of him. "Because if you say the word 'overreact', I'm not sure what'll happen, Russ. *Nothing* about how I feel about what Owen did to me is overreacting."

Russ pressed his lips together firmly and gave a quick nod.

Wade gripped his forehead and said, "You know, I really think what I need right now is some space." He put his hand out toward Russ again, as though warding off his approach. "I need to get away from you right now. Think this through."

Russ's fingertips went cold, and blood rushed in his ears. This was it. Wade's horrible surprise and it was his own damn fault. "Seriously? Because of some videos?"

"They aren't 'some videos', Russ. They were private, intimate moments."

"They were rape!"

"*My* rape, Russ. Mine. Not yours. You had no right—" he narrowed his gaze and shook his head.

"Where will you go?" Russ whispered, a tremor passing through him.

Wade's lips curled into a disgusted snarl. "I'd like to say the farm, but since I can't drive anymore…" Wade huffed a disbelieving sound, and shook his head at his helplessness.

Russ didn't want him gone; he wanted to snap his fingers and work it out. But he knew Wade needed to be in charge of his life to whatever extent he could. And maybe, by helping him do that, he'd prove himself again. "I'll drive you."

"No," Wade said. "The last thing I want is to be in a small

space with you right now."

Breath knocked out of him, he took a moment before whispering, "I can call Doug or Kari. They'd come for you."

Wade ran his hands through his hair and said, "I just want to be alone."

"I could leave."

Wade didn't reply. He fled into their bedroom and slammed the door.

In the ensuing silence, Russ leaned back against the wall, an unfamiliar thrum of defeat coursing through him.

Now what? he wondered.

Sliding down to sit on the floor, he stared at his black dress shoes before closing his eyes and pressing his fingers against his eyelids. Flashing images assaulted him: Wade arching up against restraints, cum spurting from his cock, and Owen milking Wade with one hand while punching Wade's balls with the other. Wade's face twisted in pain and ecstasy, primal and raw.

Russ had seen something close to it when Wade had throttled him mid-fuck, but that had been mixed with aggression and repressed rage. He didn't know how to feel. Wade's experience had never been about Russ, never been for him, and yet wasn't he affected by it every day? Hadn't he just been trying to protect Wade?

He licked his dry lips and stared at his shoes, fighting the urge to make sure Wade was okay in their room. He had to let him go a little, loosen his grip, and hope that Wade came back to him on his own.

WADE PACED THE floor of their room. The lights were off and the curtains drawn, the way he usually liked it, but he wished he was outside, somewhere with a lot more space to hold everything he was feeling. He wanted to remember what it was like to have secrets that no one knew—secrets that not even *he* knew.

He stopped by the window and pulled aside the curtains to gaze out at the courtyard. Late autumn had touched everything with a finger of death. It was all gray and brown, though the grass made an effort for green. He pressed his forehead against the cool glass. How did it feel for the trees to let go of their leaves? Were they proud to be naked for everyone to see?

Wade felt naked, but he didn't feel proud.

There'd been nothing beautiful about the rape and torture. But until today he'd thought he had some dignity left. He'd thought at least he was the only one who truly *knew* what happened, and he could share it or not. He'd thought he still had that measure of control.

This, though. This was different.

Videos had been made showing him at his most vulnerable, most terrified. And Russ had watched them, stripping Wade of his authority over what'd happened to him.

Wade pulled away from the window, pacing the length of the room again. Vomit pressed against the back of his throat and he ruthlessly swallowed it down.

That cold digital recording didn't hold the sensation of Owen's fat cock shoving past his bleeding anus. They didn't record the feel of Owen's hands cutting off his air supply, or Owen's hipbones slamming into his ass as he'd fucked him over and over again. The videos didn't capture what it was to be afraid beyond all knowing or how hard it'd been every time he'd surrendered to the horrible pleasure.

All they did was show the rapes from the outside. They stole his right to be the author of his story.

And *Russ* had watched the videos. He'd *watched them.*

Wade sat down on the bed, his chest aching, and his cock thudding. The ever-present terror-fueled need to cum rushed to life under his skin, and he wished he could let himself tumble screaming into those memories, to rip them apart, and to own them. He wanted to remember it all until he wasn't afraid the fear would consume him. Because those memories belonged to him. No one else.

Wade sat up and opened the bedside table drawer, the one he hadn't looked into since the first day he'd been home. He touched the butt plug still resting where he and Russ had put it months ago. Swallowing against rising panic, he felt the thickness between his fingers. He recalled a day when he'd worn the plug for his entire shift at Early Risers and the frantic, desperate sex he'd had with Russ in his office afterward.

Wade dropped the plug into the drawer again and lifted the blindfold. Bringing it to his eyes, he started to shake as the room was blocked from his view. He counted to ten slowly under his breath. A memory bloomed of wearing the blindfold while Russ had screwed him silly in their big bed. Wade continued counting, but the world spun out of control when he reached twenty-nine. He pulled the blindfold off and shut the drawer, before falling back on the mattress to stare at the ceiling.

Wade took deep breaths.

After a few minutes, he unzipped his pants, pulled his hard cock out, and studied it. A slick bubble of pre-cum drew up at his piss-hole and he smeared it over the head of his cock. He closed his eyes; a strong determination filled him, rooting him from the bottom of his toes to the top of his head. He was as solid as a tree trunk and he wasn't going anywhere.

Forcing his mind back to the basement room, he concentrated. Fear swelled in him, hard and violent, and he dove as far as he could into his sweaty, endless nightmare.

Two clothespins on his cockhead. Agony. Rattling against each other. Trapped. Owen's hand jerking his shaft. Pain. Clamps on his bruised nipples. Raw. Aching to his center.

Suddenly, the memory changed. Yes, Wade was still on the table, pain spreading though the core of him, but he was also simultaneously standing next to the table watching, safe from everything that was happening.

Dr. Salinas's voice in Wade's mind was soft. "You can change this," he said. "Own it. Make it whatever you want it to be. You have the power now."

Wade had done it a few times in therapy, stepped in and changed the scene, freed himself, or ended his pain. But this time, alone in his and Russ's bedroom, with Russ moving restlessly outside the door, he chose another route he'd been experimenting with.

"Russ," Wade whispered, and then it was Russ in his mind, hurting him, jerking him, staring into Wade's eyes, and unlike Owen who'd been lost in his own insanity, Russ stayed right there with Wade while he hurt, and, God, did he *hurt*—

—broken connections

—pain, soaring flight, and

—reprocess, reconnect

"Oh, God!" he yelled, cumming hard, spurting onto his fist and his shirt. His legs kicked uncontrollably as he arched. Russ banged on the door, calling his name, but Wade was speechless as he almost blacked out from the orgasm.

"Wade! Let me in!"

Blue dots swirled in his vision and his breath came wild and hard. "I'm okay," he panted. "I'm fine." Aftershocks shook him as he stared down at his still milking hand.

What he'd lived through with Owen was the most intimate experience of his life—the most primal, raw, and real. He'd been stripped of everything civilized, and left with only his instincts. He'd been consumed by pain, pleasure, and a will to survive. That, he realized now, was the most basic and honest place he'd ever traveled.

And he'd shared that with a lunatic, not with the man he loved.

He heard the jiggle of the door handle again, then a scraping sound, and as he looked over, the door swung open. Russ had picked the lock.

Russ's startled, confused eyes darted from Wade's cock to his face and back.

"Wade?" his voice was tentative, broken a little in a way Wade wanted to repair.

He reached out for Russ. "It's okay. C'mere," he said, voice slurred from his shattering climax. "C'mere. I'm sor—"

"Don't apologize." Russ stalked toward the bed and sat down beside him a little warily. He stared at Wade's cock and the mess of cum on his chest. "I'm the one who messed up."

"Yeah, you did. And I love that about you."

"You do?" Russ looked adorably confused, and Wade tugged at him.

"I don't need your protection. I'm strong. But I love that you want to protect me anyway."

Wade pulled Russ down for a kiss, and then after satisfying himself with Russ's taste, he gently pushed Russ's head down, whispering, "Speaking of messes, there's one to clean up. And I think you owe me."

"Wade," Russ murmured, obviously unsure.

"Shut up and blow me, babe," Wade said, counting on Russ's guilt to work in his favor.

Twenty minutes later, gripping the head of the bed as Russ fucked him, the stretch and burn of his scarred anus driving him crazy, Wade demanded, "Bite me." And when Russ firmly sank his teeth into Wade's neck and pinched his nipples at the same time, Wade came again, ass clenching down on Russ's cock, and cum spurting on the headboard.

Breathless, scared, but determined to win at the only thing that ever really mattered, Wade clung to the headboard and held on tight.

It wasn't enough, but it was a start.

"HEY," WADE SAID when Russ plopped down next to him on the bench in front their apartment building. His hands were jammed into his pockets and he sat tense and ramrod straight.

Cars sped past and traffic lights changed color. The two of them sat alone quietly.

"Are you all right?" Russ asked, feeling awkward. He remembered how Wade had slammed back onto his cock the night before, like a wanton, desperate thing—like he was trying to fuck himself into a place he couldn't seem to reach.

"Yeah," Wade answered, not looking at him, staring straight ahead.

"Okay, well, I'll just—" Russ motioned back toward their building. "Leave you to it."

He'd thought last night, at least, after Wade had curled up against him and fallen asleep, that Wade had decided to forgive him for making the wrong decision about the recordings. Maybe not.

He moved slowly, stopping in his tracks when Wade said, "Wait. Sit down, Russ."

Russ swiveled to meet Wade's eye. He wondered if he looked as unsure as he felt. Wade's face was all tired-sadness, though, and he reached toward Russ with his hands out. As Russ took a seat next to him, Wade laced Russ's fingers in his own, and then peered into his eyes.

"Last night, the sex we had—" Wade paused. "It was the first time we did it here in the apartment."

Russ nodded.

"And it wasn't how I wanted it to be, or what I was expecting, but it means a lot to me that you trusted me to let it happen."

"Baby—" Russ said, but Wade held up his hand to stop him from going on.

"I love you. I love everything about you. I love that you try to take care of me, even if you were wrong in how you did it this time." He smiled sadly. "Look, Russ, I'm screwed up. I know that. You got a bum deal."

"Wade—"

"Shh. But I'm getting better. And knowing you'd travel this road with me? Well, it's a compliment. I want you to know that."

"It's not a compliment, you idiot. It's because I need you. I love you."

"I know. And that's an even bigger compliment. The biggest one of my life. And I want to live up to it. I do."

"You will. You already have."

Wade touched Russ's chin, and forced it up a little, reminding Russ of the difference in their heights. "No, I haven't. Not yet. But I will."

Russ put his hand on Wade's cheek, feeling the soft skin over Wade's cheekbone, the transition into the freshly shaved beard, and he whispered, "If I've got you, I'm good. No matter what."

He meant it more than anything. He'd walk away from anything else in the world but Wade. Even his law firm. Even his clients. Even his life.

"Do I have you, Wade?" Russ asked, softly.

Wade gazed at him, his eyes full of love and deep wonder. "You always have me. I promise." That was the only vow that he'd ever need. "And now I need to ask you something."

"Anything."

Wade smiled sadly, reaching out and to take Russ's hand. "I need you to hurt me."

"What?" Russ stared into Wade's hazel eyes, looking for the hidden meaning. But there was none. Wade wasn't joking.

"I think I heard you wrong."

Wade shook his head. "You didn't. We need to talk."

Those words had never meant anything good.

Russ followed Wade back up to their apartment, his gut churning, and his palms sweaty.

Chapter Eighteen

THE NEXT DAY Russ sat on the front steps of their house waiting for Kari to drop Wade off.

They'd had a strange discussion the night before, one that Russ had been distracted by all day at work. Staring out over the yard, watching the early November wind shake the limbs of the trees, He still wasn't sure how he felt about what Wade had proposed.

He'd been persuasive as ever in his argument. But Russ still felt ill when he remembered the damage he'd seen on Wade's body immediately after his rescue—the bruises, the cuts, the infections. He didn't think he could stand to see Wade hurt ever again.

Except, as Wade pointed out, he could.

Wade had always responded to bites, smacks on his ass, pinches, and scratches during the course of sex. And Russ had always been rough enough in his lust to satisfy that without even thinking about it. The events in L.A. changed everything. Now sex with Wade had to be about holding back—for both of them.

But...

He rubbed a hand over his face.

Kari's car kicked up dust as she turned the corner by their mailbox, and Russ watched the dinky red Honda putter closer. On the passenger side, Wade unbuckled his seat belt, leaned over, and kissed Kari's cheek before opening the door and climbing out. Smiling, he met Russ's gaze and joined Russ at the front steps. They both waved as Kari backed down the drive.

"Hey," Wade said, once her car was out of sight, a hint of caution in his voice.

Russ rubbed at his nose. "How was…what was it? Badminton with Nicole and Eric?"

Wade snorted. "Hardly, you goon. Skeeball. At the arcade."

"Skeeball? And you didn't invite me?" Russ frowned.

"Eric was there and you made him cry last time by winning all the tickets."

"It wasn't *all* the tickets. He won some, too."

"Five. Because you wouldn't move over and let him play."

Russ shrugged. "That arcade should have more than one skeeball game. Everyone knows it's the best."

"Right," Wade said, nodding with a soft smile on his lips. "It was the arcade's fault Eric was reduced to tears by your inability to share."

"I'm competitive, all right? That's why I'm a great defense attorney," Russ said.

Wade pressed his lips in a thin line and sighed, sticking his hands in his jacket pockets and huddling in on himself.

Russ went on, "But you're right. I'll take him there sometime soon. Let him spend a mint on skeeball."

"Really?"

"Why not? I can afford it."

Wade kept his eyes focused on the far end of the yard and gave a small smile. "That'd be nice, Russ. He'd love it."

Russ ran his hand over his head and shook his shoulders out. He didn't want Wade angry with him because he'd gotten a little too into a skeeball game last spring before…well, *before.*

"So, have you thought about it?" Wade asked softly.

Russ nodded. He'd thought of little else all day. He'd even

had to ask a couple of clients to repeat themselves because he couldn't focus. There was a reason he'd always thought relationships would be a detriment to his work—and it turned out he'd been right. But he was in so deep with Wade he didn't care. Work was a distant second in terms of his priorities. A past version of him—the ambitious one that'd eschewed love—would be disgusted to see him now.

"And?" Wade twisted himself smaller, bending over his long legs as though trying to get warm.

"Inconclusive," Russ said.

"Because you don't want to," Wade said, keeping his focus on the yard as his neck splotched red.

"It's not as black-and-white as that."

"Before Los Angeles I don't think it would have been off the table." A hint of defensiveness entered Wade's tone.

"Probably not," Russ agreed. "But L.A. happened. For better or worse, it changed me."

"I know, and I'm sorry."

"Wade, when are you going stop apologizing for things that aren't your fault?"

Wade shrugged. "When I stop feeling like they're my fault."

Russ watched late-falling leaves twirl down from the oak near the mailbox. "And doing this will help you stop feeling like it's your fault?"

"I don't know. I think it'll help me feel differently about it, though. I think it'll change the way I feel about what happened to me and allow me to move on from it." Wade sighed. "I don't even know what I *mean* exactly. I know this will be with me forever. I just don't want it to own me anymore."

"You want to own *it*," Russ said, echoing something Wade had touched on in his rambles the night before.

"Exactly. Part of the therapy I've been doing with Dr. Salinas is about taking control of the traumatic experience—walking into the memory and changing the events of it, or changing the outcome. At first, I'd just save myself, or make it stop. But now I'm approaching it differently."

"How?"

Wade took a hand out of his pocket and put it out for Russ to take. Their fingers fit well, twining together in a tight, solid unity.

"I've been replacing Owen with you, Russ. Instead of Owen hurting me and making me cum so hard I lose consciousness…it's you. And it's different. Because I *want* you to be there. I *want* you to see me like that—raw and falling apart. If I have to share that experience with anyone? If I *have* to give that away? I want it to be to *you*. Not him."

Russ swallowed hard, a pressure in his chest and throat confused him. It felt like pride and love all mixed up with possessive need.

"I want you to be the one stripping me down to nothing but sensation and reaction."

Russ's eyes filled. He blinked hard to get himself under control.

Wade touched his knee. "And it's working. It's working better than anything I've done yet."

"How?"

"Each time I reimagine the events with you instead of Owen, I feel empowered and strong. Instead of raped and violated. I leave those sessions feeling like, with your help, I've taken complete control of what happened to me. But you're not really there, Russ. And I want you to be."

"What does Salinas say?" Russ asked. His heart trip-hammered, not sure what he hoped for.

Wade shook his head. "I haven't asked him. I didn't know if

you'd even be willing, and I didn't want to bring it up to him if it wasn't even an option."

Russ let go of Wade's hand, put his arm around him and drew him close. Their breath puffed into the cool November air, joining together and floating away. "I want to be there and talk to him myself."

"Is this a yes?" Wade asked, his voice rising to a note of enthusiasm Russ had missed.

"It's an 'I want to talk to Dr. Salinas."

"Hard ass," Wade muttered.

Russ chucked Wade's chin up, peered into his eyes and then kissed his lips. "I told you I'd do anything for you. I meant that. But not at the expense of your health."

Wade smiled, his eyes crinkling at the edges, and he threw both arms around Russ's neck.

Holding onto Wade, Russ tucked his face into his warm neck, smelling his shampoo and salty skin. He didn't think it was healthy to love a person so much. If he could go back in time and tell himself to never fuck Wade at that holiday party, he would.

No, he thought, kissing the knife scar on Wade's soft skin. *You wouldn't.*

RUSS WATCHED DR. Salinas sort through a pile of papers on his desk. Wade sat next to him, clutching his hand. When Dr. Salinas finally found what he was looking for, he took the chair opposite. Russ tugged on his tie.

"So," Dr. Salinas said. "I'm glad you joined us today. I understand you have some concerns you want to address?"

Russ gave a tight-lipped smile. An awkward silence filled the room, and then Wade nudged him.

"Tell him," Wade said.

"Tell him what?"

"Why you wanted to come in."

Russ was used to talking to attorneys and criminals, it wasn't as though he didn't handle confidential and personal information daily. But this was different. This was *his* confidential and personal information.

"Russ?" Wade prompted.

"Right." Russ cleared his throat. "Wade wants it rough in bed and I'm not sure that's a good idea."

Wade groaned and covered his face with his hands. "Let's back up," he said.

"Do we have to?" Russ asked, feeling claustrophobic in the dark therapy room, nestled next to Wade on the suddenly too small couch.

"It would help to have some more background," said Salinas, and Russ silently cursed the obviously amused jerk.

"Fine," Russ said, sitting up straight and going into lawyer mode. "If it pleases the court, I'd like to present a transcript of a conversation I had with Wade several nights ago—"

"There is no transcript," Wade said.

Russ tapped his temple. "I remember it well enough to re-count the highlights."

Wade sighed and waved his hand. "Go on then."

Between the two of them, they outlined the situation to Dr. Salinas. Wade reminded him of the more successful sessions they'd had recently, and explained what he'd been doing differently in them.

Dr. Salinas's eyebrows went up, but he remained quiet.

Then Wade came to the heart of the matter.

"I'd like to attempt a recreation of some of what I went through in L.A.—only, this time, with Russ. It'd be in our safe space, our home where only loving things have ever happened between us, and it'd be a consensual, safe situation that I'm in control of. Not only that, but I'm asking for these things to happen. It's a choice."

Russ watched Dr. Salinas's eyes grow distant in thought, and the man's head bobbed up and down slowly as he considered.

"And, Russ, you're amenable to Wade's proposition?"

"I don't know. That's why I'm here. Is it healthy? Is it safe? Will it do what Wade wants it to do?"

"Let me take that one question at a time," Dr. Salinas said, raising his hand.

Russ's leg jiggled in place, and he pulled at his tie again. He didn't like to think about Dr. Salinas knowing what he and Wade did together. He wasn't a prude. In the past, he'd crowed often and loud about his conquests. But Wade was different. What they had was special.

"Is it healthy?" Dr. Salinas repeated. "Wade's been steadily improving since he started working with you on your sex life, taking back what he felt he'd lost. He's reporting fewer and fewer zone outs. I believe he's on a path up from the valley. Could he tumble back? Sure. But hopefully not all the way to the bottom. The work he's done has set him up to avoid that kind of serious set back."

Russ fought the urge to point out that it wasn't impossible he'd go all the way back to the start. He reminded himself Wade *was* improving and Dr. Salinas was Russ's own choice of doctor. If Russ didn't trust him, then what was the point of the session? What was the point of any session?

"Is it safe?" Dr. Salinas went on. "Well, it really depends on how it's set up. The two of you are already working from sexual blueprints, which is something that came out of the BDSM community. I'm not sure how much you know about that community, but I've had my fair share of clients from the subculture, and one of their main tenets is Safe, Sane, and Consensual. A safe word should always be in place—I understand you've been using one—and consideration should be given when doing any sort of pain play—"

"Wait," Russ said, holding up his hand to stop Dr. Salinas's words. "You're not even fazed by this."

"No, I'm not," Dr. Salinas said. "Like I said, I've worked with many people involved in the BDSM subculture, and my sessions with Wade have indicated he'd respond to that kind of intensity in sexual encounters. I believe he probably leaned in that direction before he was raped."

Russ swallowed and nodded. He had. They did. They'd done all kinds of filthy, kinky things before Los Angeles.

Dr. Salinas smiled gently. "It's healthy for him to be seeking a way back to his native sexuality."

Russ stared at Dr. Salinas, taking in everything about the man and didn't see any cracks in his confidence at all.

"Do you disagree, Russ?" Dr. Salinas asked. "You're welcome to give an opposing viewpoint."

Russ shook his head. Wade *had* always liked it rough and sometimes risky. Before he'd left for Los Angeles, they'd played with restraints, blindfolds, and some pain. Wade had loved it.

Wade scooted closer to Russ, putting a hand on his back. "The real question, babe, is if you want to try it," he said, gently.

Russ wasn't discussing that here.

Dr. Salinas took up the slack, "If that isn't something you want to do. You have every right to draw your own boundaries. The entire concept of this kind of sexual work is that it's consensual on both sides, and that both people want it. There's nothing wrong with being unwilling to explore this option with Wade."

"You used to enjoy these sorts of things," Wade prodded. "Spanking me, using that crop you found in my closet on me, and I loved it, too."

"It was fun back then. It feels different now."

"Because of what happened?" Wade's eyes shaded slightly. "Because of what you saw on the videos you watched?"

Salinas made a soft noise that somehow expressed his awareness of the videos along with a compassionate understanding of them both.

Russ recalled what he'd seen and shuddered. He appealed to Salinas. "I don't want to hurt him. He's already been hurt so much."

Wade stroked a hand over Russ's hair. "This wouldn't be hurting me, babe. It'd be helping me."

Russ turned it over in his mind. Salinas sat patiently and Wade petted him like he was the traumatized one in the relationship.

"If we do this," Russ said, his voice thick and gravelly. "If we proceed, then we'll need to negotiate a solid, detailed plan that we're both all right with. I refuse to do just anything he did to you simply because he did it. I won't. But the sorts of things we engaged in before? Then okay."

Wade relaxed next to him. "Thank you, babe," he whispered.

Russ's heart twisted in his chest. He hoped he'd made the right choice.

PART THREE

Chapter Nineteen

W ADE KNELT NAKED in the large bathtub in their master suite, just like they'd spelled it out in the plan.

The plan.

Russ had read it over ten times in the last two hours alone, wanting to make sure it was exactly the way he remembered, and, at times, wishing he'd argued Wade down from some aspects of it. Like the part they were about to perform.

The plan encompassed the whole weekend—beginning with Friday evening and ending on Sunday night. Russ and Dr. Salinas had felt that Wade should start with a smaller period of time, but, in the end, Wade had gotten his way, arguing that he could always downscale if the experiment wasn't working out, but if he didn't get everything in the plan to begin with, then there would be no negotiating up if things were going well, and he could lose a therapeutic advantage.

Now, at seven o'clock on Friday evening, Russ swallowed the last of the final eight ounce glasses of water. He'd consumed four in the prior five hours, making sure that his piss was clear, before downing another. He wanted to be waterlogged, but not risk hyper-hydration, so he was careful.

As Wade knelt in the tub with his head bowed, Russ turned the tap in the bathroom sink to a slow trickle. He stood naked in front of Wade, reaching out to card through Wade's hair as he waited for the urge to hit. It didn't take long, and he swallowed hard. He'd never done this before. He'd never wanted to, and he still didn't feel any desire to do it. But Wade said he needed it. And Dr. Salinas hadn't disapproved, claiming that if Wade experienced certain events and sensations in the form of loving consent, then his brain would be that much closer to reprocessing and reframing them.

Lifting Wade's chin with one hand, and grasping his own penis with the other, Russ gazed down into Wade's eyes, looking for the permission he needed. Wade took a deep breath, shifted on his knees, and then nodded, closing his eyes just as the first spurt of Russ's urine hit his neck.

Wade jerked, and then looked up at Russ, his hazel eyes bright with an intense emotion that Russ couldn't categorize, and then Wade leaned into it.

Russ fought to control the stream, keeping it as slow and steady as he could without cutting it off entirely, as Wade nearly rolled into it, ducking his hair under, seeming to luxuriate in Russ's warm piss streaming down his face, neck, shoulders, and chest. Wade arched up, showing his hard cock, bright and already leaking pre-cum. Russ aimed lower and washed it away with his piss. He found himself transfixed as his urine darkened Wade's pubic hair and ran over Wade's thighs.

Wade moaned and turned around, bending over so that his ass was on display. His hole was already lubed and open from where Wade had fingered himself while Russ swallowed his last glass of water. A surge of heat hit him and a rush of blood filled his cock. An animalistic sense of ownership thrummed through his entire body at the sight of Wade covered in his urine.

His dick burned as he continued to piss a tight stream over Wade's back and down Wade's ass. Only the pressure of his overfull bladder overrode his body's system of blocking off urine in favor of semen.

"Please, Russ," Wade begged, arching his ass up. "Do it."

His nipples ached in response, and his overactive reptilian brain, the one engaged by the sight of Wade begging for his piss, thought the best solution for this pain was to bury his cock in Wade's sweet, tight hole.

Russ took a deep breath, bent his knees to get the right angle, and lined up. His piss stopped as he pushed inside. He paused with just his cockhead popped through Wade's sphincter. Wade lifted his head to cry out and reached back with his hand to hold Russ's thigh, keeping Russ from thrusting in.

Russ was grateful he did, because Wade being covered with his piss, smelling of his urine, left Russ disoriented and overwhelmed. He nearly pulled out altogether, momentarily afraid of his own reaction, and then Wade pinched his thigh and begged, "Please Russ. Piss in me."

It took effort. He was fully hard now, and he had to reach down and squeeze his own balls painfully to soften enough to start the urination again. It trickled out and slowly Wade filled up inside. Eventually, the heat of his own piss pushed against the head of his cock, and he slid a little farther in. The urine sloshed around him, and he fucked in and out, shallowly.

Wade squirmed and clenched his fists, crying, "Yes, Russ. Yes!"

Pulling out all the way, Russ's cock thudded as piss ran out of Wade's spasming hole. It sluiced down over Wade's balls to the tub below. He grunted and slammed back inside with a long thrust that buried his penis inches deep.

Wade howled, quivering around Russ's cock. He hunched over him, laying himself over Wade's back. He clasped Wade's hands in his, and rutted into his ass while piss gushed out over his own balls and down the front of his thighs. Wade moaned.

A proprietary thrill ran through Russ's gut as he rutted. He whispered in Wade's ear the words they'd agreed on. "You're clean now, Wade. I've washed every part of you."

Wade shuddered, quivered, and clenched every muscle in his body, going tight and tense beneath Russ. Russ felt Wade's struggle, the urge to fight or run, and then Wade shifted beneath him and burst free of the fear. A vibration coursed through Wade's body, and Russ smoothed it with his hands, rubbing over Wade's piss-slick arms and down his wet chest and stomach. He never missed a stroke, pushed by his own unexpectedly primal urges.

Saving up saliva, Russ turned Wade's head to get access to his mouth, pushing it between Wade's lips with his tongue. Wade swallowed it eagerly. Russ licked Wade's lips, sucked his bottom lip in, and then returned to fucking him as hard as he dared. Wade relaxed on Russ's cock, running his tongue over Russ's spit on his lips, tasting it.

"More," Wade whispered, collapsing to the floor of the tub, taking Russ's long, deliberate thrusts with a blissed-out expression. His hand moved on his own cock as a smile bloomed on his face.

Russ pulled out, pinched the head of his cock again to soften it enough, and groaned as he relaxed his refilling bladder to piss on Wade's back, into his open hole, and down his thighs. His cock and his balls felt too tight, and he pinched his scrotum to keep himself from growing too hard and cutting off the thin stream.

Wade lifted his head as Russ pushed two fingers into his hole and spread them, holding Wade open to piss inside again. Shuddering all over, Wade's hand moved fast and rough on his own cock, and Wade's balls drew up, so close to cumming. He listened for the safe word, but it didn't come, so he thrust his fingers deep inside, pissing onto Wade's back. Just as he felt the first clutch of Wade's orgasm, he pushed aggressively against Wade's prostate, and angled himself to piss on Wade's straining face.

Wade crowed, and shook convulsively, his spasming asshole pushing the piss out around Russ's fingers. Russ pulled his fingers out, and thrust his cock in their place. Digging into Wade's wet hips, he shot hard and deep, crying out as the pleasure pummeled him.

Panting and quaking through aftershocks, he kissed all along Wade's piss-damp shoulders and neck, only pulling out when he was soft enough to wash his cum out with a final burst of urine. His heart pounded anxiously, sanity restored after orgasm, but Wade lay grinning on the floor of the tub, ass up, and a peaceful expression on his face.

As Russ lay down next to him in the puddle at the bottom of the big tub, Wade opened his eyes, and there was a brightness in them Russ had missed so long he hadn't ever dreamed it would come back.

"Okay?" Russ whispered, his fingers in Wade's hair, touching the wet tendrils.

"Yeah. I feel clean," Wade said. "Except now I need a shower."

Russ laughed.

"You?" Wade asked.

"I'm good," Russ said.

He was also unnerved, surprised at how unexpectedly intense his reaction had been. Who knew that he'd turn caveman? It was ridiculous, and creepy, and yet a damned turn-on, too. But only because Wade wanted him to do it. It'd been amazing to see Wade open up to his piss, to watch him get hard, to see him so trusting.

Wade seemed to know all that Russ didn't say, his eyes taking on a gleam of understanding, and he leaned in to kiss him gently, whispering "Thank you," against his lips.

THE RIDING CROP had been Wade's for years before he met Russ. He'd never found anyone he trusted to use it on him, though, so it had been a fantasy he'd never gotten to indulge in. He'd kept it hanging in his closet next to his belts and there it had remained until Russ had stumbled on it while helping Wade pack up for the move into his apartment. A wicked gleam had come into his eye immediately.

Within moments of Russ discovering the crop, Wade had been on his hands and knees on the closet floor, a pair of his clean socks shoved into his mouth to muffle his cries, and his ass smarting from the stinging slap of the crop against his bare skin. Then Russ had relentlessly finger-fucked him in between strikes until Wade had been sweaty, arching, and begging around the sock crammed in his mouth.

Russ had spread his ass cheeks then, rimmed him until Wade saw stars and screamed in a way that the sock could not cover up, and then he'd jerked Wade's aching cock hard and fast, occasionally striking Wade's ass with the crop, until Wade seized up and came all over the carpeted floor of his closet.

Wade remembered that he'd still been trembling and groaning with his orgasm, when Russ grabbed him by the hair, forced him back onto his heels, and stood in front of him, jerking off onto Wade's face, some of his semen landing in Wade's open, gasping mouth.

It'd been unbelievably hot.

Since L.A., Wade clearly hadn't been ready for anything like that, and Russ had balked during their planning session, saying he didn't know if he could hit Wade with *anything*, not even with Wade's consent, anymore. But Wade had insisted, demanded it, and Dr. Salinas had interceded, reminding Wade that they both had a right to boundaries. If Russ wasn't going to do it, then Wade needed to accept that.

Oddly, it had been reminding Russ of the tapes that had changed things. Wade said pain in sex had always brought him to a place where he just *gave in* to the feelings in his body, and at those words, Russ's head had come up, and he'd really listened to Wade.

Wade had said, "Look, you were the first person to ever give me that the right way, Russ. And then Owen gave it the wrong way. And I want *you* there in my mind. When I fall into a memory like that, and I'm aching hard and sick with it, I want to think of *you*. I want to orgasm because of *you*. I want to let myself give in to it because you're there and it hurts, but it's safe. You saw on those tapes how I fought and lost, Russ. I want to lose to you. Not him. I don't want to lose to him ever again. Not in my mind and not in my bed."

Russ's tongue had darted out nervously, but he'd nodded, and the crop had been added to the plan. Sometimes Wade thought Russ was too easy.

But that thought evaporated when the bright, burst of pain landed on his ass, and he jerked against the restraints holding him prone to the bed. The blindfold did its job beautifully, blocking out all light, and Wade shifted, his cock already aching and hard, not getting nearly enough friction against the smooth sheets.

"One," Russ said, his voice low enough that Wade had to listen for it. "Hold your ass still."

Wade tried to comply and then yelled as another strike landed on his left ass-cheek. He tugged his legs against the restraints holding them straight and apart, and then pulled at the leather that bound his arms to the hooks on the back of the headboard. Wade had installed them himself earlier in the afternoon.

A series of blows fell and Wade shifted trying to move into them and away from them at once, and then Russ placed a hand on his lower back, stilling him, saying, "Hold still." Wade shivered as Russ ran the leather piece on the crop over Wade's balls gently, reminding him of how low they were pulled by the extra band they'd added to the ball stretcher to make it all last as long as Wade could stand, and said, "I don't want to miss and hit these." And then he lightly slapped them with the crop, sending rockets of gut-turning pain through Wade's body. Even his fingernails felt the wrench of it, and he catapulted into a memory—

Agony that tore his body open, Owen wielding the crop again and again, his balls exposed, vulnerable, and then **pain** *like he'd never known—*

"Shh," Russ was hushing him, his breath white noise in Wade's ear. "Shhh, Wade. You with me?"

"Yeah," Wade said, the darkness under the blindfold making him unsure. Was this a hallucination? Was he back with Owen in the basement? Was Russ real?

"Good," Russ said. "Five more."

The pain burned up his butt as Russ counted out the blows, reaching just one short of the number they'd agreed on, and then Wade felt Russ pull his ass cheeks aside, felt Russ blow on his hole, and then there was a shocking slap of the leather against his sensitive anus, and he screamed, kicking against the restraints, and nearly cumming in a whirl of shocked pain and a flare of fear, but the ball stretcher held him back.

"That's it," Russ murmured, rubbing soothing hands up and down Wade's back, and over the stinging, burning skin of his ass. "You're doing a great job. Just hold on right there, deep breaths.

That's good."

Wade struggled to comply, his body tense and braced for another blow, even though he knew none would come for a while.

There was the sound of the lube being uncapped, and then Wade felt Russ's slick fingers dip down into the crack of his ass. Russ knelt between Wade's legs, and Wade groaned and pushed back as Russ's fingers—two of them to make it harder to cope—squeezed into his asshole.

"Can't," Wade said, when Russ tried to work a third in. He was tense from the crop and Russ pulled all his fingers out.

"Hold on," Russ said, keeping his hand on Wade's side as he looked for something in the bedside drawer. A moment later, Wade felt the cool, smooth, lubricated tip of the anal plug pressed against the muscle of his anus, and Russ said, "Take it, Wade. Prove to me you can do this."

Wade tried to open for it, and as it slid slowly inside—

Hot, pain, burning hurt, wet and slick, blood

—"Come on, Wade. Take it in. You can do this. Come on, baby."

Wade shuddered as the widest part of the plug forced past his sphincter, and he groaned as he squeezed down on it, and struggled against the restraints for a comfortable position. The plug was curved for pressure on his prostate, and when Russ twisted it a little the always shocking-good of that stimulation made him clench and moan.

"That's it," Russ said, kissing Wade's ass cheeks, and down the backs of his thighs, with sharp, biting kisses. "That's it. You're doing great. Stay with me."

"With you," Wade said, shivering and aching, his hips flexing, rutting his cock against the bed, which rocked the plug against his prostate, too.

Russ moved and the bed shifted, and then Wade felt Russ's

fingers card softly through his hair, before gripping it firmly, and lifting his head. Russ positioned himself near Wade's face—Wade could feel the heat of his body, and smell the soap-scent of his skin—and Russ's fingers gripped his jaw. "Suck me, Wade."

Russ's cock was thick and the angle, blocked by Wade's out-stretched arms, led to Wade doing little more than sucking the head eagerly, but Russ's appreciative sounds made it clear that Wade was doing a great job.

"The second set," Russ said, and Wade barely had time to register the words before the crop fell onto his aching ass, and Wade yelled around the head of Russ's cock, and then the next blow fell, and the next. He rutted against the bed, the anal plug massaging his prostate maddeningly, the pain from the blows taking his breath away, and his mouth stuffed with Russ's cock.

"Come on, Wade," Russ said, tugging at Wade's hair with a sharp pull. "Cum."

But Wade wasn't there yet, couldn't reach it, the ball stretcher holding him back, and then Russ whapped the crop down on him in a rain of strikes that brought Wade to the edge of his ability to cope. *Searing hurt, agony, pain, Owen—*

No.

Russ.

Russ's scent, taste, voice. Russ calling to him, begging him to cum.

Wade grasped for reality, seeking Russ with every sense, licking Russ's cock, smelling his musky crotch, feeling his heat, envisioning him, and the pain came again, and again, and he screamed, broke out of his mind, and felt the sting of semen pulling up his cock from his balls, held too far away. Oblivion came as he surrendered, gave in, and shot a hard, pulsing load that wracked him all over and left him sobbing, face down in the pillow.

He struggled to breathe through intense aftershocks while Russ talked to him, called him beautiful and amazing, and rubbed his back. Wade could hear the slap of Russ's hand jerking himself off as Russ kissed his neck, and then moved so that his own semen spattered onto Wade's burning, aching ass. He shuddered again as Russ smeared it over his skin, and then fell down beside him, whispering, "Amazing baby. You're amazing."

Wade felt like he'd been carved out, made clean, rebooted. As Russ undid his restraints, Wade smiled into the blackness of the blindfold.

It had been enough.

RUSS WATCHED WADE sleep. He was exhausted, but Wade was more so. He'd collapsed face down on their bed after throwing off the soft robe he'd worn while scarfing down the sandwich Russ made for him. Now he breathed deeply, a bit of drool coming out of the corner of his mouth, and his face reflected a sated relaxation.

It'd been a long day, both physically and emotionally demanding. Russ had found space inside of himself he hadn't known was there. As it turned out, he had a surprising amount of room for meeting Wade's needs, no matter how difficult for Russ personally, or how worried he'd been about following Wade into heights of shared experience he'd never sought before.

Instead, like a moth, he'd flown fast after Wade's rising flame, driving them both higher and hotter, until they'd combusted.

Wade's face as he came apart, his surrender, had been beyond any sex that Russ had ever had, and while he suspected he'd never drive Wade into the same level of primal emotion Owen had managed in his insanity, he believed they'd come close enough. More importantly, he sensed Wade felt the same way.

Wade's eyes when Russ had removed the blindfold had been

wild with emotion, and he'd said the same thing over and over, until Russ had kissed him quiet: *thank you, thank you.*

The scar on Wade's neck was still slightly raised, but in the dim light from the bedside table, Russ could see that the angry purple had faded. He nearly reached out to touch it, but stopped himself. He didn't want to wake Wade. He needed his sleep.

Russ climbed out of bed and headed into the bathroom for his final preparations before he joined Wade for the night. As he brushed his teeth, he looked at the plan for tomorrow. It was written in Wade's loose hand, and the early parts of the day were all things they'd reviewed, but Wade had added afternoon information that Russ hadn't seen yet.

Saturday

Morning: The Care of Wade:

Sleep

Massage

Long bath

Cuddle on the couch/bed/wherever

Afternoon: The Care ~~and Feeding~~ of Russ

(for taking such good care of me):

Homemade Chicken and Dumplings

Massage

Long bath (no legal journals allowed)

Pie (or cake, I brought both—stay out of the refrigerator,

Russ! It's for tomorrow.)

Grease 2 (ha! no, I'm kidding, but you can choose the

movie—just not Grease 2!)

Sandwich built to specifications

Pie (or cake)

Russ spit out his toothpaste and let his eyes drift to the evening plans. He knew those by heart already. They included a pretty difficult scene that would probably result in Wade needing Sunday morning to be identical to Saturday morning.

Russ was okay with that.

As he took a leak, his balls twinged, reminding him that he wasn't seventeen anymore. Coming more than twice a day was really beyond the pale and too much for him to ask of them.

He washed his hands, and headed back to bed, pausing only to look at the picture of the meadow for a minute.

It was exactly the same but over the last few months of being alone with Wade in the bed beneath it, the picture had changed to him. He could admit that Wade was right. It was the better picture for their room. It was, in fact, beautiful. Like learning to love the new Wade.

Wade moved into Russ's arms without waking up, and Russ breathed in the scent of his hair. Life with Wade had always been like the painting—never what he thought he wanted, but, in the end, despite his doubts, whatever Wade brought was better.

Half asleep, Russ burned with love for the new and old Wade both.

THE DAY HAD gone just as Wade wanted it to go, and when evening finally fell, Russ was calm in the certainty that they were both rested and ready. It was going to be a difficult night.

The kitchen table was the perfect height. They'd both known this beforehand, of course, having purchased it with the idea in mind that they might want to screw on it. Russ knelt on a sofa cushion he'd thrown down, preparing Wade's ass with his fingers—to begin the fuck he'd only have to stand up, bend a little at the knee, and he'd slide right inside.

Wade's ankles were bound to his wrists, which were, in turn, tied beneath the kitchen table to o-rings. Wade had installed them while Russ watched that morning. The position left Wade's ass at the edge of the table, his knees bent up almost to his chest, and his arms twined around his naked legs to bring his wrists in alignment with his ankles. He was well and truly held in place, though he could move his torso and head a little, which was what Russ wanted, in order to see a full range of physical response from Wade.

He stood up, looked at his handiwork, and licked his lips. Wade was gorgeous—his eyes hot and wild, his cheeks red, and his lips red and wet where Wade kept sucking them into his mouth to chew on nervously.

This particular scene had been the easiest one for Russ to agree to, though he'd been able to tell both at the time of the plan, and now while watching for Wade's every muscle-twitch and fleeting expression, that this was the scene that scared Wade the most.

Russ knew why.

It was going to hurt in a way that made his own pulse thrum in empathy. But it was what Wade wanted, and it was similar to things he'd hinted at wanting to try before he'd left for Los Angeles. Underneath Wade's fear, Russ saw the excitement, too, at fulfilling that fantasy with Russ, and of taking the scenario back from Owen.

"Ready?" Russ asked.

There wasn't much prep to this one. He'd fingered Wade open, and smeared his own cock with lube, but Wade hadn't wanted a lot of run up to it. He said the pain needed to be raw and harsh, not masked by endorphins from arousal. Russ had agreed. It was Wade's show, and he could do it either way.

Russ pumped his cock a little, bringing himself to a straining hardness, and then wrapped his fist around Wade's thick dick, thumbing at the head as he lined up and pushed inside. As always, the grip of Wade's ass was fantastic. The veins and muscles stood out on Wade's neck as he swiveled his hips trying to accommodate the rough push of Russ's fat length.

Russ pulled back out, and then settled into a slow, shallow fuck that tugged the head of his cock against Wade's scarred anus. Sweat broke out on Wade's forehead, and his nipples stood at erect, desperate attention.

"Fuck, babe," Wade muttered, anxiously. "So intense."

Russ pushed in all the way, and held tight.

Wade moaned and clenched around him, pre-cum stringing from the head of his dick to slick up the treasure trail under his belly button. Russ fondled Wade's balls, already tight and high.

"Okay?" he asked. It was one of the only times they'd fucked without the ball stretcher to hold Wade back, and he needed to hear some assurance.

"Mm-hmm," Wade said, a whine in his voice. "Can you just—" Wade grunted, and clenched again.

Russ smoothed his hands over Wade's chest, tugging lightly on his dark chest hair, tweaking his nipples, and then he said, "If you're sure."

"Dammit, Russ."

He almost laughed then, but he bit it back, and reached over to the bowl at the edge of the table. Choosing a binder clip, a regular office one that Wade had provided, he tested the spring of it. Fear flashed in Wade's eyes.

He fucked in and out of Wade's ass slowly as he considered. Wade tossed his head on the table, finally saying, "Russ! Come on!"

"Here we go. Shh, I've got you." He leaned forward and

spread the chest hair away from Wade's peaked nipples. Pinching the right one to hardness, he placed the clamp carefully. As he let go, Wade's ass spasmed on his cock and a slow moan leaked from his throat. Russ repeated the action on Wade's left nipple and left the black clamps in place with his nipples trapped in their harsh bite.

"Talk to me, baby," Russ said.

"Hurts," Wade whispered.

"Uh huh. And?"

"Aches. All the way into my chest. It's intense. Hard to deal. *Fuck.*"

"Mm," Russ said, and flicked the clamps lightly, watching Wade squirm, feeling each reaction in the grip of Wade's ass on his cock. "Tell me."

"Burns. Hurts."

"Okay, and here's more."

He slid his hands down to Wade's cock and balls, pinching at his now loose scrotum, finding a suitable place just beneath the root of Wade's cock. Wade's breathing was shallow already, and Russ said, "Tell me."

"Hurts. Please, more."

"All right."

He took another clip and clamped it onto the loose skin between Wade's balls and hard cock, and watched Wade grunt and twist. Wade's ass clamped down around him, convulsing and squeezing as he moved and fought the pain.

"Mm, you know what you have to do, Wade," Russ said. "You need to talk."

"Fuck!" Wade cursed, and then Russ pinched another bit of skin beneath the other clamp on Wade's scrotum, and added a second clip. "Fuck!" Wade screamed.

"Enough?"

Wade shook his head.

Russ added one more clamp and felt Wade's insides clench so hard it almost hurt Russ's dick. Wade's neck was bright red, his chest flaming, his eyes so hot and wild that Russ thought he could feel their heat. His cock was so hard that it leaked strings of pre-cum that now filled his belly button. It flexed all on its own, in eager, wanton desire. Wade's chest moved up and down in short, shallow huffs as he coped with the pain.

"Doing okay?" Russ murmured, rubbing his hands up and down Wade's thighs. He swallowed thickly at the expression on his love's face—hurting, trusting, breaking, and yet strong. Russ's dick twitched against the slick, gritty-velvet walls gripping him tightly.

"Please," Wade said. "Now. Ready."

Russ fucked Wade slowly a few times, the tight, sweet pull of his ass bringing him close to the brink. Wade's startled, vulnerable, wide-eyed expression was taking him there even faster.

"Tell me," Russ said.

"Fuck, so good. Now, Russ! Please! Make me hurt!"

As he pumped hard and fast into Wade's spasming ass, Russ released the clamps on Wade's chest. Blood rushed back into his sensitive nipples and Wade screamed, his face screwing up in a vital, primal expression. Russ groaned and nearly came. Wade clenched all over and tears of pain leaked from his eyes. Those hazel eyes glowed with heat, and he stared, sweaty and red-faced, at Russ as he struggled not to scream.

Licking the sweat off his upper lip, continued to slam into Wade's ass hard enough to rattle Wade's teeth and jerked his entire restrained body back and forth on the table.

Wade cried. "Don't stop!"

Russ rubbed Wade's swollen, dark nipples with one hand, and jerked Wade's cock with the other, clanging the clamps on Wade's balls together as he did.

Wade cursed again, and then said, "Coming! Oh, fuck! Russ!"

Russ cried out as his own orgasm hit when Wade's did, going almost blind with pleasure as Wade's ass spasmed all around him. Collapsing on top, kissing his nipples, he shuddered through aftershocks that made his balls ache.

Wade's ass was still milking his cock, when Russ righted himself. After Russ could breathe without shuddering through an aftershock, he removed the clamps from Wade's scrotum, undid the straps holding Wade's wrists to his ankles, and slid slowly out of Wade's ass.

As Russ helped Wade straighten his legs out, he massaged them so that they didn't cramp.

"Thank you," Wade whispered, his eyes wild and surprised. "Good. It was good."

Russ licked his lips and said, huskily, "I noticed. The 'fucks' were flying out of your mouth."

Wade chuckled but he seemed subdued, at peace, a limp, achy, bliss overlay him. Russ wanted to get him somewhere softer, like their bed, but Wade seemed incapable of moving. Running his hand along Wade's cheek, he sought out his gaze. Wade smiled softly and then shuddered again.

"Call me your sweet cum dumpster," Wade murmured.

"You're my filthy sweet cum dumpster," Russ whispered in his ear. "Filled with my cum."

Wade shivered and smiled. "Thank you."

Russ smoothed fingers over Wade's nipples, and then he leaned down to examine the dark marks where the clamps had bit into his ball sac. After determining everything was okay. He kissed him, and then stepped over to the kitchen sink for a warm towel to clean them both off.

When he came back, Wade was sitting up, propped up with his arms, and he grinned at Russ. "That was really hard." He sounded pleased.

"But you did great," Russ whispered, wiping his own cum from between Wade's ass-cheeks.

"Yeah. I did. Didn't leave this room for even a minute. Wrote this directly onto my brain and heart."

A small smile broke on his own face and he continued to clean Wade up before helping Wade off the table and supporting him as they made their way up to bed.

WADE WOKE UP in the wee hours of the morning with his nipples pleasantly sore and his balls too. He rolled over to look at Russ and grinned to himself. Russ was on his back with his mouth open in oblivious unconsciousness. He adored the sight of his man getting much needed rest after taking Wade further than either of them had believed Wade would ever want to go a couple of months ago.

After the shower, earlier, they'd ended up tangled up in bed together, Russ's cock buried in Wade's body, spooned in an unscripted act of intense intimacy. In their sleep, they'd parted, but Wade would cherish those moments forever.

He kissed Russ's shoulder and nuzzled his sleeping face. He loved Russ so much.

After a few minutes of watching Russ sleep, Wade carefully got out of bed, slipped on blue jeans and a t-shirt before carefully opening the door without waking Russ. He took a moment to stand outside their room and looked down the hallway leading to the other rooms upstairs. A smile started on his face as he walked slowly toward the first room and stepped inside.

It was a bedroom-cum-office and it had a brand new desk in it, as well as some empty bookshelves. He imagined himself studying there once he'd returned to school, and Russ reviewing client files on a cozy Sunday morning. And he imagined Russ turning him over the desk for a good screw. The idea didn't terrify him anymore.

He walked down to the room at the very end of the hall and leaned against the doorjamb. It held two twin-sized beds in it, untouched since the delivery men left them before his life had been turned upside down. He'd intended the room to be a place for Nicole and Eric to crash, and to maybe one day fill with kids of their own. But, of course, no one had stayed in it even once. Wade wanted to change that. He wanted to make this house the home it was meant to be.

Wade smiled. That day was still a long time from now, but it was getting closer. Close enough that he didn't think he was wrong anymore to dream about it. He headed back toward the front stairs, pausing to admire each room in the home he'd chosen with Russ.

As he walked through the kitchen, he glanced at the table, amused that Russ had already cleaned up completely. No one would ever guess the dirty sex they'd just had on top of it only hours ago. Wade shifted on his feet, a twinge in his balls letting him know that he'd cum too many times in the last day, and that his nethers were not up for more, no matter what his brain might think.

He didn't think he'd want to go as far as they had over the weekend very often, but contentment swelled in him to know that they *could* go to those harder places if he felt the urge. The memory of Russ's expression of possessive adoration and rampant lust when they'd done the last scene had seared itself into Wade's brain, and his heart ached with love.

Opening the back door, the cool night air rushed over him. He grabbed the jacket hanging on a hook and threw it on before slipping on his leather sandals. As he stepped outside, he shivered, but he had something he needed to say, and he had to get away from the house to say it.

The moon overhead was full and it lit his way, a pale, thin light that just gave him enough of a sense of direction to trudge over the wet grass of the yard, back to the dark property line.

The wind smelled of wood smoke and he turned back to look at his home—his and Russ's. He took in both stories, the light from their upstairs bathroom making the window of their bedroom a dark honey-yellow. Wade turned his attention to the dark, star-filled sky.

"Hey, Owen." He cleared his throat. "So, uh, I wanted to say some things to you. But you're dead." Wade said it again, because it was so final. "You're dead."

He sniffed, but the tingle in his nose was the cold, not tears. He took in a deep, full breath, and looked up at the moon and the stars. He felt like he was almost as big as they were, like he could float up into the night or dissolve into it.

He stuffed his hands into his pockets and listened to the wind.

"I feel bad for you. You didn't know the first thing about love. You wanted to. Really, you did. And somehow in your psychosis you convinced yourself that you loved me." Wade pushed his lower lip up. "But you didn't. I'm convinced you didn't even like me."

He nodded slowly to himself. "You were scared. I get that. You were always scared: of your bisexuality, of your dad, of Russ when he was your boss, of me when I sucked you off. You were so fucking scared all the time."

He sighed, ran a hand through his hair. It wasn't working. He needed to spit it out.

"Look, here's the thing: you wanted to fundamentally alter me—physically, emotionally, sexually. I know deep down, despite caring about me, despite wanting me, you hated me, because you hated yourself."

Wade squatted down beside the garden, tilling his fingers into the dirt. "And you know what? That's not my fault. It's not even my problem. Do you have any idea how great it feels to say that? It's not even my *problem*, Owen. It never was." He glanced up to the sky again. "And now that you're dead, it's definitely not." He stood up, shaking the dirt free of his fingers. "I don't need to be out here talking to you. I don't really need this, but, even though you're dead, I kind of feel like you do. So, I hope it helps."

Wade looked up to the sky and said, "Wherever you are, I hope you don't hate yourself anymore, and I hope you're not sick anymore either. I like to imagine you're finally free of that. Because right now—right this second—I feel free of you. And it feels great."

Wade saw the light of their bedroom come on, and then a light deeper in the house, and then the light in the room that would one day be some little kid's.

He knew they weren't out of the woods yet. There was still healing to be done. But he also knew the difference between consent and violation, between devotion and betrayal, between love and hate. He felt it in his heart, in the twinges in his body, and the soaring of his soul, still flying from the leap he and Russ had made together.

"Russ is looking for me," he said. "Russ who loves me just the way I am. Scars, damage, and all. Goodbye, Owen. I'm done with you."

Wade jogged toward their house as it came alive with light. He knew Russ was probably frantic, wondering where he'd gone, but as he rushed onward, he was burned with light and joy.

Russ was his beacon.

The kitchen flared to life and the porch lights blazed on. Wade's heart soared higher in flight. He was free and every window was Russ shining his way home.

Epilogue

L OS ANGELES IN May was still bright, warm, and full of
color—even at dawn. Wade leaned back a little when Russ
wrapped his arms around him from behind, his chin digging into
Wade's shoulder slightly.

"Technically, it's Santa Monica," Russ reminded him.

"Yes, Santa Monica in Los Angeles County."

"We could still leave, skip out of here, and never set eyes on
this devil town again."

Wade smirked, looking down at the bougainvillea climbing
the trellis just below, the morning breaking over the ocean, and
the light of the Ferris wheel. It was a very pretty devil town. And
the hotel room surpassed even Russ's standards.

"You know, I've never been one to run away from risk,"
Wade said.

Russ sighed. "A little self-preservation is good."

Wade shrugged. He closed his eyes and breathed in the scent
of ocean.

"Putting yourself back in the jaws of hell—" Russ started in
his attorney voice. "Oh, fuck it, why do I bother? This is half of
why I love you."

Wade laughed softly.

The evening before, he and Russ had walked almost a mile
with their pants legs turned up, strolling in the surf. Russ had
undone a few extra buttons on his shirt, rolled his sleeves up, and

not uttered a single complaint about anything at all—not the temperature of the water, or the cigarette butts in the sand.

Wade knew Russ was nervous about their plans for the trip, but one glance at Russ's face had revealed something completely different: Russ was happy. He was happy to be on the beach with Wade, absorbed in the moment, and not wanting for anything more. The knowledge had made Wade's head spin, and he'd grabbed Russ and kissed him hard. It'd been a beautiful moment.

So, no, he didn't want go home.

Besides, the trip was *about* self-preservation. It was about putting a place with an event, and letting go. Wade was satisfied with the closure he'd given himself on the subject of Owen. But his lack of knowledge about where he'd actually been held continued to plague him. The basement room remained in his mind as a hell without dimensions—someplace that could sneak up on him at odd times, like during hide and seek in the barn with Eric.

It was the main thing to haunt him anymore: a traveling room that he'd trip and fall into.

Interestingly, at least according to Dr. Salinas, once Wade was stuck in the memory of the room, nothing bad happened to him there. He no longer relived the pain and suffering he'd gone through with Owen—well, not often anyway. Instead, he'd just be trapped there, away from the ones he loved, with no idea of how to get back.

A year out, the rest of the trauma seemed more or less resolved, depending on the day and the circumstances Wade found himself in. Between the work he continued to do with Dr. Salinas by replacing Owen with Russ in his mind, replacing rape with consent, and the work he occasionally still did with Russ, too, he wasn't triggered to those particular memories as often anymore.

Life had become almost normal again. Wade had started a

few classes to pursue his teaching dreams, and they'd moved into their house for good a year prior. It was Wade's safe haven, and he loved the home he and Russ had made together.

In addition, there wasn't the same amount of day-to-day planning to their sex life. Wade could and did generally enjoy impromptu sex now, but there were times he'd ask for something more, something to help process trauma, and Russ would oblige. It was during those sessions Wade felt he made the biggest strides in integrating his experiences in a way he could stand to live with.

The basement room, though, was different. Wade assumed the power it still had over him came from all of the unknown particulars surrounding it. He didn't know anything about the driveway leading up to the house where he'd been held, or the number of steps down to the basement room, or the roads he'd traveled to get there. He hoped that if he could set the house in a definitive place, it would stop haunting him, and maybe he'd trust himself to drive again.

And then, who knows where he would trust himself to go from there? Maybe they could finally talk about starting a family.

"I'm not going home, Russ."

"Then we should get a move on," Russ said. "If we have to take breaks or deal with zone-outs, we should start now."

"It's barely six in the morning," Wade said, a fast rush of blood in his veins.

"It's about an hour and fifty minutes away," Russ said, already in motion behind him, packing up their things for the day and tidying the room. "If we leave now, we'll miss traffic, and if there are problems, we'll have time to deal with them."

Wade wrapped his arms around his chest, his eyes steadfastly on the horizon, the morning sun breaking from the east, and he cleared his throat.

"Hey, hey, hey," Russ said, soothingly. "It's just a house. It's just a place and that's all it is."

"Right," Wade agreed with a nod of his head, digging deep to find that center of himself he could depend on. "Just a house."

Two hours later, Wade held himself tightly in the passenger seat, staring out his window as the landscape passed by. There were browns, greens, purples, and various shades of yellow and blue. There were houses, and stores, and other cars. There were on ramps and off ramps, and long, empty concrete overflow beds, and then they came around a bend, and Wade caught his breath.

"Okay?" Russ asked.

"Somewhere near here," Wade said softly, some vague memory of the lay of the land kicking in. "He offered me the lemon cookies."

Wade still couldn't stand the smell of lemon. Dr. Salinas said that taste and smell were wired through the most ancient part of the human brain, and that it would be unlikely he'd ever shake that association.

Russ made a soft noise and shifted his hand from the steering wheel to Wade's knee.

Wade took slow breaths, dragging in calm to replace the rise of panic. "I ate them all," he said.

He used to berate himself mentally for being so greedy, wondering if the drugs would've completely knocked him out if he'd only had two, but he didn't do that anymore. There was no point. Nothing came undone by taking on the blame.

The rest of the drive was in silence. Russ cleared his throat a few times, but he didn't speak, and Wade had nothing to say.

They were met in Bakersfield by a representative for the Kern County Sheriff's office, but it wasn't until they drove close to the Ojai Valley Community Hospital, where Wade had been taken immediately upon discovery in Owen's house, that Wade recognized anything at all. He recalled the ambulance loading area from when they'd taken him out to rush him in, and he recalled being hustled into another ambulance when he was well enough to be transferred to Cedars Sinai a few days later.

Travis Whittaker, the deputy who'd been asked to drive them up to the abandoned property and escort them into the house, was a young guy. At most twenty-two years old. Which made him seem like a child in Wade's eyes. Wade doubted that he'd ever had any real adversity in his life, and in a weird, unaccountable burst of affection, he wanted to throw his arms around the kid and beg him to stay safe. He wanted to make Deputy Whittaker promise to stay just the way he was now for all of eternity. With a life in law enforcement, Wade doubted that would happen.

Russ seemed to sense fragility taking root inside of Wade, and he put his hand in Wade's as they rode in the scrupulously clean back of Deputy Whittaker's unmarked Crown Victoria. The curved, crawling drive up to the house in the mountains brought back another memory for Wade—the excruciating pain of the ambulance ride, bumping along as they'd taken the rough, unpaved road down.

"All right?" Russ asked.

Wade nodded. He didn't have a lot of words, but he didn't think he needed to say anything, and he was right. Russ squeezed Wade's hand and then brought it up to his lips to brush a kiss on his thumb.

"Your case was the talk of the department," Deputy Whittaker said, leaning forward a little over his steering wheel to peer out of the windshield. "We don't get a lot of sickos up this way. Usually it's all petty stuff—theft, a murder or two. This was huge."

Wade stared at the shell of Deputy Whittaker's pale, pink ear.

"I mean, a hostage situation with sexual predation, all going up in gunfire? Wow. The perp was killed with the first shot, but the guys in the station were so disgusted they put a few extra bullets in him for good measure."

Russ spoke up. "You'll need to cut the commentary, Deputy. Just drive and escort. Or I'll—"

"Russ," Wade cut in before whatever legal threat could come out of his mouth. "It's fine."

Russ looked ready to dispute it, but Deputy Whittaker shrugged good-naturedly and said, "I understand. Traumatic experience and all. I shoulda kept a lid on it from the get go. I get chatty. It's a problem."

Russ muttered, "We all have our burdens," in a way that made it very clear what he thought of Deputy Whittaker.

Wade felt a small smile tug on the side of his lips for the first time all day, and he shook his head, watching out the window as the trees grew thicker and then thinned out when they approached the house.

It was a pretty small place, a modest Old Tahoe cottage. Wade wasn't sure what he'd been expecting. He was surprised, though. A part of him had always half expected it to be a typical L.A. bungalow set up in the hills. Though Russ had told him that Owen had chosen a hard-to-get-to location up in the mountains. He'd never realized just how isolated it was until now.

The dark wood of the porch gave way to a white front door and some windows that were all dark. No light shone within. The house felt soulless and empty as he climbed out of the car, and walked toward it with his jaw set.

"They cleared the place out a long time ago," Whittaker said, walking out in front of Wade, clapping his hand over his chest for a moment, searching for something. He reached into his left breast pocket and procured the key.

"Here we go. I'll go in first, make sure it's all clear. We don't get many vagrants up this way, but I'd hate for you to get a scare."

Wade swallowed, he could feel Russ right behind him, and he shoved his hands into his pockets.

Russ came along side and said, "Not exactly my idea of home-sweet-home." He was gazing out toward the peaks that trailed away from the edge of the mountain the house was perched on. "No movies, no drive-thrus. The grocery's a half hour away."

"Russ," Wade said, softly. "Not now."

Russ nodded.

Deputy Whittaker arrived at the front door moments later and said, "It's all good. I'll let you men explore at your own pace. If you need me, I'll be right here on the porch. Just a holler away."

Wade stepped over the threshold and looked around at the entryway that gave way to an empty den and kitchen. He took his time moving through the house, looking into bedrooms he didn't know if Owen had ever used, and then he came to the door that could only lead down to the basement.

He turned to Russ and found him inches away, gazing at him intently, as though watching for any cracks.

Wade thought his voice sounded rusty when he said, "So, this is the door."

Russ nodded and lifted his eyebrows, never taking his gaze from Wade's face.

"I guess I should open it."

Russ just looked at him, and Wade gave way just a little, a small crack appearing in the hard shell he'd put up since they'd woken that morning in the hotel bed. He knew he could turn around now, walk away, and Russ wouldn't think less of him. It'd be okay to chicken out.

"All right then," Wade said. "I'm going to open it."

"Okay."

Wade turned the knob and looked at the carpeted stairs leading down to another door at the bottom that was open. He counted—twelve steps. twelve steps down. He felt Russ's hand on his lower back, not pushing him forward, just steadying him, and he took a deep breath and let it out.

The descent felt like it took forever, but when he passed through the entry way and entered the room, already lit with the fluorescent fixtures that Wade remembered so well, he froze in place. The dimensions were right. It was white and big enough, but also, weirdly, too small. In the corner was the shower, the toilet, and the drain. All the rest of the room was bare—no sign of the implements Owen had used, except for the holes in the wall where the boards and hooks had been drilled in.

"The bed was there," Wade said pointing. "I was almost never in it."

Russ said nothing, but his hand didn't leave Wade's back.

"Over there—he'd tie me to the ceiling and beat me until I passed out, or until I couldn't take it anymore."

Wade noticed how calm he sounded and how calm he felt. He sought inside himself for the panic that used to be overwhelming and found nothing but a deep sense of sorrow. He'd lost a lot in this room, but not everything. Owen—sick as he was—was the one who'd lost it all, every single shred of humanity and decency and, in the end, his life. Wade pressed his lips together. It was a sad end to a man who could've been so much more. Mental illness had stolen everything from Owen.

He sighed. "What happened in here was wrong."

"Yes," Russ agreed.

"But I'm not angry about it anymore. It's just a story I lived."

Wade heard Russ swallow. He turned to him, and looked into his intense gray eyes. Wade smiled and brought his hand up to touch Russ's chin, and then he said, "I'm just glad I lived to tell it. And now I get a new story. With you."

Russ nodded.

Wade turned back to the room. It was, when all was said and done, a really horrible little room. But it had nothing to do with him anymore.

"I'm ready to go," he said. "There's nothing left to see."

A few minutes later, sitting in Deputy Whittaker's car with Russ's hand in his, he watched the house being locked up.

"Well?" Russ said, softly.

"It's just a house," Wade said. "In the end, it's just a house."

Whereas what he and Russ had back in Atlanta was a home.

"Do you think it'll stay put?" Russ asked, obliquely referencing Wade's insistence that the room traveled and haunted him.

Wade shrugged. "Only time will tell, I guess. But I don't see why it'll be going anywhere. It's nothing special. Just a place I never have to be again."

THAT NIGHT WADE twisted in the hotel sheets underneath Russ's hunching body, taking Russ's cock and staring into his eyes. He shuddered and sucked on Russ's lower lip, before grabbing his face and kissing him hard. Clutching Russ, his hands moving over Russ's sweat slick back, Wade was grateful and deeply in love.

California in May was bright and full of color. It was red for blood and green for hope. It had hosted his pain and agony, but in the light coming through the sliding glass door to the balcony, it also hosted his love, and his urgent burning desire for life.

For Russ.

THE END

Letter from Leta

Dear Reader,

Thank you so much for reading *The Difference Between*! I hope you were able to find healing in the book along with Russ and Wade.

Be sure to follow me on BookBub or Goodreads to be notified of new releases. And look for me on Facebook for snippets of the day-to-day writing life, or join my Facebook Group for announcements and special giveaways. To see some sources of my inspiration, you can follow my Pinterest boards or Instagram.

If you enjoyed the book, please take a moment to leave a review! Reviews not only help readers determine if a book is for them, but also help a book show up in site searches.

Also, for the audiobook connoisseurs out there, many of my other books are available in audio. I hope to eventually add my entire backlist, including *The Difference Between*, to my audiobook roster over the next few years.

Thank you for being a reader!
Leta

Standalone

ANY GIVEN LIFETIME
by Leta Blake

He'll love him in any lifetime.

Neil isn't a ghost, but he feels like one. Reincarnated with all his memories from his prior life, he spent twenty years trapped in a child's body, wanting nothing more than to grow up and reclaim the love of his life.

As an adult, Neil finds there's more than lost time separating them. Joshua has built a beautiful life since Neil's death, and how exactly is Neil supposed to introduce himself? As Joshua's long-dead lover in a new body? Heartbroken and hopeless, Neil takes refuge in his work, developing microscopic robots called nanites that can produce medical miracles.

When Joshua meets a young scientist working on a medical project, his soul senses something his rational mind can't believe. Has Neil truly come back to him after twenty years? And if the impossible is real, can they be together at long last?

Any Given Lifetime is a stand-alone, slow burn, second chance gay romance by Leta Blake featuring reincarnation and true love. This story includes some angst, some steam, an age gap, and, of course, a happy ending.

WAKE UP MARRIED, EPISODES 1 – 3
by Leta Blake & Alice Griffiths

Join the fun in this soapy serial as Will & Patrick's fake marriage turns into true love! Written by best-selling author Leta Blake and newcomer Alice Griffiths!

Episode One: Will & Patrick Wake Up Married

After a drunken night of hot sex in Vegas, strangers Will Patterson and Dr. Patrick McCloud wake up married. A quickie divorce is the most obvious way out—unless you're the heir of a staunchly Catholic mafia boss with a draconian position on the sanctity of marriage. Throw their simmering attraction into the mix and all bets are off!

Episode Two: Will & Patrick Meet the Family

Meeting the family is challenging for every new couple. But for Will and Patrick, the awkward family moments only grow more hilarious—and painful—when they must hide the truth of their predicament from the people they care about most. Throw in the sexual tension flaring between them and you've got a recipe for madcap laughs and surprisingly heartwarming feels.

Episode Three: Will & Patrick Do the Holidays

A couple's first holiday season is always a special time. Thanksgiving, Christmas, and New Year's Eve are magical when you're in love. Too bad Will and Patrick's marriage is a sham and they're only faking their affection for each other. Or are they? Sparks fly in this episode of the *Wake Up Married* serial. Will the sexual tension between Will and Patrick finally explode in a needy night of passion? Or will they continue to deny their feelings?

THE RIVER LEITH

by Leta Blake

Amnesia stole his memories, but it can't erase their love.

Leith is terrified after waking up in a hospital bed to find his most recent memories are three years out of date.

Worse, he can't even remember how he met the beautiful man who visits him most days. Everyone claims Zach is his best friend, but Leith's feelings for Zach aren't friendly.

They're so much more than that.

Zach fills Leith with longing. Attraction. Affection. **Lust.** And those feelings are even scarier than losing his memory, because Leith's always been straight. Hasn't he?

For Zach, being forgotten by his lover is excruciating. Leith's amnesia has stolen everything: their relationship, their happiness, and the man he loves. Suddenly single and alone, Zach knows nothing will ever be okay again.

Desperate to feel better, Zach confesses his grief to the faceless Internet. But his honesty might come back to haunt them both.

The River Leith is a standalone MM romance with amnesia trope, hurt/comfort, bisexual discovery, "first time" gay scenes, a second chance at first love, and a satisfying happy ending.

SLOW HEAT

by Leta Blake

A lustful young alpha meets his match in an older omega with a past.

Professor Vale Aman has crafted a good life for himself. An unbonded omega in his mid-thirties, he's long since given up hope that he'll meet a compatible alpha, let alone his destined mate. He's fulfilled by his career, his poetry, his cat, and his friends.

When Jason Sabel, a much younger alpha, imprints on Vale in a shocking and public way, longings are ignited that can't be ignored. Fighting their strong sexual urges, Jason and Vale must agree to contract with each other before they can consummate their passion.

But for Vale, being with Jason means giving up his independence and placing his future in the hands of an untested alpha—as well as facing the scars of his own tumultuous past. He isn't sure it's worth it. But Jason isn't giving up his destined mate without a fight.

This is a gay romance novel, 118,000 words, with a strong happy ending, as well as a well-crafted, **non-shifter** omegaverse, with alphas, betas, omegas, male pregnancy, heat, and **knotting**. Content warning for pregnancy loss and aftermath.

Gay Romance Newsletter

Leta's newsletter will keep you up to date on her latest releases and news from the world of M/M romance. Join the mailing list today and you're automatically entered into future giveaways. letablake.com

Leta Blake on Patreon

Become part of Leta Blake's Patreon community in order to access exclusive content, deleted scenes, extras, bonus stories, rewards, prizes, interviews, and more. www.patreon.com/letablake

Other Books by Leta Blake

Any Given Lifetime
The River Leith
Smoky Mountain Dreams
The Difference Between
Heat for Sale
Stay Lucky
Stay Sexy
Omega Mine: Search for a Soulmate
Bring on Forever
Angel Undone

The Home for the Holidays Series
Mr. Frosty Pants
Mr. Naughty List

The Training Season Series
Training Season
Training Complex

Heat of Love Series
Slow Heat
Alpha Heat
Slow Birth
Bitter Heat

'90s Coming of Age Series
Pictures of You
You Are Not Me

Co-Authored with Indra Vaughn
Vespertine

Cowboy Seeks Husband

Co-Authored with Alice Griffiths
The Wake Up Married serial
Will & Patrick's Endless Honeymoon

Gay Fairy Tales
Co-Authored with Keira Andrews
Flight
Levity
Rise

Audiobooks
Leta Blake at Audible

Free Read
Stalking Dreams

Discover more about the author online:
Leta Blake
letablake.com

About the Author

Author of the bestselling book *Smoky Mountain Dreams* and the fan favorite *Training Season*, Leta Blake's educational and professional background is in psychology and finance, respectively. However, her passion has always been for writing. She enjoys crafting romance stories and exploring the psyches of made up people. At home in the Southern U.S., Leta works hard at achieving balance between her day job, her writing, and her family.